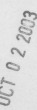

The
Rake

This Large Print Book carries the Seal of Approval of N.A.V.H.

LESSONS IN LOVE

The
Rake

Suzanne Enoch

Thorndike Press • Waterville, Maine

Published in 2003 by arrangement with Avon Books, an imprint of HarperCollins Publishers, Inc.

Thorndike Press® Large Print Core.

The tree indicium is a trademark of Thorndike Press.

The text of this Large Print edition is unabridged.
Other aspects of the book may vary from the original edition.

Set in 16 pt. Plantin by Ramona A. Watson.

Printed in the United States on permanent paper.

Library of Congress Control Number: 2003107413
ISBN 0-7862-5800-4 (lg. print : hc : alk. paper)

For my fellow Ladies of Avon,
whose friendship, warmth, assistance,
and encouragement is not only awesome,
but unprecedented.

And for Sharon Lyon,
who suggested gift boxes.

As the Founder/CEO of NAVH, the only national health agency solely devoted to those who, although not totally blind, have an eye disease which could lead to serious visual impairment, I am pleased to recognize Thorndike Press★ as one of the leading publishers in the large print field.

Founded in 1954 in San Francisco to prepare large print textbooks for partially seeing children, NAVH became the pioneer and standard setting agency in the preparation of large type.

Today, those publishers who meet our standards carry the prestigious "Seal of Approval" indicating high quality large print. We are delighted that Thorndike Press is one of the publishers whose titles meet these standards. We are also pleased to recognize the significant contribution Thorndike Press is making in this important and growing field.

Lorraine H. Marchi, L.H.D.
Founder/CEO
NAVH

★ Thorndike Press encompasses the following imprints: Thorndike, Wheeler, Walker and Large Print Press.

Prologue

Lady Georgiana Halley burst through the drawing room doors. "Did you hear what that man did this time?"

Lucinda Barrett and Evelyn Ruddick exchanged glances that Georgiana could have read from a mile away. Of course they knew precisely whom she was discussing. How could they not, when he was the worst man in England?

"What now?" Lucinda asked, putting down the cards she'd been shuffling.

Shaking raindrops from the hem of her gown, Georgiana plunked herself into the third chair at the gaming table. "Elinor Blythem and her maid got caught in the rain this morning. They were walking home when *that man* drove by in his coach at full tilt and sent a cascade of street water straight at them." She pulled off her gloves and slapped them onto the table. "It's fortunate the rain had just begun, or he might have drowned her!"

"He didn't even stop?" Evelyn poured her a hot cup of tea.

"And get wet himself? Heavens, no." Georgiana dropped a lump of sugar into the tea and stirred vigorously. Men were so maddening! "If the morning had been dry, he would have stopped to let Elinor and her maid ride with him, but for most men, 'nobility' is not a state of mind or of station. It is a state of comfort."

"A state of monetary comfort," Lucinda amended. "Don't spill."

Evie refilled her own cup. "While you two are entirely too cynical, I have to agree that society seems to forgive arrogance when a gentleman has money and power. True nobility has all but vanished. In the days of King Arthur, inspiring a woman's admiration was at *least* as important as the ability to slay a dragon."

In Miss Ruddick's optimistic imagination, nearly everything tied into tales of chivalry — but this time she had a point. "Yes, exactly," Georgiana said. "When did the dragons become more important than the maidens?"

"Dragons guard treasure," Lucinda said, jumping on the analogy, "which is why females with large dowries can rate almost as highly as dragons."

"It should be *we* who are the treasures, dowries or not," Georgiana insisted. "I think the difficulty is that we're more complicated than wagering or horse races. Understanding a female is utterly beyond the capacity of most men."

Lucinda bit into a chocolate tea cake. "I agree. It certainly takes more than a sword swinging in my direction to get my attention." She chuckled.

"Lucinda!" Blushing bright red, Evie fanned her face. "For heaven's sake!"

Georgiana sat forward. "No. Luce is right. A gentleman can't win a female's heart the same way he wins a . . . a boat race on the Thames. They need to know there are different rules involved. For instance, I wouldn't want anything to do with a gentleman who makes a habit of breaking ladies' hearts, no matter how handsome he was or how much wealth and power he had."

"And a gentleman should realize that a lady has a mind of her own, for goodness sake." Evelyn set down her teacup with a clatter as an exclamation point.

Lucinda stood and went to the desk at the other end of the room. "We should write these down," she said, pulling several sheets of paper from a drawer and returning to distribute them. "The three of us wield a great deal of influence, particularly with the so-called gentlemen to whom these rules would apply."

"And we would be doing other ladies a service," Georgiana said, her anger ebbing as the plan began to take shape.

"But a list won't do anything for anyone but ourselves." Evelyn took the pencil Lucinda handed her. "If that."

"Oh, yes it will — when we put our rules into practice," Georgiana countered. "I propose that we each choose some man and teach him what he needs to know to properly impress a lady."

"Yes, by God." Lucinda thumped her hand on the table in agreement.

As she began writing, Georgiana chuckled darkly. "We could get our rules published. 'Lessons in Love,' by Three Ladies of Distinction."

Georgiana's List

1. *Never break a lady's heart*

2. *Always tell the truth, no matter what you think a lady wants to hear*

3. *Never make a wager over a lady's affections*

10

4. *Flowers are nice; but make sure they're the lady's favorite kind. Lilies are especially lovely.*

Chapter 1

By the pricking of my thumbs,
Something wicked this way comes.
— *Macbeth*, Act IV, Scene i

Lady Georgiana Halley watched Dare enter the ballroom and wondered why the soles of his boots didn't smoke, he was so well traveled on the path to Hell. The rest of him certainly smoldered, dark and devilishly seductive, as he made his way toward the gaming rooms. He didn't even notice when Elinor Blythem turned her back on him.

"I really do hate that man," she murmured.

"Beg pardon?" Lord Luxley loped by her, the country dance sending him leaping in a circle with her at the center.

"Nothing, my lord, I'm only thinking aloud."

"Well, share your thoughts with me, Lady Georgiana." He touched her hand, turned, and vanished for a moment behind

Miss Partrey as they wound through the line again. "Nothing pleases me so much as the sound of your voice."

Except, perhaps, for the gold clinking in my purse. Georgiana sighed. She was becoming far too jaded. "You are too kind, my lord."

"That is an impossibility where you are concerned."

They circled around again, and Georgiana scowled at Dare's broad back as the scoundrel strolled out of sight, probably to go smoke a cheroot and drink with his blackguard friends. The evening had been so pleasant before Dare had intruded. Her aunt was hosting the soiree, so she couldn't imagine that anyone had even invited him.

Her dance partner joined her again, and she favored the handsome, golden-haired baron with a determined smile. She would just have to put that devil Dare out of her thoughts. "You are energetic tonight, Lord Luxley."

"You inspire me," he said, sounding winded.

The dance came to a close. While the baron dug in his waistcoat for a handkerchief, Georgiana caught sight of Lucinda Barrett and Evelyn Ruddick, standing with their heads together at the refreshment table. "Thank you, my lord," she said to her partner, curtsying before he could offer to take her on a stroll around the room. "You've exhausted me beyond recall. If you'll excuse me?"

"Oh. I — of course, my lady."

"Luxley?" Lucinda exclaimed from behind her ivory-ribbed fan as Georgiana joined them. "How did that happen?"

Georgiana gave in to a genuine smile. "He wanted to recite the poem he'd written in my honor, and the only way to stop him after the first stanza was to agree to a dance."

"He wrote you a poem?" Evelyn looped her hand around Georgiana's arm and led the way to the chairs lining one side of the room.

"He did." Grateful to see Luxley select one of the debutantes as his next victim, Georgiana accepted a glass of Madeira from one of the footman. After three hours of quadrilles, waltzes, and country dances, her feet ached. "And you know what rhymes with Georgiana, don't you?"

Evelyn wrinkled her brow, her gray eyes twinkling. "No, what?"

"Nothing. He just put 'iana' after every ending word. In iambic trimeter, yet. 'Oh, Georgiana, your beauty is my sunlightiana, your hair is finer than goldiana, your —' "

Lucinda made a choking sound. "Dear Lord, stop that at once. Georgie, you have the most astounding ability to make gentlemen do and say the most ridiculous things."

Georgiana shook her head, pushing a goldiana curl out of her eyes as it came loose from one of its ivory clips. "My money has that ability. Not me."

"You shouldn't be so cynical. After all, he did go to the effort of writing you a poem, awful or not," Evelyn said.

"Yes, you're right. It's very sad that I've become so jaded at a mere four-and-twenty, isn't it?"

"Are you going to choose Luxley for your lesson?" Evelyn asked. "It seems to me, he could stand to learn a few things — namely about how dim women aren't."

Taking a sip of sweet Madeira, Georgiana smiled. "To be honest, I'm not sure he'd be worth the effort. In fact —" A movement by the stairs caught her attention and Dare reentered the ballroom, a woman on his arm. Not just any woman, she noted with a slight scowl: Amelia Johns.

"In fact what?" Lucinda followed her gaze. "Oh, dear. Who invited Dare?"

"Not me; that's for certain." Miss Johns

couldn't be above eighteen years old — a good twelve years younger than Dare. In years of sin though, he surpassed her by centuries. Georgiana had heard rumors that the viscount was courting someone, and with her family's money and her pert brunette innocence, Amelia was no doubt the target, the poor thing.

Dare took both of Amelia's hands in his, and Georgiana gritted her teeth. The viscount said something brief and, with a jaunty grin, released the girl and strolled away. Amelia's face flushed, then paled, and she hurried from the room.

Well, that blasted well made one thing clear. Georgiana stood, facing her friends again. "No, not Luxley," she stated, surprised at her calm determination. "I have a different student in mind — one in serious need of a good lesson."

Evie's eyes widened. "You're not thinking about Lord Dare, are you? You hate him. You barely speak to him."

Across the room Dare's deep laugh sounded, and Georgiana's blood heated to near boiling. Obviously he didn't care a fig that he'd wounded a young girl's feelings — or worse, broken another heart. Oh, yes, he badly needed a lesson. He was the reason they'd made the lists in the first place. And she knew the exact lesson she intended to teach him. In fact, she could think of no one better qualified to deliver it than she. "Yes, Dare. And, obviously, I'll have to break his heart to do it, though I'm not certain he even has one. But —"

"Shh," Evelyn hissed, making a cutting gesture with her hands.

"Who has one what?"

Her spine stiffening at the low drawl, Georgiana turned around. "I wasn't talking to you, my lord."

Tristan Carroway, Viscount Dare, looked down at her, his light blue eyes amused. He couldn't have a heart, if he was able to smile that charming, sensuous smile right after reducing another woman to tears and flight.

"And here I was," he said, "only approaching to tell you how remarkably lovely you look this evening, Lady Georgiana."

She smiled, seething inside. Now he was complimenting her, while poor Amelia was without a doubt in some dark corner, weeping. "I did choose this ensemble with you in mind, my lord," she said, smoothing her silk burgundy skirt. "Do you truly like it?"

The viscount was no fool, and though his expression didn't change, he took a half step back. She hadn't brought her fan along tonight — though Lucinda's was in easy reach if she changed her mind about rapping him across the knuckles.

"I do, my lady." His sweeping glance took her in from head to toe, leaving her with the unsettling sensation that he knew whether her shift was silk or cotton.

"Then this is the one I'll wear to your funeral," she said with a sweet smile.

"Georgie," Lucinda murmured, taking her arm.

Dare lifted an eyebrow. "Who says you'll be invited?" With a devilish grin, he turned on his heel. "Good evening, ladies."

Oh, did he ever need to be taught a lesson! "How are your aunts?" Georgiana asked his backside.

He stopped and, with a slight hesitation, turned around. "My aunts?"

"Yes. I don't see them this evening. How are they?"

"Aunt Edwina is quite well," he said, his expression wary. "Aunt Milly is recovering, though not as quickly as she would like. Why?"

Ha. She had no intention of explaining the reason behind her question. Let him wonder until she had the details of her plan figured out. "No reason. Please give them my compliments."

"I will. Ladies."

"Lord Dare."

As soon as he was out of sight, Lucinda released Georgiana's arm. "So that's how you make a gentleman fall in love with you. I'd wondered what I'd been doing wrong."

"Oh, hush. I can't simply fall into his arms. He would know something was afoot."

"How are you going to accomplish it, then?" Even the usually optimistic Evelyn was skeptical.

"Before I do anything else, I need to speak with someone. I'll tell you what I can tomorrow."

That said, Georgiana went in search of Amelia Johns. Dare had vanished, but she kept an eye out for his tall form anyway. One of his more annoying traits was that one never knew when or where he might turn up.

Drat. That reminded her that she'd forgotten to ask him whether he'd been invited this evening or had bullied his way into her aunt's party.

A thorough search revealed no sign of the pretty young debutante, and with a preoccupied frown Georgiana went to find her aunt and resume her hostess duties.

Being Aunt Frederica's live-in companion came with both certain privileges and responsibilities, and spending the evening being charming when she would rather have gone upstairs to plot was one of the latter.

Making Tristan Carroway fall in love with her was risky for more than one reason, but it was a lesson he badly needed to learn. He'd toyed with one heart too many, and she would make certain he never did it again. Ever.

Chapter 2

❧

Fair is foul, and foul is fair
— *Macbeth*, Act I, Scene i

Tristan Carroway, Viscount Dare, looked up from the London *Times* as the brass knocker banged against his front door. The price of barley was falling again, just two months short of when Dare's summer crop would be ripe.

He sighed. The losses would probably wipe out the profit he'd managed to wring from the late-spring harvest. It was time for another meeting with his solicitor, Beacham, about selling to the American market.

The knocker sounded again. "Dawkins, the door," Tristan called, taking a swallow of hot, strong coffee. At least one good thing had come out of the Colonies. And with the prices he paid for their coffee and tobacco, they should be able to afford his damned barley.

As the rapping sounded once more, he folded the paper and stood. Dawkins's eccentricities were amusing, but the butler had best be polishing the silver somewhere and not sleeping in one of the sitting rooms, as the old fellow had an alarming tendency to do. As for the rest of the servants, they no doubt had their hands full with his entire family in residence. Either that, or they'd all fled without bothering to give notice.

With the way his luck had been running lately, a herd of solicitors and dunners probably waited at the door to take him into custody for unpaid bills. "Yes?" he said, pulling it open. "What —"

"Good morning, Lord Dare." Lady Georgiana Halley curtsied, the skirt of her dark green morning dress flowing around her and a matching bonnet framing her sun golden hair.

Tristan snapped his jaw shut. Ordinarily, a woman so lovely standing on his doorstep would be a good thing. There was nothing the least bit ordinary, however, about Georgiana Halley. "What the devil are you doing here?" he asked, noting that her maid waited a few steps behind her. "You're not armed, are you?"

"Only with my wits," she returned.

He'd been wounded by her wits on more than one occasion. "And I repeat, why are you here?"

"Because I wish to call on your aunts. Please stand aside." Gathering her skirt, she brushed past him into the foyer.

Her skin smelled of lavender. "Won't you come in?" he asked belatedly.

"You're a very poor butler, you know," she said over her shoulder. "Show me to your aunts, if you please."

Folding his arms across his chest, Tristan leaned against the doorframe. "Since I'm a poor butler, I suggest you go find them yourself."

In truth, he blazed with curiosity to discover why she had chosen to call at Carroway House. She'd known its location for years, yet today was the first time she'd deigned to darken his doorstep.

"Has anyone ever told you that you're unbearably rude?" she returned, facing him again.

"Why, yes. You have on several occasions, as I recall. If you care to apologize for that, however, I'll be happy to escort you wherever you wish to go."

A flush crept up her cheeks, coloring her delicate, ivory skin. "I will never apologize to you," she snapped. "And you may go straight to Hades."

He hadn't expected her to apologize, yet he couldn't help suggesting it every so often. "Very well. Upstairs, first door on the left. I'll be in Hades, if you should require my services." Turning on his heel, Tristan exited the hallway for the breakfast room and his newspaper.

As her footfalls receded up the stairs, he could hear her cursing him under her breath. He allowed himself a small smile as he sat back, the paper unopened before him. Georgiana Halley had come across Mayfair to call on his aunts, though she'd seen them at her own home less than a fortnight earlier, just before Aunt Milly's latest attack of gout.

"What the devil is she up to?" he murmured.

Given their past, he didn't trust her as far as he could throw her. Tristan stood again, leaving the remains of his breakfast on the table in case one of his servants should decide to make an appearance and clear it away. Damnation, where was everyone this morning?

"Aunt Milly?" he called, topping the stairs and angling to the left. When he'd invited his aunts to live with him three years before, he'd given up the domain of the morning room, and they and every imaginable foot of bombazine and lace had taken full advantage of that fact. "Aunt Edwina?" He pushed into the bright, frilly room. "Why, I hadn't realized you had a visitor this morning. And who might this charming young lady be?"

"Oh, shut up." Georgiana sniffed, and turned her back on him.

Millicent Carroway, garbed in a frighteningly bright-colored version of an Oriental kimono that clashed with every other hue in the room, poked her walking cane in his direction. "You know very well who's come to visit us. Why didn't you tell me she'd sent her regards last night, you evil boy?"

Tristan dodged the cane and swept in to kiss his aunt on her round, pale cheek. "Because you were asleep when I returned, and you informed Dawkins that I shouldn't disturb you this morning, my bright butterfly."

Bubbling laughter issued from her ample chest. "So I did. Fetch me a biscuit, Edwina dear."

The angular shadow in the near corner rustled into motion. "Of course, sister. And you, Georgiana, have you taken breakfast yet?"

"I have, Miss Edwina," Georgie replied, with such warmth in her honeyed voice that Tristan was startled. He and she and warmth didn't often appear together. "And please, stay where you are. I'll see to Miss Milly."

"You are a treasure, Georgiana. I've often said so to your Aunt Frederica."

"You're too kind, Miss Edwina. If I were truly a treasure, I would have come to call on you before now, instead of making you travel across Mayfair to see Aunt Frederica and me." Georgiana rose, treading hard on Tristan's toe as she strolled to the tea tray for the plate of biscuits. "How do you take your tea, Miss Milly? Miss Edwina?"

"Oh, do dispense with the miss this and miss that, if you please. I don't need to be reminded that I'm an ancient spinster." Milly chuckled again. "And poor Edwina is even more ancient."

"Nonsense," Tristan interrupted with a smile, refraining from leaning down to rub his foot. Apparently Georgiana had taken to wearing iron-heeled walking shoes, for she couldn't weigh more than eight stone, if that. She was tall but slender, with the rounded hips and pert breasts he was so partial to on a young lady. On her, in particular — which was what had gotten him into trouble with her in the first place. "You are both as young and as lovely as springtime."

"Lord Dare," Georgiana began, sounding pleasant and polite as she distributed tea and biscuits, though she offered none to him, "I was under the impression that you had little wish to join us this morning."

So she wanted to be rid of him. All the more reason for him to stay, though he had no intention of allowing her to think he was the least bit interested in whatever she might be gossiping about. "I was looking for Bit and Bradshaw," he improvised. "They're to accompany me to Tattersall's this morning."

"I thought I heard them in the ballroom earlier," Edwina said. In her ever-present black clothes and seated in the one corner of the room the morning sun didn't reach, she looked like one of Shakespeare's infamous shades with spectacles. "For some reason all of the footmen were in there, as well."

"Hm. I hope Bradshaw's not trying to blow something up again. If you'll excuse me, ladies?"

As she returned to her seat Georgiana tried to step on him again, but he was ready this time and backed out the door before she could connect. He had every intention of finding out why she wanted to chat with the aunties, but he would have a

27

better chance of doing that later, after she'd gone. At the moment, he needed to inform his brothers that they would be accompanying him to the horse market.

From the landing leading to the third floor, where the ballroom and the music room were located, the sound of applause reached his ears. That explained where the servants were, but didn't alleviate his anxiety about what Bradshaw might be up to. He shoved the ballroom's double doors open without ceremony — and nearly received an arrow through his skull.

"Damnation!" he bellowed, ducking reflexively.

"Jesus! Dare, are you all right?" Dropping a crossbow, Second Lieutenant Bradshaw Carroway of His Majesty's Royal Navy strode across the wide, empty floor, shoving aside servants, and grabbed Tristan by the shoulder.

Tristan threw him off. "Obviously," he snarled, "when I said no lit gunpowder in the house, I neglected to explain that I also meant no deadly weapons in the ballroom." He jabbed a finger in the direction of the still figure sitting in one of the deep windowsills. "And you'd best not be laughing."

"I'm not."

"Good." Movement caught his attention as the servants began fleeing out the other entries. "Dawkins!"

The butler skidded to a halt. "Yes, my lord?"

"Mind the front door. We have a guest, with the aunties."

He bowed. "Yes, my lord."

"Who's here?" Bradshaw asked, yanking the arrow out of the doorframe and inspecting the tip.

"No one. Put your new toy somewhere the Runt won't find it and come along. We're going to Tattersall's."

"Are you going to buy me a pony?"

"No, I'm going to buy Edward a pony."

"You can't afford a pony."

"One must keep up appearances." He faced the depths of the ballroom again. "You coming, Bit?"

To no one's surprise, the black-haired figure shook his head. "I've some correspondence with Maguire."

"At least go for a walk with Andrew this afternoon."

"Probably not."

"Or a ride."

"Maybe."

Tristan frowned as he padded downstairs beside Shaw. "How is he?"

His brother shrugged. "You're closer to him than I am. If he won't talk to you, where do you think that leaves me?"

"I keep hoping it's something I've done, and that he's chatty with everyone else."

· Shaw shook his head. "He's a Sphinx to everyone, as far as I know. I do think he smiled when I almost impaled you, if that helps."

"That's something, I suppose."

Concerned as he was about the middle Carroway brother's continuing reticence, the presence of Georgiana Halley in his house was nearly as troubling. Something was going on, and he had the distinct feeling that the sooner he discovered what it was, the better it would be for him.

At the moment, though, he needed to go purchase a pony for his youngest brother, with money he didn't have to spare. But if his family had one proud tradition, it was their skill with horses, and he'd already put the Runt off longer than he wanted.

"So who's with the aunties?" Shaw asked again.

He stifled a sigh. They would all find out, anyway. "Georgiana Halley."

"Geor . . . Oh. Why?"

"I have no idea. But if she intends on burning the house to the ground, I'd rather

30

be elsewhere." An exaggeration, but the less discussion concerning Georgiana and himself, the better.

Though she had long made a point of staying as far away from most of the Carroways as she could manage, Georgiana had always had a liking for Milly and Edwina. "So, with Greydon married," she explained, "my aunt has no real need for a companion. She and her daughter-in-law Emma are getting on splendidly, and I don't want to be in the way."

"You don't mean to return to Shropshire, though, do you, dear? Not during the Season."

"Oh, no. My parents still have three other daughters waiting for their debuts. They hardly want me dragging back there to set a poor example. Even Helen is one female too many, and she's married."

Edwina patted her arm. "You are not a poor example, Georgiana. Milly and I never married, and we have never suffered from the lack of a husband."

"Not that we ever lacked beaux, of course," Milly broke in. "Just never found the right ones. I don't miss marriage one bit. Though I admit that with this bad foot, I do miss dancing."

"That's why I'm here, really." Georgiana sat forward, taking a deep breath. This was it; the first move on the chessboard to begin the game. "I thought you might like having someone here to help you get about, and I would like to feel at least a little useful, so I —"

"Oh, yes!" Edwina interrupted. "Another female in the house would be splendid! With all the Carroway boys in London until Midsummer's Eve, believe you me, it would be a relief to have someone civilized to chat with."

Georgiana smiled, taking Milly's hand. "So, Milly, what do you say?"

"I'm sure you have better things to do than follow an old, gouty spinster about."

"Nonsense. I would make it my task to see you dancing again," Georgiana answered firmly. "And it would be my pleasure."

"Oh, say yes, Milly. We'll have such fun!"

Milly Carroway smiled, color touching her pale cheeks. "Then I say yes."

Georgiana clapped her hands together, hiding her relief in enthusiasm. "Splendid!"

Edwina stood. "I'll have Dawkins prepare a room for you. I'm afraid with all the brothers in town, the west rooms are occupied. Do you mind the morning sun?"

"Not at all. I rise early." Not that she would do much sleeping, knowing that devil Tristan Carroway was under the same roof. She was insane, to do this. Yet if she didn't do this, who would?

While her sister bustled from the room, Milly remained in her well-cushioned chair amidst an imposing pile of overstuffed pillows, one foot bandaged and resting on an equally well padded stool. "I'm so pleased you're coming to stay with us," she said, sipping her tea. Dark eyes regarded Georgiana over the porcelain rim. "But I was under the distinct impression that you and Tristan didn't get on well. Are you certain you wish to do this?"

"Your nephew and I have had our differences, yes," Georgiana admitted, choosing her words with great care. Dare would no doubt be after his aunts for information about her visit later, and she needed to begin spinning the threads of her trap. "That is no reason, though, for me to avoid spending time with you and Edwina."

"If you're certain then, my dear."

"Yes, I'm certain. You've given me a purpose again. I hate feeling useless."

"Do I need to write your aunt to ask her permission for your change of address?"

Georgiana drew a quick breath. "Oh, of course not. I am four-and-twenty, Milly. And she'll be pleased to know I'll be here with you and Edwina." With a last smile, she stood. "In fact, I need to tell her, and to take care of a few things this morning. Do you wish me here this evening?"

Milly chuckled. "I still wonder if you have any idea what you're getting yourself into, but yes, this evening will be lovely. I'll inform Mrs. Goodwin to lay another place at table."

"Thank you."

Georgiana collected her maid and made her way back to her aunt's coach.

Milly Carroway hobbled to the window to watch the dowager duchess's carriage depart.

"Sit down, Millicent!" Edwina exclaimed, as she slipped back into the room. "You'll ruin everything."

"Don't worry, Winna. Georgie's gone to get her things, and Tristan's at Tattersall's."

"I can't believe it was so simple."

Resuming her seat in the cushioned chair, Milly couldn't help smiling at the pleased, eager look on her sister's face, despite her own reservations. "Well, she's saved us the trouble of going to Frederica and asking to borrow her for the Season, but try not to get your hopes up."

"Oh, nonsense. That fight Georgie and Tristan had was six years ago. Would you rather he settled for one of those simpering debutantes? Those two are a perfect match."

"Yes, like a flame and gunpowder."

"Ha. You'll see, Milly. You'll see."

"That's what I'm afraid of."

That had gone so smoothly, Georgiana could scarcely believe she'd actually done it. She'd barely suggested that she'd move in; then they'd done the rest for her. As she returned to Hawthorne House, however, reality began to seep back in.

She'd agreed to become a resident for an indefinite stay at Carroway House, where she'd see Tristan every day. And she'd put into motion a plan that she wasn't entirely certain she would have the courage to see through to its end. A plan to put Dare in his place and to teach him the consequences of breaking hearts.

"Well, no one deserves it more than he does," she muttered.

Her maid, seated on the opposite side of the coach, blinked. "My lady?"

"Nothing, Mary. Just thinking aloud. You don't mind a change of residence for a while, do you?"

"No, my lady. It'll be an adventure."

Getting her maid to acquiesce to her plan was one thing; however, convincing her aunt would be another entirely.

"Georgiana, you've gone mad." Frederica Brakenridge, the Dowager Duchess of Wycliffe, set down her cup of tea so hard the steaming liquid sloshed over the rim.

"I thought you were fond of Milly and Edwina Carroway," Georgiana protested, trying to maintain her expression of innocent surprise.

"I am. I thought you were distinctly *not* fond of Lord Dare. For six years you've been complaining about how he stole that kiss from you to win a wager, or some such nonsense."

It took all of the control Georgiana had not to blush. "That seems rather trivial after all this time, don't you think?" she said lightly. "And besides, you have no need of me, and my parents have even less need of me. Miss Milly could use a companion."

Aunt Frederica sighed. "Whether I need you or not, Georgiana, I enjoy your company. I'd hoped to lose your companion-

36

ship to marriage; with your income, there's no reason for you to go from one old lady to the next until you're infirm enough to need a companion yourself."

There was a powerful reason for that — but it was not one she intended to disclose to anyone. Ever. "I don't wish to marry, and I can't very well join the army or the priesthood. Leisure doesn't sit well with me. Being a companion to a friend seems the most tolerable occupation — at least until I'm of an age where Society will accept that I truly have no desire to marry and intend to devote my time and money to charitable works."

"Well, you seem to have it all planned. Who am I to interfere?" Frederica asked, with a wave of her fingers. "Go, then, and give my best to Milly and Edwina."

"Thank you, Aunt Frederica."

To her surprise, her aunt grabbed her hand and squeezed it. "You know you're welcome here whenever you wish to return. Please remember that."

Georgiana stood and kissed her aunt on the cheek. "I will. Thank you."

She still needed to speak with Amelia Johns at the Ibbottson ball on Thursday. But in the meantime, she had a plan to put into motion.

Chapter 3

Oh, God! What mischiefs work the wicked ones,
Heaping confusion on their own heads thereby.
— *Henry VI*, Part II, Act II, Scene i

As Tristan went downstairs for dinner, the house seemed uncommonly quiet. True, his family was gathered in the dining room to eat, but the silence didn't seem to be the usual chaos-removed calm. Rather, it almost felt as if Carroway House was holding its breath.

Or more likely, he decided as he straightened his coat and pushed open the dining room door, Lady Georgiana Halley's visit had set his perceptions out of kilter. He stepped inside the room — and stopped.

She sat there, at his table, chuckling at something Bradshaw had said. The surprise must have shown on his face, because Georgiana lifted an eyebrow as she met his gaze.

"Good evening, my lord," she said, her

smile unaltered, though her green eyes cooled.

He doubted anyone but he had even noticed the change. Tristan snapped his jaw closed. "Lady Georgiana."

"You're late for dinner," his youngest brother, Edward, piped up. "And Georgie says that's rude."

The Runt had never met the chit before today, yet they were already on a first-name basis. Tristan took his seat at the head of the table, noting that some idiot had placed Georgiana just to his right. "So is staying for dinner without being invited."

"She *was* invited," Milly stated.

As she spoke, he realized that both his aunts were present for the first time in days. Cursing Georgiana under his breath for taking his attention away from his family, he stood again. "Aunt Milly. Welcome back to the chaos." He rounded the table to kiss her on the cheek. "But you should have called for me. I would have been happy to carry you in here."

Blushing, his aunt flipped a hand at him. "Oh, nonsense. Georgiana came back with that wheeled contraption over there, so she and Dawkins just rolled me into the dining room. It was quite fun."

He straightened, returning his gaze to Georgiana. " 'Came *back*'?" he repeated.

"Yes," she said sweetly. "I'm moving in."

His mouth started to fall open again, and he clenched his jaw against it. "No, you're not."

"I am."

"You're n—"

"She is," Edwina interrupted. "She's come to help Milly, so be quiet and sit down, Tristan Michael Carroway."

Ignoring the snickers from his younger brethren, Tristan slid his gaze back to Georgiana. The minx smiled at him again.

Evidently, the evil that he'd done in his life was so excessive that his eternal punishment was getting started early. Eternity simply wasn't long enough in his case. Pasting an uncaring smile on his face, he dropped into his chair again. "I see. If you think she can truly be of assistance to you, Aunt Milly, then I have no objection."

Georgiana scowled. "You have no objection? No one asked —"

"I would like to point out, though, Lady Georgiana," he continued, "that you have decided to stay in a household with five single gentlemen, three of them adults."

"Four," Andrew broke in, coloring. "I'm seventeen. That's older than Romeo was when he married Juliet."

"And it's younger than I am, which is what counts," Tristan countered, sending his brother a stern look. The lack of discipline usually didn't bother him, but damn it all. Georgiana didn't need any more ammunition to use against him. She'd already collected bucketfuls.

"Don't worry over my reputation, Lord Dare," Georgiana said, though he noted that she avoided his gaze. "The presence of your aunts provides me with all the respectability I require."

For some damned reason, she was determined to stay. He'd figure out why later, when he didn't have a half dozen people hanging on every word he and Georgiana exchanged. "Then stay." He sent her a dark look. "But don't say I didn't warn you."

Though he was far from immune to Georgiana's considerable charms, he had developed the talent of appearing to be unmoved. Bradshaw, two years younger and with a reputation vying for the blackness of his own, wasn't nearly as skilled. On the other side of the spectrum, Robert, twenty-six, might have been dining alone for all the response he made. Andrew simply drooled, while Edward suddenly seemed

41

fascinated with learning table manners.

Tristan made it through dinner without suffering an apoplexy, then escaped to the billiards room to smoke and curse. Anything between himself and Georgiana was finished; she'd made that abundantly and repeatedly clear. Whatever in damnation was going on, he didn't like it. And he liked even less that he was going to have to go to Georgiana to get his answers — unless he could pry them from Milly and Edwina, who had no doubt succumbed to the chit's charms as well, and had no idea what she might be up to.

"She's gone up to bed."

Tristan jumped. Bit leaned against the doorframe, arms crossed over his chest, and Tristan scowled at him, wondering for a brief moment how long his brother had been there. "What? Robert the Sphinx has decided to speak, unasked? Is it a miracle, or are you trying to make trouble?"

"I just thought you should know, in case you were tired of hiding. Good night." Robert pushed upright and vanished back into the hallway.

"I am *not* hiding."

He simply had rules for himself where Lady Georgiana Halley was concerned. If she attacked, he would respond in kind; if she insinuated herself into a group of which he was already a part, he would not object. And she could break her damned fans across his knuckles whenever she pleased, because it was his private opinion that for some reason she continued to want to touch him. The contact rarely elicited more than a wince, and it gave him the opportunity to purchase replacements for her, which, of course, annoyed her even more.

But this insistence of hers on living under his roof was different. There were no pages in this rule book, and he bloody well needed to make some before anything happened.

Tristan resignedly snuffed out his cheroot and headed upstairs.

Georgiana sat before the fire in her bedchamber, an unopened book on her lap. She hadn't slept at all last night; contemplating her plan had kept her up and pacing until dawn. Tonight, though, was even worse. *He* was in this same house, perhaps only a floor away, perhaps only a hallway away.

A quiet knock sounded at her door, and she nearly leapt out of the chair. "Calm down, for heaven's sake," she muttered to herself. She'd asked Dawkins the butler for a glass of warm milk; it wasn't as though Dare would come calling at her private rooms in broad daylight, much less at this hour of the night. "Come in."

The door opened, and Dare strolled into her bedchamber. "Comfortable?" he drawled, stopping before the fireplace.

"What — Get out!"

"I left your door open," he said in a low tone, "so keep your voice down unless you want an audience."

Georgiana took a deep breath. He was right; if she succumbed to her sudden panic at being in a room alone with him, she would both ensure her own ruin and destroy any chance of teaching him the lesson he so desperately needed to learn. "Fine, I'll say it more quietly, then: *Get out.*"

"First tell me what the devil you're up to, Georgiana."

She'd never been a very good liar, and Dare was far from being a fool. "I don't know why you think I'm 'up to' anything," she retorted. "My circumstances have changed over the past year, and —"

"So you're here out of the goodness of your heart, to care for the aunties," he said, resting one arm along the mantel.

"Yes." She wished he didn't look so much at ease in her bedchamber, and so full of sin at every blasted minute. "What else would you suggest I do, under the circumstances?"

He shrugged. "Get married. Go torture your husband, and leave me out of it."

Georgiana set her book aside and rose. She didn't want to press that particular topic; she would, in fact, have preferred that he'd never mentioned it. If she didn't address it, however, he would never believe any kind word she said to him now or in the future, let alone fall in love with her. "Marriage, Lord Dare, is not an option for me, now is it?"

For a long moment he looked at her, his expression dark and unreadable. "To be blunt, Georgiana, the state of your virginity would be less important to most men than the size of your income. I could name a hundred men who would marry you in a second, given the chance."

"I hardly need — or want — a man who desires only my money," she said hotly. "Besides, I have made an agreement with your aunts. *I* do not break my word."

Dare pushed upright from his lazy slouch. He seemed taller than she remembered, and before she could stop herself, she took a step backward. A muscle in his lean cheek twitched, and he turned for the door.

"Get me the invoice for that rolling chair," he said over his shoulder, "and I'll reimburse you for it."

"No need," she returned, trying to regain her composure. "It's a gift."

"I don't take charity. Give me the invoice tomorrow."

She stifled an irritated sigh. "Very well."

After the door closed, she stayed where she was for a long while. The night he had taken her virginity, as he put it, she had thought herself in love. To discover the next day that he'd done it to win a wager — one of her stockings, yet — had hurt more than she thought possible.

Whatever his reasons for not boasting of his victory to the *ton*, she had never forgiven him. So now she would teach him exactly how much it hurt to be betrayed. Then, perhaps, he would understand what it meant to be honorable, and he could make a decent husband to a poor, naive girl like Amelia.

With that in mind, she climbed into bed and tried to fall asleep. Amelia Johns needed to be let in on the game, or she herself would be as guilty of heartlessness as Tristan Carroway was. Perhaps she should do so at once; waiting until the Ibbottson ball would only give Dare an additional three days to ruin Miss Johns's life.

Miss Amelia Johns seemed surprised to see Georgiana when she called at Johns House the next morning. Her brunette hair in a fetching bun with strategic curls escaping to caress her neck and cheeks, and garbed in a muslin day dress the color of sunshine, she looked the portrait of fairy-tale innocence. "Lady Georgiana," she said, curtsying, her arms full of flowers.

"Miss Johns, thank you for seeing me this morning. I can see that you're busy; please don't let me keep you from your task."

"Oh, thank you," the girl replied, smiling, as she set down her burden beside the nearest vase. "These roses are Mama's favorite. I would hate for them to wilt."

"They're lovely." The girl hadn't asked her to sit, but Georgiana didn't want to appear impatient, so she slowly took a seat on a couch halfway across the wide morning room.

Amelia stood over the vase, her alabaster brow furrowed as she tilted the yellow blooms this way and that, searching for the perfect angle. Good heavens, the girl didn't stand a chance against Dare.

"May I offer you some tea, Lady Georgiana?"

"No, but thank you. Actually, I wanted to discuss something with you. Something of a . . . personal nature." She glanced at the maid fluffing pillows of the overstuffed furniture.

"A personal nature?" Amelia giggled engagingly. "My goodness, that sounds so intriguing. Hannah, that will be all for now."

"Yes, miss."

Once the maid was gone, Georgiana relocated to a chair closer to Amelia. "I know this will seem highly unusual, but I do have a reason for asking," she said.

Amelia paused in her flower arranging. "What is it?"

"You and Lord Dare. There is a connection between you, is there not?"

Large blue eyes filled with tears. "Oh, I don't know!" Miss Johns wailed.

Georgiana hurried to her feet and put an arm around the younger girl's shoulders. "There, there," she said, in her most soothing voice. "This is what I was afraid of."

"A . . . afraid of?"

"Oh, yes. Lord Dare is famously difficult."

"Yes, he is. Sometimes I think he means to propose to me, and then he'll twist the conversation around until I don't know whether he even likes me or not."

"You do expect a proposal, though?"

"He keeps saying that he needs to marry, and he dances with me more than any of the other girls, and he took me on a drive through Hyde Park. Of course I expect him to propose. My entire family expects it." She sounded almost indignant that Georgiana might have any doubt regarding Dare's intentions.

"Yes, I should think that's quite reasonable." Georgiana stifled a scowl. He'd done the same with her, six years earlier, and she'd expected the same thing. All she'd received, though, was ruin, a stolen stocking, and a broken heart. "And in that case, I have something to confide in you."

Amelia wiped at her eyes with a pretty embroidered handkerchief that matched her dress. "You do?"

"Yes. Lord Dare, as you may know, is the dearest friend of my cousin, the Duke of Wycliffe. Because of that, I have had numerous opportunities over the years to observe the viscount's behavior toward females. I must say that without exception

I have always found it appalling."

"Exceedingly appalling."

So far so good. "And so, I have decided that Lord Dare needs to be taught a lesson about how to comport himself toward the gentler sex."

Puzzlement showed on Amelia's innocent face. "A lesson? I don't understand."

"Well, I happen to be staying at Carroway House for a short time, to help Lord Dare's aunt recuperate from the gout. I plan to take this opportunity to demonstrate to Dare just how poor his behavior toward you has been. It may look a bit strange. It may even appear for a short time that Dare is fond of me, but I assure you that my only purpose is to teach him a lesson which in the end will both encourage him to propose to you and will make him a better husband."

It sounded logical — to her, anyway. She watched Amelia's transparent expression to see whether the girl thought so, as well.

"You would do that for me? We don't even know one another."

"We are both females, and we're both appalled at Dare's behavior. And it would give me immense satisfaction to see that at least one man has learned how properly to treat a lady."

"Well, Lady Georgiana," Amelia said slowly, going back to fiddling with the bright roses, "I think if you could teach Tristan a lesson that would convince him to marry me, that would be a very good thing." She paused, a small frown furrowing her brow. "Because we are being honest with one another, I have to admit that he confuses me very often."

"Yes, he excels at that."

"You know him better than I, and you are closer to his age, so I suppose you must be wiser, as well. So I am glad if you can teach him this lesson. The sooner the better, because I have my heart set on becoming his viscountess."

Ignoring the insult to her advanced age, Georgiana smiled. "Then we have an agreement. As I said, at first things may seem a bit strange, but be patient. Everything will work itself out in the end."

Georgiana hummed as she and her maid climbed back into her hired carriage and returned to Carroway House. Dare wouldn't know what had hit him until it was far too late. Once she was finished with him he would never even *think* of lying to vulnerable young ladies about his feelings, or of stealing stockings from them while they slept. After this, he would be glad to take

Amelia Johns for a wife and never even think of looking elsewhere.

"So, Beacham, tell me your news."

The solicitor looked ill at ease as he took a seat opposite Tristan at the office desk, but Dare didn't consider that a bad sign. He had never seen Beacham when the fellow *didn't* look nervous.

"I have done as you requested, my lord," Beacham said, thumbing through a stack of papers until he found the one he wanted. "At last report, in the Americas barley was selling for seven shillings more per hundred pounds than it does here."

Tristan did some quick figuring. "That's 140 shillings per ton, with shipping costs at what, a hundred shillings per ton? I hardly think it's worth the time or the effort for an overall profit of twelve pounds, Beacham."

The solicitor grimaced. "That's not the precise fig—"

"Beacham, we're moving on now."

"Ah. Yes, my lord. To where are we moving, my lord?"

"To wool."

Beacham removed his spectacles, wiping the lenses with a handkerchief. Spectacle removal was frequently a good sign. "Except for Cotswold sheep, the wool market is quite sluggish."

"I breed Cotswold sheep."

The spectacles returned to the bridge of his nose. "Yes, I know that, my lord."

"We all know that. Get on with it. My entire summer yield to the Americas, less expenses."

The spectacles didn't come off this time, and Tristan reflected that he'd spent far too much time wagering, looking for his opponents' weaknesses and give-away signs. On the other hand, over the past year he'd made more money for the estate through wagering than by regular means.

"I would anticipate a profit of approximately 132 pounds."

"Approximately."

"Yes, my lord."

Tristan let out his breath, then caught it again as a feminine figure in yellow-and-rose muslin crossed in front of the open office door. "Good. Let's proceed, then."

"Ah, it *is* still a risk, my lord, once time and distance are figured into the equation."

With a brief smile, Tristan pushed to his feet. "I like risk. And yes, I know it's not enough to make any difference at all in my situation. It will look as though I'm making

53

money, though, which is at least as important."

The solicitor nodded. "If I may be blunt, my lord, I could wish your father had had as keen an understanding of income."

They both knew that his father had spent where he should have saved yet had pinched pence on small, insignificant items, which had served only to alert and alarm both his creditors and his peers. The result had been an unmitigated disaster.

"And I appreciate your being the only solicitor in Dare's employ not to spread rumors." Tristan headed for the door. "Which is why you're still in my employ. Prepare the correspondence, if you please."

"Yes, my lord."

Tristan caught up with Georgiana at the music room door. "And where did you go, this morning?" he asked.

She jumped, guilt obvious on her pretty face. "None of your business, Dare. Go away."

"It's my house." Her reaction intrigued him, and he changed what he'd been about to say. "I have a coach and a curricle. Both are at your disposal. You don't need to hire hacks."

"Don't spy on me. And I do as I want." Georgiana hesitated, as though she wanted to go into the music room yet didn't want him following her in there. "I am assisting your aunts as a friend. I am not in your employ, and who, where, when, or how I go anywhere is up to me. Not you, my lord."

"Except in my home," he pointed out. "What do you want with the music room? My aunts aren't in there."

"Yes, we are," Milly's voice came. "Behave yourself."

To his surprise, Georgiana took a step closer. "Disappointed, Dare?" she breathed. "Did you anticipate being able to torment me longer?"

He knew how to play this game. "Any 'anticipation' where you're concerned, Georgiana, had already been satisfied in my case, hasn't it?" Tristan reached out to finger one of the soft golden curls framing her face.

"Then I'll give you something else to anticipate," she said, her jaw clenched. He barely had time to note that she carried a fan before it cracked across his knuckles.

"Damnation! You little minx," he grunted, snatching his hand back as the broken ivory and paper fluttered to the floor. "You can't go about hitting gentlemen."

"I have never hit a gentleman," she

sniffed, and disappeared into the music room.

Tristan stalked back downstairs, refusing to rub his smarting fingers. Now he would have to cut short his luncheon at White's to go purchase her another blasted fan. He gave a grim smile. Slender as his purse was, buying fans for Georgie was one thing he refused to give up. Nothing annoyed her quite so much as his gifts.

Tristan looked at the herd of young, single ladies gathered at one side of the Ibbottson ballroom. The not-quite-so-young part of the herd stood closer to the refreshment table, as though nearness to food would render them more enticing to the circling pack of male wolves. He had yet to see Georgiana stand anywhere near that meat market, unless she happened to be conversing with some poor unfortunate who'd joined it.

What he would never be able to imagine even in his wildest dreams was the Marquis of Harkley's golden-haired daughter reconciled to the hopeless spinster section. The idea that she might be forced there because of his actions six years ago was ridiculous. Georgiana was intelligent, well educated, witty, tall, and beautiful. She was also fabulously wealthy, which in and of itself was enough to entice most suitors.

Hell, if he'd known at the time in what poor condition his father would be leaving the Dare properties and title, he might have — would have — made a more serious play for her affections. If she hadn't discovered the idiotic wager and convinced herself that was the sole reason he'd been in pursuit, they might have found their present circumstances vastly altered.

"Isn't that your Amelia?" Aunt Edwina said from beside him.

"She isn't *my* anything. Let's please make that clear." All he needed was another misunderstanding coming between him and a potential spouse. With his money woes, he was on the verge of becoming unmarriageable himself. In fact, he was more likely to end up beside the punch bowl and the sweetmeats than Georgiana was.

"So you've settled on a different one?" His aunt wrapped her fingers around his arm and perched up on tiptoe. "Which one?"

"For God's sake, Auntie, none of them. Stop being such a matchmaker." She looked downcast and he sighed. "It'll probably be Amelia. I would like a chance to browse the entire fruit bowl before I select my peach, though."

She chuckled. "You are becoming reconciled to marriage."

"However can you tell?"

"Last month, marriage was apothecary shops and poison. Now it's fruit bowls and peaches."

"Yes, but peaches have pits."

A wheeled chair rolled onto his toe and stopped there. "What has pits, dear?" Milly asked.

Milly Carroway was a substantial woman, and her weight combined with that of the chair was enough to make him see spots. The chair's driver smiled at him, her eyes alight with green devilment. Keeping his gaze steady on hers, he wrapped his fingers around her hand and the back of the chair, and pushed.

She flinched as though he'd struck her, but the wheel rolled back off his toe, and he could breathe again. He would have supposed her treading on his feet was better than being attacked with fans, but that didn't take into account large aunts and large wheeled chairs.

"Peaches do," he said.

"And what does that have to do with anything?"

"He's going to marry a peach," Edwina offered. "He's just afraid of pits."

"I am *not* afraid of pits," he retorted. "It's just a matter of wisdom."

"So a woman is a piece of fruit?" Georgiana broke in. "What does that make you, Lord Dare?"

He lifted an eyebrow. "Let's leave that question rhetorical, shall we?" he drawled.

"Where's the fun in that?"

Georgiana was in high spirits. On any other occasion he would have enjoyed the exchange, but since he intended on spending the evening convincing himself that he could tolerate the peach known as Amelia Johns, he didn't want to expend the energy necessary to keep up with his tormentor.

"Why don't we continue the amusement later?" he suggested, patting Aunt Milly on the shoulder. "If you'll excuse me, ladies?"

Tristan made his way toward the herd of waiting females. Several heiresses were among them, ready and willing to trade their dowries in order to bring a title into the family. Amelia Johns seemed the least offensive of the lot, though they all shared a simpering mediocrity.

"My lord."

He stopped short at the sound of the female voice behind him. "Lady Georgiana," he said, facing her.

"I, ah, recall from several years ago that there was one thing you did quite well," she said quietly, a blush touching her smooth cheeks.

She couldn't be discussing what he thought she was discussing. "Beg pardon?" he asked, which seemed safer than risking his knuckles again.

"Your waltz," she said, her voice clipped and abrupt, and her color deepening. "I recall that you waltz well."

Tristan tilted his head at her, trying to read her expression. "Are you suggesting that I ask you to dance?"

"For your aunts' sake, I think we should at least appear to be friends."

This was unexpected, but for the moment he was willing to play along. "At the risk of being turned down then, Lady Georgiana, will you waltz with me?"

"I will, my lord."

As he held out his hand, he noted that her fingers shook. "Would you prefer to wait for a quadrille? We'll look just as friendly."

"Of course not. I am not afraid of you."

With that she gripped his fingers and allowed him to lead her onto the dance floor.

Tristan hesitated as he faced her, taking her hand more firmly in his and sliding his arm with slow care around her waist. She shivered again, but lifted her free hand to his shoulder.

"If you're not afraid," he murmured, swaying her into the dance, "then why do you tremble?"

"Because I don't like you, remember?"

"You haven't allowed me to forget."

For a moment she met his gaze, then looked down at his cravat again. Across the room he caught sight of her cousin, the Duke of Wycliffe, looking at the two of them in obvious amazement, but he had no answer except to shrug.

"I think Wyciffe may faint," he offered, to have something to say to her.

"I said we should dance to reassure your aunts of our ability to get along," she returned. "That doesn't mean you have to converse with me."

If they couldn't converse, at least he did enjoy dancing with her; she was lithe and graceful, as much a pleasure to waltz with as she had been six years before. That was part of the problem with having her in his house now — he'd never fallen completely out of lust with her. She had been eager and willing and passionate, and he was perversely pleased to have been her first, even with the eternity of torture she seemed determined to inflict upon him because of it.

"If we're being friendly, allow me to recommend that you not close your lips so tightly," he murmured.

"Do not look at my lips," she ordered, glaring at him.

"Shall I look at your eyes, then, or your nose? Your lovely bosom?"

She flushed scarlet, then lifted her chin. "My left ear," she stated.

Tristan chuckled. "Very well. It's a nice ear, I have to admit. And fairly level with the right one. All in all, quite acceptable."

Her lips twitched, though he pretended not to notice. After all, he was gazing at her ear. And though he wasn't looking at the rest of her, he could certainly feel her. Her azure skirt swirled against his legs, the fingers of her hand clenched and unclenched against his, and as he turned her, their hips brushed.

"Don't hold me so closely," she muttered, her fingers tightening in his again.

"Sorry," he said, putting the proper distance between them once more. "Old habit."

"We haven't waltzed for six years, my lord."

"You're difficult to forget."

Emerald ice looked into his eyes again. "Is that supposed to be a compliment?"

Good Lord, he was going to get himself killed. "No. A statement of fact. Since our . . . parting of ways, you have broken seventeen fans on me, and now left me with two crushed toes. That is difficult to forget."

The waltz ended, and she quickly pulled away. "That was friendly enough for one evening," she said, and with a curtsy glided away.

Tristan watched the sway of her hips as she left. Friendly enough or not, she'd managed to make him forget he was to dance the first waltz of the evening with Amelia. Now that silly chit would probably ignore him for the rest of the evening.

He gazed at her until she vanished behind the next set of dancers. Only one crushed toe and a waltz this evening. And if his suspicions were correct, the mayhem had only just begun.

Chapter 4

Noble madam,
Men's evil manners live in brass; their virtues
We write in water
— *Henry VIII*, Act IV, Scene ii

Georgiana's friends pounced on her as soon as she reached the edge of the dance floor.

"So it's true!"

"I heard that —"

"You actually did it, Georgie? I can't believe —"

"Please," Georgiana said, "I need to get some air."

Together, Lucinda and Evelyn practically dragged her over to the nearest window. Pushing it open, she pulled in a deep breath of fresh night air.

"Better?" Evelyn asked.

"Nearly. Give me a moment."

"Take several moments. I need one or two myself, after seeing you waltzing with Dare. He actually *smiled* at you, you know."

"I saw it, too. Is he in love with you yet?"

"Hush," Georgiana cautioned, closing the window again and taking a seat beneath it. "And no, of course not. I'm still laying the trap to catch his attention."

"I almost didn't believe it when Donna Bentley told me you'd moved into Carroway House. You said you'd tell us what you had planned."

Georgiana heard the reproach in Lucinda's voice, but she couldn't do much to remedy it. "I know, but it happened more quickly than I expected," she said.

"No doubt. But what about the rumors?"

"His aunts are dear friends of the duchess," Georgiana countered. "I'm helping Miss Milly while she recovers from the gout."

"It does make perfect sense, when you put it that way," Evie said, looking relieved. "And I haven't heard anything different."

Lucinda sat beside her. "Georgie, are you certain you want to go through with this? I know we made those lists, but now this is very real."

"And besides, everyone knows you hate Lord Dare." And everyone thought it was merely because he had kissed her and then she'd found out that he'd done it to try to win a wager. No one knew differently: not her aunt, not her friends, not the noblemen of the *haut ton* — no one but Tristan Carroway. And she intended to keep it that way.

"Don't you think that's all the more reason for me to teach him a lesson?" she asked.

"I suppose so, but this could be dangerous, Georgiana. He is a viscount, with several large properties. And he also has a certain reputation."

"And I am cousin to the Duke of Wycliffe, and the daughter of the Marquis of Harkley."

Dare had had the opportunity to hurt her reputation six years ago, and he hadn't done it. Revenge after he discovered her present plan, though, was something else entirely. Georgiana shuddered. If Dare had any notion of fair play at all, nothing would happen.

"I have to admit," Evelyn said, taking her hand, "it's exciting, in a way. To know about your plan, when no one else does."

"And no one else *can* know, Evie," Lucinda said, glancing over her shoulder as though she feared they were being overheard even now. "If anyone realizes this is a game, Georgiana could be ruined."

"I would never say anything," Evelyn

protested. "You know that."

Georgiana squeezed back. "I'm not worried about that. You are my dearest friends."

"It's just that subterfuge is so unlike us," Evelyn continued.

She was right about that. Georgiana grinned. "Just don't forget, you two have to do this next."

"I'm waiting to see whether you survive or not," Lucinda said, her dark eyes serious despite her smile. "Just be careful, Georgie."

"I will be."

"Lady Georgiana."

The gentleman who emerged from the salon next door was Dare's polar opposite, thank goodness. She wasn't up for another sparring match yet. "Lord Westbrook," she said, relief making her smile.

The marquis sketched a bow. "Good evening. Miss Barrett, Miss Ruddick, greetings to you both."

"Lord Westbrook."

"I see you've taken on another task for yourself," he said, returning his calm brown gaze to Georgiana. "The Carroways must be grateful for your assistance."

"It's mutual, I assure you."

"Am I being too optimistic in thinking

you might have a space left on your dance card for me?"

She gazed at the handsome, chestnut-haired marquis for a moment. Since Dare was supposed to fall in love with her, she would have to pretend to be somewhat enamored of him, but she liked John Blair, Lord Westbrook. He was more of a gentleman than most of her other suitors — and far more of one than the blackguard Viscount Dare. "I happen to have the next quadrille free," she said.

He smiled. "I'll return for you in a few moments, then. My apologies, ladies, for interrupting your conversation."

"Now that man," Lucinda said, gazing after him as he disappeared into the crowd, "doesn't need any lessons."

"Why is he still unmarried, then, do you think?" Evelyn asked.

Lucinda glanced at Georgiana. "Perhaps he's set his sights on someone in particular, and he's just waiting for her to come around."

"Oh, nonsense," Georgiana said, rising to go find Milly and Edwina.

"Then why are you blushing?"

"I'm not." And besides, Westbrook didn't need her money. So without that enticement he might decide she was markedly less appealing if he were to find out about her indiscretion with Dare. "Come with me and chat with Miss Milly and Miss Edwina. They say they're in dire need of some civilized female conversation."

"Ah, our specialty," Lucinda said, taking her arm.

"Where are you going?"

Georgiana tried not to jump as she settled Milly into the wheeled chair the next morning. Footmen on either side of her panted from the exertion of bringing Milly and the chair down the curving staircase to the main floor. She finished tucking the blanket around her charge's hips and her bad foot, then straightened to face the viscount.

"We're going for a walk in the park," she said, nodding her thanks to the servants and turning the chair toward the door. Dressed in her ever-present black, Edwina accepted a black shawl and parasol from Dawkins and prepared to join them. "And I thought we'd discussed your not spying on me at every moment."

His gaze slipped the length of her to her feet and back again, swift but thorough, as though he couldn't quite quell his all-too-male instincts enough to keep

69

his eyes on her face.

"Here," he said after a moment, digging into his coat pocket and producing a long, thin box. "This is for you."

She knew what it was; he'd been giving them to her for nearly six years. "Are you certain it's wise to keep arming me?" she asked, careful not to touch his fingers as she took the box and opened it. The fan was a soft blue, with a dove appearing on the delicate rice paper as she opened it out. It bothered her that he always knew what she would like.

"At least this way I know what'll be coming at me," he returned, glancing at his aunts and back again. "Speaking of which, wouldn't you rather take the barouche this morning?"

"We wish to exercise ourselves, not your horses."

"We could exercise together."

Georgiana blushed scarlet. With his aunts present she didn't dare hand him the retort he deserved — and he knew it, dash it all. "You might get hurt, in that case," was the best she could muster, scowling as she snapped the fan open and closed.

"I might be willing to risk it." He leaned in the morning room doorway, his light blue eyes amused. "And you may receive more exercise than you intend, anyway, pushing that contraption through Hyde Park."

"Thank you for your concern," she said, "but it's not necessary." She needed to try to be pleasant to him, she reminded herself.

The viscount pushed upright. "I'll go with you. The fact that it's not necessary simply reflects to my credit."

"No, it doesn't —"

Dare's eight-year-old brother, Edward, pounded down the stairs. "If you're going to Hyde Park, so am I. I want to ride my new horse."

A muscle in Dare's cheek twitched. "We'll do that later, Edward. I can't give riding lessons and push Aunt Milly at the same time."

"I'll give riding lessons," Bradshaw interrupted from the landing above.

"I thought you'd joined the navy, not the cavalry."

"Only because I already know everything there is to know about horses."

Dare began to look irritated, and so Georgiana gave him a genuine smile. "The more, the merrier, I always say." She stepped aside, motioning him to the back of the chair.

By the time they made it down the shallow front steps and onto the drive to join Edward, his horse, and Bradshaw, they were a party of eight, including all five of the Carroway brothers. Tristan looked over his shoulder as his brother Andrew hopped down to the drive, Robert following behind him at a slight limp.

"Bradshaw's giving riding lessons," he grumbled, pushing his aunt out to the cobblestoned street, "but why are you lot here?"

"I'm assisting Bradshaw," Andrew said cheerfully, taking up position on the other side of Edward.

"And you, Bit?"

The middle Carroway brother kept his position at the back of the group. "I'm walking."

"Oh, this is so nice," Milly said, clapping her hands together. "The whole family out for a walk together, just like when you were all naughty little boys."

"I'm not naughty," Edward stated from aboard his gray pony. "And neither is Prince George."

"There are some who would disagree with you, Edward," Tristan said with a slight smile, "but I'm sure Prinny appreciates the gesture of confi—"

"Prince George is the name of my horse, Tristan," the youngest Carroway clarified.

"You may want to reconsider that. Perhaps simply 'George.' "

"But —"

"You might call him Tristan," Georgiana suggested, trying not to laugh at the exchange. "Is he a gelding?"

Bradshaw made a choking sound. "Dare's right, Edward. Naming animals after present and future monarchs is generally frowned upon."

"But what shall I call him, then?"

"King?" Andrew suggested.

"Demon?" came from Bradshaw.

"Storm Cloud," Georgiana contributed. "He is gray, after all."

"Oh, yes. And it sounds like an Indian name, from the Colonies. I like Storm Cloud."

"You would," Dare said, under his breath.

Georgiana's spirits improving, she leaned down to tuck Milly's blanket back into place. "Are you comfortable?"

"More than any of you." Milly chuckled. "Heavens, I may just take a nap."

"No, I insist that you enjoy yourself out here," Tristan said, leaning forward to kiss his aunt on the cheek. "The sunlight and fresh air will do you good. Sleep is for lag-gards."

Georgie studied the viscount's profile for a long moment. He did that without thinking, kissing and teasing with his old aunts. She hadn't expected such easy affection from him, hadn't thought he was ever anything but arrogant and cynical and self-absorbed. It didn't make sense. If he had feelings and compassion, he would never have used her as shamefully as he had. The idea that he'd changed, though, was even more absurd than believing he had a heart to begin with.

They must have made quite a sight as they reached Hyde Park: three exceedingly handsome single gentlemen in the company of two younger lads, one of them on pony back, two elderly ladies, and one female companion. All that lacked was a dog that jumped through hoops and an elephant, and they would have been a circus.

"Georgie, do you have a horse?" Edward asked.

"Yes, I do."

"What's his name?"

"*Her* name," she corrected, feeling the more females in this group, the better, "is —"

"Sheba. A grand black Arabian," Dare finished.

"Oh, smashing. Is she in London?"

Georgiana folded her arms and looked at Dare. "Ask your brother. He seems to be carrying on my part of the conversation quite well."

The viscount turned the chair up the path alongside Rotten Row. "Yes, Sheba is in town. She stables at Brakenridge House with the Duke of Wycliffe's beasts — though as long as you're staying here, you might as well move her in, too."

"Yes," Edward said enthusiastically, bouncing up and down in the saddle. "You can go riding, and I'll be your escort."

"And who will be *your* escort, stripling?"

"I don't need an escort. I'm a bruising rider."

Tristan's eyes danced. "Your bottom's going to be bruised if you keep bouncing around like that."

"Here," Bradshaw offered, stepping in, "let me shorten those stirrups. And anytime you wish to go riding, Georgiana, Edward and I will be happy to escort you."

She caught Tristan's scowl, quickly blanketed. "Yes, that would be lovely," he grumbled, "man, woman, and child, all riding together cozy as bedbugs. That won't start any rumors, I'm sure."

"Oh, just tow me along behind the

horses," Milly said, chortling. "I'll lend some respectability."

Georgiana couldn't help laughing at the image. "I appreciate your willingness to sacrifice yourself for propriety, Milly, but I am here to help you — not to put your life in danger."

Despite the general laughter, Georgiana was surprised at Dare's thought for her reputation. More likely, though, he simply didn't want his family entangled with her any more than was absolutely necessary. Well, she wasn't after his family; she *liked* them. Her entangling was aimed straight at him.

On the walk back from Hyde Park, Tristan watched Georgiana link arms with Aunt Edwina, chatting and laughing and smiling with his family. Over the past few years she always seemed determined not to be amused, at least in his presence. Today she radiated warmth and good humor.

He couldn't figure it out. Last night, a waltz. And today, when he'd thought to trap her into revealing something of her true purpose, his entire ramshackle family had invited themselves along and spoiled his plans.

If she was merely in search of a way to

occupy herself, the *haut ton* boasted several elderly ladies more in need of voluntary companionship than his aunts. She couldn't possibly be comfortable or happy under his roof; she came from one of the wealthiest families in England, after all. His household still managed to be respectable, but lavish feasts and extravagant soirees had vanished with his father's death.

He decided to press his luck. "I almost forgot. The Marquis of St. Aubyn offered me his box at the opera tonight. I have four seats, if anyone would care to attend. *The Magic Flute*, I believe, is the piece."

Andrew snorted. "I can understand why Saint bowed out, but *you're* going to the opera? Voluntarily?"

"Did you lose a wager, or something?" Bradshaw contributed.

Damn Bradshaw for mentioning wagering in Georgiana's presence. "A show of hands, if you please."

As he expected, Bradshaw and Andrew lifted their hands, followed by Edwina and Milly. Georgiana didn't, though he knew she liked the opera. But she wasn't the only one who could play bluff-and-guess.

"All right, you four it is. Just don't behave too respectably, or you'll damage my reputation."

"Aren't you going?" Georgiana asked, understanding beginning to dawn in her eyes.

He lifted an eyebrow, relishing the thought that he'd outmaneuvered her. "Me? At the opera?"

"But Milly will need assis—"

"Andrew and I will manage," Bradshaw said amiably. "We can drag her and the chair behind the coach."

"Oh, heavens!" Milly laughed again as they reached the foot of the short drive. "You boys will be the death of me."

Despite Milly's protests, her cheeks were rosy and her hazel eyes clear. It was the best she'd looked in weeks, and Tristan couldn't help smiling as he and Bradshaw lifted her out of the chair at the foot of the steps and carried her up to the morning room, Andrew and a footman following with the chair. The contraption was a damned good idea, and for that reason if no other, he was glad Georgiana had come to visit.

The ladies all retreated into their sitting room, and Tristan went down the hall to his office. He hated doing accounts, but with his precarious position, he needed to be involved in every aspect of money management. Purchasing Edward's pony and reimbursing Georgiana for the wheeled chair represented the total amount of his incidental funds for the month — and it was only the seventh. The wool sales would help, but he couldn't expect to see that money for two or three months, at best.

He was stupid to have volunteered his stable for Georgiana's mare. He was already paying for feed for Edward's new pony, in addition to the four coach and carriage horses, and his and his brother's mounts. A feisty Arabian would eat twice as much as little Storm Cloud. "Blast," he muttered, penciling in the estimated expense.

This was why he'd finally listened to the aunties when they'd suggested he find a rich heiress looking for a title. This was why he'd been courting Amelia Johns despite his desperate wish to flee in the opposite direction.

Tristan scowled as he pushed away from his desk. He'd barely spoken to Amelia in the past few days, and the last time he'd done so was to inform her that under no circumstances would he attend her bloody vocal recital. He needed to be more attentive, before some cash-starved earl snatched her up and he had to begin the courting process all over again with some other, even more simpering, chit.

Dawkins scratched on the door. "The mail, my lord," he said, holding out a silver salver laden with correspondence.

"Thank you." As the butler exited, Tristan sorted through the large stack. Besides the usual flood of correspondence from Andrew's school chums, the estate manager at Dare Park had sent his weekly report, as had Tomlin at Drewsbyrne Abbey. Only two bills, both of which he'd already anticipated, thank God, and a perfumed letter for Georgiana.

Not perfume, he decided as he sniffed it again, more carefully. Men's cologne. What sort of dandy would scent his own correspondence? He flipped it over, the heavy scent making him sneeze, but the correspondent had omitted a return address.

He wasn't surprised that her acquaintances knew to send correspondence to Carroway House; after one evening the entire *ton* likely knew how much clothing she'd brought with her and what she'd had for breakfast. But he hadn't anticipated that he would be handing her letters from her male admirers.

"Dawkins!" The butler, no doubt anticipating the summons, stuck his head back through the door. "Inform Andrew and Lady Georgiana that they have correspondence, if you please."

"Of course, my lord."

Andrew galloped in first, then vanished again with his stack of letters. Several minutes passed before Georgiana appeared. As she walked into the room, Tristan looked up from the accounts he'd been unable to concentrate on while he wondered who in damnation had sent her a letter.

If there was one thing he didn't want, it was to seem interested, so he nudged at the smelly thing with his pencil and went back to scrawling figures. As she started out of the room, though, he looked up. "Who's it from?" he asked, trying to sound as if he didn't care whether it was from her brother or the president of the Americas.

"I don't know," she said, smiling.

"So open it."

"I will." With that, she exited again.

"Damnation," he grumbled, and erased the chicken scratches he'd put on the ledger.

Outside the doorway, Georgiana stifled a chuckle as she stuffed the smelly thing into her pocket. Sending letters to oneself was so . . . juvenile — except in this case, it had worked.

Chapter 5

Get thee to a nunnery!
— *Hamlet*, Act III, Scene i

By the time the household finished dinner and the quartet left for their evening at the opera, Georgiana was ready to reconsider her obligations to the Misses Carroway. She had no engagements this evening herself, feeling that her duties to Milly and Edwina should come before soirees and balls.

And now that she'd been abandoned by the aunties, she was left with an entire evening of nothing to do but think about being all but alone in a large house with Tristan Carroway.

He was an arrogant, impossible man; and the worst part was that she could still see how Amelia Johns could be enamored of him. If she could forget for a minute how awful he'd been to her, she could even imagine herself with him again, in his arms with his knowing hands and knowing mouth —

"Georgie," young Edward said, galloping into the library where she'd taken refuge, "do you know how to play '*Vingt-et-un*'?"

"Oh, goodness. I haven't played that in years."

"Don't interrupt Lady Georgiana," Dare's deep drawl came from the doorway. "She's reading."

"But we need four players!"

She forced a smile, but could feel the blush creeping up her cheeks. "But you and I only make two."

"No. Bit and Tristan and I make three. We need you."

"Yes, we need you," Tristan echoed.

She tried to read his expression to see whether he was being anything less than innocent, so she could retaliate, but she couldn't tell what he might be thinking behind those light blue eyes.

If she declined Edward's invitation, she would look like a coward and a snob; even worse, Dare would be sure to call her one or both names, since he had no inclination to be a proper gentleman. One of them would have to rise to the occasion, and better she than he. "Very well," she said, closing her book and standing. "I would love to play."

She ended up in the drawing room

seated between Edward and Robert, which meant that she had to face Dare's knowing gaze all evening.

As Edward dealt the cards she turned to Robert, mostly to avoid looking at Tristan. She knew little of the middle Carroway brother, except that years ago Robert had been talkative and witty and very funny. Everyone knew he had nearly been killed in the war, and she had seen him in public only rarely since his return. Except for a slight limp, though, he looked as fit as he ever had.

"How did you manage to get talked into this?" she asked with a smile.

"Luck."

"If you don't mind my asking," she pressed, despite his uncommunicative response, "how did you get your nickname? Bit, isn't it?"

"*I* named him Bit," Edward said, setting down the remainder of the deck and examining his cards. "When I was a baby that's how I said his name."

Young Edward must think her and his brothers ancient. "Do you have nicknames for any of your other brothers?"

The youngster squinted his dark gray eyes in concentration. "Well, Tristan is Dare, and sometimes he's Tris; and

Bradshaw is Shaw; and sometimes we call Andrew, Drew, but he doesn't like that very much."

"Why not?"

"He says it's a girls' name, and then Shaw calls him Drusilla."

She tried not to laugh. "I see."

"And they call me the Runt."

"That's awful!" Georgiana glared at Tristan. How typical, that he would use such a demeaning name on a member of his own family.

"But I am the runt! I like it!" Edward squirmed upright, sitting on his folded legs to give him more height in comparison to his tall brothers.

"He likes it," Tristan drawled, drawing another card from the pile at the center of the table and setting it before her.

"I can't imagine why," she sniffed.

"*Vingt-et-un*," Bit said, spreading out his cards for their view.

Tristan scowled at his brother, light blue eyes dancing. "Never trust the quiet ones."

There it was again, that fond look with which he favored his family members from time to time. Georgiana cleared her throat, surprised to find that the intimacy and ease among the brothers could make her feel awkward — and annoyed at Dare for appearing to possess those kinder qualities.

In a strange way, it made him more . . . enticing. She was the seducer, she reminded herself. She was not there to be seduced. "I'm surprised you're not at one of your clubs tonight, my lord. Surely your skill with cards could be put to better use there."

He shrugged. "This is more fun."

Apparently playing cards with an eight-year-old and a near mute was also more fun than attending the opera or going to Vauxhall Gardens or visiting one of his mistresses, or any of the other ways he typically spent his nights. If he was trying to impress her with his domesticity, though, it was a wasted effort. Nothing he did for the rest of his life would ever impress her, because she knew precisely what kind of man he truly was.

"So are you ever going to confess who sent you that letter this afternoon?" he asked, when they'd been playing for over an hour.

"It was unsigned," she said, gathering the deck for her deal.

"A mystery, then," he returned, leaning forward for his glass of brandy. "Any suspects?"

"I . . . have my suspicions," she hedged,

as she dealt them each two cards, faceup. For heaven's sake, she'd only meant to plant the idea that she might have determined suitors willing to breach the masculine stronghold of Carroway House; she hadn't expected the Spanish Inquisition.

"Who?" Tristan leaned his chin on his hand, gazing at her, while Robert signaled for an additional card.

Georgiana's first instinct was to remind him that her business was none of his. The purpose of this exercise, though, was to make him fall in love with her. That being the case, she really needed to stop insulting him with every breath. "I wouldn't wish to falsely implicate anyone," she said, trying not to sound arch. "I will therefore reserve my response until further evidence should appear."

" 'Further evidence,' " he repeated. "You mean the man himself? By all means, have him call on us."

She scowled. "He wouldn't be calling on *you*, for heaven's s—"

"*Vingt-et-un!*" Edward shouted, bouncing up and down. "You two are never going to win if you keep making moony eyes at each other all night."

Robert made a choking sound.

"Well," she squeaked, feeling even less eloquent than Bit, "you've left me no hope of winning, Edward. I think I shall retire for the evening, gentlemen."

The men stood when she did, Tristan nodding stiffly as she made what she hoped was a dignified exit. Once in the hallway, she gathered her skirt in her fists and fled up the stairs.

"Georgiana!"

Tristan's deep voice stopped her on the landing.

"Well." She faced him, determined to make light of Edward's comment. "That was a surprise, wasn't it?"

"He's only eight," Dare said flatly as he climbed toward her. "And if this keeps up, he won't see nine. Don't let an infant's prattling upset you."

"I . . . I . . ." She cleared her throat. "As I said, it just surprised me. I'm not upset. Really."

"You're not upset," he repeated, gazing at her skeptically.

"No."

"Good." Grimacing, he ran his fingers through his dark hair, a gesture she had once found very attractive. "Because it's not true. I want you to know that."

At his serious tone, she leaned against

the railing. "You want me to know what, my lord?"

"That I'm not mooning after you. I'm thinking of getting married, in fact."

Ah-ha. "You are? Who is she? I'll tender my congratulations."

"Don't do that," he said, too quickly, his expression deepening to a scowl.

Georgiana stifled a smile. "Whyever not?"

"I haven't — quite — exactly — proposed to her yet."

"Oh. Well, I'm glad we got this straightened out, anyway. Good night, my lord."

As she continued up the stairs, she could feel his gaze on her back. Poor Amelia Johns. A broken heart would do Tristan Carroway considerable good, if only to teach him not to toy with other people's dreams and hearts.

When she reached her room, she dashed off another letter to Lucinda and enclosed a second letter, in a harsher hand and written with a different pen, addressed back to herself. She hoped Lucinda would be a bit more conservative with the cologne. The scent of the first one still lingered in the air, and she could swear that it had turned the flames blue when she threw it in the fireplace.

Georgiana rose early. Thankfully for her exercise regimen, both Milly and Edwina tended to sleep late. After a night at the opera, no doubt she wouldn't see them before noon. Summoning Mary and donning her riding dress, she hurried downstairs. Her cousin's groom stood waiting outside, Sheba saddled and ready beside him.

"Good morning, John," she said, smiling as he helped her into the saddle.

"Good morning, Lady Georgiana," he answered, remounting his gray gelding. "Sheba's up for a good gallop this morning, I think."

"Glad to hear it, because Charlemagne feels the same way." Dare, mounted on his splendid, rangy bay, clattered around the corner of the house to stop beside her. "And so do I. Good morning, John."

"Lord Dare."

Despite her annoyance, she had to admit that he looked very compelling. She could practically see her reflection in his black Hessians, and with his dark coloring and light blue eyes, his rust coat gave him an almost medieval grandeur. His black breeches didn't have a wrinkle in them, and he sat Charlemagne as though he'd been born on horseback. There were rumors that that was where he'd been conceived.

"You're awake early this morning." Blast it, she wanted some fresh air to clear her head. Dare and a clear head were incompatible.

"I couldn't sleep, so I gave up the attempt. Shall we? Regent's Park, perhaps."

"John will escort me. I don't need your assistance."

"John will escort me, as well. We don't want me falling out of the saddle and breaking my neck, do we?"

She burned to hand him a cutting response, but the longer they argued, the shorter her ride would be. "Oh, very well. If you insist on coming along, let's go."

Sweeping a deep bow from the saddle, he clucked to Charlemagne. "How could I refuse that invitation?"

They set out at a trot for Regent's Park, the two of them side by side and John a few yards behind. *Flirt,* she reminded herself. *Say something nice.* Unfortunately, nothing came to mind. "Does Bradshaw intend to continue his naval career?" she finally asked.

"He says he does, but he's already itching to be made captain of his own ship. If that doesn't happen soon, we all assume he'll become a pirate and steal a vessel."

He said it in so mild a voice that she blurted a laugh before she could stop herself. "Have you informed him of your theory?"

"Edward has. The Runt wants to be first mate."

"And will Robert go back to the army?"

His lean face became bleak for a moment. "No. I won't allow it."

His uncharacteristic tone and choice of words left her silent. Reconciling the two sides of Tristan Carroway was becoming confusing: He seemed so caring about his brothers and his old aunts, and yet when it came to women like Amelia, he behaved like a heartless rake.

Which of the two was the real Lord Dare? And why was she even asking that question, when she knew the answer? He had broken her heart and ruined her hopes for the future. And he'd never even apologized for it.

He was an idiot, Tristan decided. They'd been having an actual pleasant conversation, and he'd even made her *laugh*, for God's sake, and then he'd blurted out his response about Bit before he could clamp his jaw around it.

Whatever she was up to, it seemed to involve being nice to him, and he certainly had no objection to that. But he knew very well how much she hated him, and he couldn't think of a damned reason why she should have a change of heart about that now.

This game of hers would be easier to decipher if he wasn't still allowing his lust for her to color every thought and conversation. Six years hadn't erased the feel of her skin or the taste of her mouth from his senses, and he'd long ago realized that neither time nor an endless parade of lovers and mistresses would ever do so. It was deuced frustrating, and having her sleeping beneath his roof was making it even more so.

"Aunt Milly's been improving since you arrived," he said, attempting to change the subject before his overheated brain made him say something he would regret.

"I'm glad to hear th—"

"Georgiana! I say, Lady Georgie!"

Tristan looked down the street. Lord Luxley, that damned pretty-faced stuffed shirt, galloped toward them, knocking over an orange cart in his hurry to reach them. If that idiot had sent the letter Georgiana'd been so smug about, he would eat his hat. The baron suffered from a woeful lack of intelligence.

He watched Georgiana's gaze travel from the oranges rolling all over the street to Luxley's face. "Good morning, my lord," she said, in the cool tones she usually reserved for Tristan.

"Lady Georgiana, you look like an angel. I'm so pleased to see you this morning. I have" — and he began digging through various pockets — "something I wish to give you."

Her expression unchanged, she held up one hand, calling for him to stop. "I think you also have something to give that cart vendor."

"Hm? What?"

While Tristan continued to watch her, intrigued, she gestured at the old woman standing next to the overturned cart, weeping as the morning rush of carriages and coaches crushed her produce into orange pulp all over Park Road. "Over there. Lord Dare, what is the price of an orange these days?"

"Two pence each, I believe," Tristan answered, tripling the price.

She glanced at him, acknowledging his exaggeration, then returned her attention to the baron. "I think you need to give that woman at least two shillings, Lord Luxley."

Finally, Luxley looked over at his victim.

"That orange girl?" His lip wrinkled in distaste. "I think not. She shouldn't have left her cart in the middle of the street like that."

"Very well, then. You have nothing I wish to receive," Georgiana said coolly. Reaching into her pocket, she produced a gold sovereign. Clucking at Sheba, she moved past the stunned, red-faced Luxley, and leaned down to hand the money over herself.

"Oh, bless you, my lady," the old woman gushed, grabbing her gloved hand and pressing it to her cheek. "Bless you, bless you."

"Lady Georgiana, I must protest," Luxley blustered. "You've given her far too much. You can't wish to spoil the —"

"I think Lady Georgiana has done exactly as she intended," Tristan broke in, bringing Charlemagne between her and the baron. "Good day, Luxley."

They started up the street again, leaving a slack-jawed Luxley behind them. After a moment of silence, Georgiana sent Dare a sideways glance from behind the brim of her blue bonnet. "It's probably a good thing you interrupted him just then, Tristan, or I would have had to punch him."

"I was only thinking of the injuries to myself if I had to separate the two of you in a brawl. And of the damage you'd do to poor Luxley, of course."

Her smile touched her green eyes. "Of course."

Good lord, she'd granted him two smiles in one morning. And she'd called him by his Christian name for the first time in six years. Thank God he'd been on his way out to arrange a picnic with Amelia, or he would have missed spending this morning with her.

He wondered what she would think if she knew that he kept her stocking in a mahogany box in the top drawer of his chest. As far as society was concerned, he'd won the first part of the wager by gaining a kiss, and failed abysmally at the second part. His silence might have saved her reputation, but it hadn't saved what might have grown between them.

Tristan shook himself. "Shall we?" He kneed Charlemagne.

With a laugh, Georgiana and Sheba were off like a shot beside him. "To the trees!" she shouted, the wind blowing the bonnet back off her curling golden hair.

"Sweet Lucifer," he murmured, mesmerized at the sight. His big bay was stronger and faster than Sheba, but even Charlemagne seemed to realize that today they were in this for the pursuit, and not the victory.

If Georgiana was playing some sort of game, it was a damned interesting one.

She reached the trees first. Laughing in triumph, she faced him as he drew up beside her. "My dear Lord Dare, I think you let me win."

"I'm not certain how I should answer that," he said, patting Charlemagne on the neck, "so I'll only say that you and Sheba move as though you were made for one another."

Georgiana lifted a fine eyebrow. "A compliment, now. I'm almost inclined to be impressed by your manners. Next time we race, though, do try harder."

He grinned. "Then I'm afraid you've enjoyed your last victory."

"I'd put my money on Lady Georgiana, anytime," a voice came from the trees, and the Marquis of Westbrook emerged onto the path, ducking overhanging branches as he approached on his gray gelding.

Her smile faltered. "I don't participate in wagers, my lord," she said, a slight tremor in her voice.

Westbrook didn't bat an eye. "Then I'll

only place my confidence in you."

Tristan narrowed his eyes at the smooth reply. The marquis had to know of the wager involving himself and Georgiana; everyone knew of it. So he'd made his little *faux pas* deliberately.

"Thank you, Lord Westbrook."

"John, please."

Georgiana's lips curved upward. "Thank you, John," she amended.

They seemed to have forgotten Tristan was even there. He loosened the reins in his fingers and shifted his right foot. Charlemagne sidestepped in that direction, crowding Westbrook's gray.

"Beg pardon," he said, as the gray stumbled.

"Control your animal, Dare," the marquis said in an annoyed tone, wrenching his mount back around.

"I don't think Charlemagne liked you saying my Sheba could beat him," Georgiana said. When she glanced at Tristan, he had little doubt that she knew what he'd done. Yet she hadn't given him away.

"Charlemagne doesn't like transparent flattery," Tristan amended, turning his gaze to Westbrook.

"Your mount should be reminded that he's a horse. Animals should know their place."

Ah, battle, Tristan thought, his blood heating at the insult. "Charlemagne does know his place, as Lady Georgiana indicated. First, I believe."

"And *I* believe Lady Georgiana was only being polite. She no doubt recognizes the inferior quality of the animal involved."

"If you don't mind, Lord Westbrook," Georgiana said, "I prefer to supply my own dialogue."

Poor fellow, already back from John to Lord Westbrook. Tristan would have pursued his victory, but he didn't want Georgiana angry at him, too. When the marquis glared at him, realizing that he'd been outmaneuvered, Tristan only grinned. As soon as Georgiana glanced in his direction, he wiped the expression away.

"My apologies, Lady Georgiana," the marquis said. "It was not my intention to offend."

"Of course it wasn't. Lord Dare frequently has an adverse effect on others."

"That's true," Tristan agreed. The description was the mildest he'd ever heard her give on his behalf.

She looked sideways at him again, then turned her attention back to Westbrook. "If you'll excuse me, my lord, I need to return to Carroway House. Lord Dare's aunts will be rising shortly."

"I shall take my leave, then. Good day, my lady. Dare."

"Westbrook."

As soon as the marquis vanished from view, Georgie turned Sheba toward the edge of the park. "What was that for?" she asked, her gaze on the path.

"I'm evil."

Her lips twitched. "Obviously."

Chapter 6

Have not saints lips, and holy palmers too?
— *Romeo and Juliet*, Act I, Scene v

"No one's been killed yet? I'm astonished." The Duke of Wycliffe stood to one side of an artistic grouping of potted palms.

Tristan glanced toward Wycliffe's petite bride, engaged in a country dance with the Earl of Resdin's son, Thomas. "Emma looks well," he said. "I assume she and your mother are reconciled?"

"They were reconciled the moment my mother realized I intended to marry," the duke said in his low drawl. "Don't change the subject. What the devil is Georgiana doing at Carroway House?"

"She's volunteered to help Aunt Milly. And I'm grateful for it; she's made a huge difference."

"You're grateful. To Georgie. My cousin. The same female who nearly punctured you with a parasol a few summers ago."

Tristan shrugged. "As you said, Grey, no one's been killed. No maimings or amputations, either." Except for the negligible damage to his knuckles and his toes, her stay had been surprisingly injury-free for him.

The duke straightened, looking past Tristan's shoulder. "Don't look now, but she's approaching. Let the maimings begin."

The familiar, charged tension that accompanied Georgiana's presence ran through him. She kept him on his toes, figuratively speaking. And now it was doubly complicated, since he didn't want to begin a fight if she was bearing an olive branch.

"Grey," she said, going on tiptoe to kiss her cousin on the cheek, "the two of you wouldn't be gossiping, would you?"

"Actually," Tristan said, before Grey could remind Georgiana yet again of their mutual antagonism, "we were admiring the cut of Lord Thomas's coat. He almost looks as though he has shoulders and a neck tonight."

She followed their gaze. "Poor fellow. He can't help that he's the mirror image of his father."

"Resdin should have known better than to propagate," Grey commented. "If you'll excuse me, I'm going to go rescue Emma."

Georgiana sighed as her cousin strolled toward the dancers. "He does look happy, doesn't he?"

"Marriage agrees with him. I thought you were chatting with your friends."

"Trying to get rid of me? That would leave you standing here all by yourself, my lord. How could I bear doing you such a poor turn?"

Tristan froze for a heartbeat. Lady Georgiana Halley was flirting. With him, of all people.

"Then perhaps you might wish to dance again?" he drawled, bracing himself for a nasty set down, or for a bolt of lightning to strike one or the other of them dead.

"That would be lovely."

He studied her expression as he took her hand to lead her onto the dance floor, but saw nothing that indicated she might intend him bodily harm. The soft violet of her dress darkened her light green eyes to exquisite emerald, and if God had any compassion at all, the next dance would be a waltz.

The orchestra struck up a quadrille. Apparently God had a sense of humor. "Shall we?"

As soon as they joined the dance, another dozen couples hurried onto the floor. Before news of his father's poor money management skills had reached every crevice of the *ton*, he might have assumed that he was the reason for the stampede. Ladies had once been known to fight over his affections. Tonight the gentlemen were in the lead, and they seemed to have their attention on Georgiana.

It had been that way since she'd turned eighteen. Over the last few years he had claimed aloud to pity the poor soul with whom she might choose to matrimonify. His private sentiments had remained less clear, even to him. Tonight, however, the ogling annoyed him a great deal.

She swooped past, then caught his hand as they changed direction. "Has someone else stepped on your toe?" she asked. "You look very dour."

"I allow no one but you to tread on me," he replied, smiling as they parted again.

Something was wrong with him. He *knew* she was up to no good: Nothing in the past six years led him to believe that she might suddenly forgive him for his duplicity and his abject stupidity. Yet there he was, glaring at the other males in the set as though he had some claim on her person. And he'd been ready to flatten Westbrook earlier just for complimenting her.

He turned to collect the hand of the next lady winding through the set, and blinked. "Amelia."

"Lord Dare. You look well tonight."

"Thank you." She wasn't angry with him? He hadn't spared her a thought in nearly a week, and at last count had missed scheduling a picnic and a ride in Hyde Park. "And you look lovely."

"Thank you."

She was swept away in the tide of dancers, and Georgiana returned to his side. Her cheeks were flushed, and she looked as though she was trying very hard not to laugh. "What is it?" he asked.

"Oh, nothing."

That wouldn't do. "What happened?" he repeated, holding her gaze as they took their turn circling the other dancers.

"If you must know," she said, catching a breath, "Lord Raymond proposed to me."

Tristan turned to find the old bastard arm in arm with some woman half his age. "Just now?"

"Yes. Don't look so surprised. It happens all the time."

"But I thought —"

The smile vanished from her face. "Don't you dare," she grated.

"You'll have to enlighten me later, then." This was damned confusing. She'd said she could never marry, yet now he found that men proposed to her all the time?

The dance ended, and he offered Georgiana his arm. To his surprise, she accepted. The aunties had joined a group of their friends beside the huge stone fireplace at one end of the room, and he headed in that direction.

"Explain," he said, as the crowd around them thinned.

"Why should I?"

"Because you're blaming me for something that —"

"I could marry someone who only wants my money in an instant," she said in a low, tight voice. "I've already told you that I won't marry for that reason. And I cannot marry for love."

"Someone who loved you would understand."

Stopping, her cheeks paling alarmingly, Georgiana snatched her hand from his grip. "I would never trust anyone who said he cared for me. I've heard it before."

With that, she rejoined his aunts, leaving him standing alone by the refreshment table. Apparently he'd destroyed much more than her maidenhead. He'd destroyed her ability to trust her heart — or anyone else's.

"I need a drink," he muttered.

Dare looked very somber as he stepped up to the refreshment table and demanded a whiskey. Georgiana scowled. She'd meant only to flirt tonight, yet instead she'd argued with him again. She was so used to it by now that *not* fighting with him was difficult.

"You and Tristan make a lovely couple, my dear," Edwina said, taking her arm and pulling her down onto one of the chairs beside the hearth. "I'm no meddler, of course, but now that you're getting along, well, anything could happen."

"Surely not," she protested, forcing a disbelieving laugh and wishing they'd chosen a spot not quite so close to the oppressive heat. After the exertion of dancing, it was sweltering.

"Oh, I know you had that fight all those years ago, but you were just a child then, and he was so wild."

"Very wicked, he was," Milly joined in, "before Oliver died and left such a mess for him."

"I . . ." Across the room, Amelia gestured to her. "Will you excuse me for just a moment?" Georgiana said quickly, rising again and doubly thankful for the distraction.

"Of course, dear. Go see your friends."

"I'll be right back."

Glancing in Dare's direction to make sure he wasn't looking, she slipped around the edges of the room, following Amelia as the younger girl ducked into the hallway. Miss Johns had some sense, anyway. If the viscount caught the two of them together, he would suspect something. Georgiana couldn't let that happen — not now, when she finally seemed to be making an impression in his thick skull.

"Miss Johns?"

"How is this helping me?" the girl asked, pouting as she pulled at one of her brunette curls. "He's practically ignored me for a week."

"I'm teaching him to realize that other people have feelings, too, and that he can't just stomp on them whenever he chooses." Georgiana stepped closer, lowering her voice. "When he saw you during the dance, did he act any differently than usual?"

"Well, he did look almost guilty for a moment. I have to admit, he's never done that, before."

"Then it's working already. Trust me,

Miss Johns. When I'm finished, he'll want nothing more than to marry you and be a very pleasant husband."

"All right," the girl said slowly. "Perhaps you could look as though you weren't having quite so much fun in his company, though."

Georgiana blanched. *Good heavens.* She looked as though she were having fun? Something was terribly wrong, then. Or perhaps in her innocence, Amelia had misread what she saw. That must be it.

"I'll do my best," she agreed. With a quick squeeze of the girl's hand, she returned to the ballroom.

Tristan looked as though he was halfway through his second whiskey. That would never do. She'd said too much, and she'd meant never to tell him how much he'd wounded her. She didn't want him to know how much of her affections he'd owned. Squaring her shoulders, she strolled to the refreshment table. "My lord, I think your Aunt Milly is probably very tired after all the activities of the past few days," she ventured.

He nodded, handing his glass to a footman. "I'll see her home, then. Stay if you wish. Edwina and I will manage."

"I confess," she said, following him as he

strode toward his aunts, "I'm quite ready to leave, myself."

Tristan slowed. "Are you certain? I don't want to ruin anything else for you, Georgiana."

"Don't be surly. I do as I please."

"Surly. That's a new one."

If there was one thing about which she could compliment Lord Dare, it was that he always paid attention to what she was saying. "You know I hate to repeat myself."

Milly seemed only too happy to depart the ball, and Georgiana swallowed a twinge of guilt. The aunts had never wronged her, and she needed to pay better attention to them. If they became merely an excuse, even for a moment, then she was as blackhearted as Dare.

At the front door she held the chair steady while Tristan lifted Milly out of it and carried her into the coach. Milly was not a small woman, yet the viscount never seemed to have any trouble carrying her about. And the way his muscles played beneath his tight-fitting black jacket . . . Georgiana drew a quick breath and looked away.

Obviously this evening had completely worn her out, as well. Otherwise, she would never have been thinking about his muscles, or the way his blue eyes had become so serious when she'd stupidly spoken about not trusting anyone.

"After you, my dear."

Georgiana started as Edwina nudged her toward the coach's open door. Tristan stepped back down, holding out his hand to her.

"Are you certain you don't want to stay?" he murmured, curling his fingers around hers.

She nodded, alarm bells going off in her head. She'd seen that dark, seductive look in his eyes before. It was a very dangerous look; it had once slain her virginity. Seating herself in the corner of the coach, she folded her hands in her lap. Dare sat opposite her, beside Edwina. All the way back to Carroway House he was uncharacteristically quiet, and she could feel his gaze on her, half-hidden in the dark.

What had she done to warrant so much of his attention, other than take her flirting up a notch and then lose her concentration and snap at him? He was *supposed* to be flattered, and his interactions with her were bound to become more pleasant. None of which explained why her mouth had gone dry, or why her heart beat so fast.

"I hope we didn't tire you out too much,

Aunt Milly," he drawled, as they rolled to a stop outside Carroway House.

"Oh, a little, but I feel as if I've been shut up for years. This was wonderful." She chuckled. "I'm certain you'll all tire of me before I'm back on my feet."

"Nonsense," Georgiana said. "I want to see you dance again, remember?"

While the footmen set the wheeled chair at the top of the shallow steps, Tristan lifted Milly and carried her up. Georgiana helped Edwina into the house, but the elder Carroway sister balked at the foot of the stairs.

"I'm not at all tired," she said. "Join me in the library, Georgiana. I'll have Dawkins bring us some tea."

That sounded better than hiding under her bed and hoping Tristan didn't stop by. He would never broach any delicate subject in Edwina's presence. "That's a splendid idea. I'll come down as soon as I help Milly."

"No, you won't," Tristan's other aunt said from over his shoulder. "I do employ a maid, dear. Have some tea. I'll see you in the morning."

"Good night then."

Georgiana and Edwina settled in the library, though it took several minutes for

112

her to calm down enough to read the book she clutched in her hands. Tristan hadn't said anything about joining them. More likely he would go out to one of his clubs for the rest of the evening. The hour was still early, by his standards. After he left, she could safely go upstairs without worrying about encountering him in the hallways.

Georgiana scowled. She was being silly. Everything was progressing exactly as she'd planned. He'd been nice tonight, and she simply wasn't comfortable with it yet.

"I don't think you're reading."

The voice was barely more than a warm whisper of air in her hair. Georgiana leapt out of her chair, a shriek catching in her throat as she twisted to face the viscount. "Don't do that!"

"Shh, you'll wake up Aunt Edwina." Dare chuckled.

She whipped back around. Edwina was asleep, her head back and her mouth hanging open, a delicate snore emanating from her chest with each breath. Georgiana frowned. "You should go, then."

"Why?" He came around the back of the chair toward her.

"Because our chaperone is asleep."

"You need a chaperone? I thought you weren't afraid of me any longer."

"I was never afraid of you, Dare."

Tristan folded his arms across his chest. "Good. Then we can chat."

"I don't want to chat," she protested, backing toward the door. "I want to go to bed."

"I *am* sorry, you know."

She slowed her retreat, her heart pounding. "Sorry about what?"

"About misleading you. There were things I wasn't —"

"I don't want to hear it. You're six years too late, Tristan."

"You wouldn't have listened six years ago. And I was very stupid. So now I wanted to at least apologize. You don't have to accept it; I really don't expect you to."

"Good."

Georgiana turned on her heel and stalked out of the room. She'd barely gone two steps, though, when his hand clamped down on her shoulder and spun her back around.

"What —"

He leaned down and touched his lips to hers, and then he was gone. Georgiana leaned back against the wall, then sank bonelessly to the floor, trying to rally her breath. Brief though the touch had been, she could still feel the warmth of his mouth on hers.

For some reason, she'd thought she would feel pain, physical pain, if he ever touched her like that again. But the kiss had felt . . . pleasant. Very pleasant. And she hadn't been kissed in a very long time.

Slowly, she pushed back upright and climbed the stairs to her bedchamber. Somehow she hadn't realized that her scheme would have such an effect on *her*. Thank goodness she knew better than to trust her heart over her head. Especially where Tristan Carroway was concerned.

Even so, she locked her bedchamber door before she crawled into bed. A minute later, she rose again and pushed one of the heavy overstuffed chairs against the door. "Much better," she muttered, and climbed back under the covers.

In the library, Edwina waited until everything quieted upstairs. Once she felt assured that Georgiana had gone safely to bed, she sat up straight and resumed reading.

Milly might have reservations about matching Tristan with Georgie, but she had none. They all enjoyed Georgiana's company, and she was warm, witty, and kind — much better than those simpering young things Tristan felt obligated to pursue.

Edwina gave in to a smile. Whatever had happened between the two of them all those years ago, they seemed to be resolving it, thank goodness. If Milly could manage to stay in her wheeled chair for another few days, they might very well succeed in making a match that pleased everyone.

Chapter 7

The gods are just, and of our pleasant vices
Make instruments to plague us.
— *King Lear*, Act V, Scene iii

Despite his reputation, Tristan always enjoyed attending the sessions of the House of Lords. It was somewhat reassuring to see that, careless as he'd been in his private life before he'd inherited the title, in public and politics he stood up well against some of the abject idiots helping determine the course of the country.

This morning, though, as he took his seat between the Duke of Wycliffe and the rarely present Marquis of St. Aubyn, he couldn't even concentrate enough to remember which country they were voting to raise tariffs against. He hoped it wasn't America, since he was attempting to sell them his wool. He raised his hand and said "aye" when Wycliffe nudged him in the ribs, but other than that his thoughts were on Georgiana.

He'd thought before of simply walking up to her and kissing her, but better sense had always prevailed. Last night, though, the memory of her taste, of her sweet, soft mouth, had been overwhelming. And so he'd kissed her, for the first time in six years. Even more surprising, she had let him do it.

"How goes your pursuit of Miss Johns?" Wycliffe murmured, sitting back as the Tories began arguing over trade alliances, and St. Aubyn began sketching the blustering old Duke of Huntford in his wife's favorite evening gown.

"I keep hoping she'll suddenly turn interesting," he said, sighing. She hadn't seemed so bland when he'd first met her. Now, though, every female seemed . . . lifeless. Except for one. Perhaps that was the problem; he needed to stop comparing poor Amelia to Georgiana. Naturally the naive, polite chit would pale in comparison.

"Just remember that you aren't the only one in pursuit, my boy. She's quite the heiress."

"Hence my persistence in the chase." Tristan frowned. "If my father had managed to die two or three years earlier, I might have been able to pull the family out of this muck without resorting to something as heroic and tragic as self-sacrifice."

St. Aubyn chuckled, glancing up from his artwork. "You might try selling off your brothers."

"I've thought about that. But who would buy Bradshaw?"

"Good point."

"What are you doing here anyway, Saint?" he pursued, looking for anything that would distract him from thoughts of Georgiana's lithe body. "Parliament isn't exactly your usual haunt."

"I registered to vote at the beginning of the Session. If I don't appear every so often, they try to declare me dead and confiscate my property. It gets to be annoying."

"I'm off to Gentleman Jackson's this afternoon," Wycliffe cut in again. "Care to join me?"

Tristan shook his head. "I've been attempting to ask Amelia out on a picnic for a week. I thought I'd give it another try today."

"What's the difficulty?"

Georgiana. "Lingering thoughts of self-preservation."

"If you're that skittish about her, you'd best proceed with less recklessness than usual. If you compromise her, you'll *have* to marry her. No escape possible."

"I'm not likely to forget that."

Wycliffe looked at him a bit strangely, but if there was one person Tristan never intended to tell about his true relationship with Georgiana, it was her mountain-sized, boxing aficionado cousin. How odd that it hadn't worked out that way with her, though. She'd been so angry when she'd learned about the wager that all he'd thought of was keeping the tale quiet. Otherwise he and Georgiana might be married now. Of course, she would also have shot or poisoned him well before today, so the point was a moot one.

As soon as the morning session ended, he stopped by Bond Street and then returned home to have a picnic packed. No doubt he wasn't the only bachelor thinking of dining in the park today. Dawkins pulled open the front door for him, and after only five knocks. Leave it to the Carroway butler to lock the door during the day and to neglect to do so at night.

"Is everyone home?" he asked, pulling off his hat and gloves. He wasn't concerned about "everyone's" presence, but he couldn't inquire if Georgiana was about without raising even Dawkins's thick eyebrows.

"Masters Bradshaw, Andrew, and Edward have gone riding," the butler said. "Everyone else is present."

And the best rider among them remained holed up in the bowels of the house. Robert would come around in his own time, though. Hopefully. "Splendid. Have Mrs. Goodwin prepare a picnic luncheon for two, will you?"

"Of course, my lord."

He pounded upstairs to change. As he emerged from his room, he nearly ran into Georgiana, heading down the hallway. "Good morning," he said, putting out a hand to keep from knocking her into the wall.

"Good morning."

Unless he was mistaken, her color was high, and her green eyes focused on his mouth. Good God, had she enjoyed the kiss? He couldn't think of anything else, either. The fan he'd bought her as a peace offering bumped in his pocket. He hadn't expected that he wouldn't need it. "Were you looking for me?"

She cleared her throat, taking a belated step backward. "Actually, yes, I was. I spoke with Milly this morning, and she would like to attempt a walk in the park. I thought perhaps a picnic there to celebrate her efforts would be . . . appropriate."

Tristan scowled, then wiped the expression away before she could notice. "What made you think of a picnic?"

"It's just so lovely today."

He met her gaze, and after a moment she looked toward the vase on the side table. She'd always been a terrible prevaricator. "So this suggestion of yours has nothing to do with the fact that I was already planning a picnic with someone?" he pursued.

Georgiana lifted an eyebrow. "Heavens, no. I hadn't realized. If you have an engagement with someone more important to you than your aunt, by all means go. *I* will supply a picnic for those of us who give a damn."

"Very subtle. Are you thinking of my aunts, or are you trying to keep me away from Amelia Johns?"

"Am . . . So that's who you're after, the poor girl. Do as you please, Dare." She turned on her heel, striding for the staircase. "You always do."

Hm. That had been fairly obvious. And uncharacteristic of Georgiana. She had to know by now whom he was courting; everyone else in London did. Perhaps she *was* trying to keep him away from Amelia. Knowing her, she would consider it her duty to protect the chit from his evil attentions. On the other hand, perhaps — just perhaps — she was jealous.

"Dawkins," he called as he started down the stairs, "make that a picnic for four, if you please. Those of us who give a damn will be in Hyde Park this afternoon."

"Very good, my lord."

Spending the afternoon with Amelia would have been torture, anyway. A picnic with Georgiana was another kind of torture, but one he at least could look forward to.

They set out in Dare's coach, the only vehicle he owned that could accommodate the two aunts, Tristan, Georgiana, a picnic lunch, a footman, and the wheeled chair. Georgiana allowed herself a moment of guilt over the fact that poor Amelia would be stuck at home on such a lovely afternoon. On the other hand, she was saving the girl from a lifetime of pain and humiliation at the hands of an unrepentant Viscount Dare. One afternoon of solitude seemed a fair trade.

Not that an unrepentant Tristan was *entirely* bad. She could stand a kiss or two from him, she supposed, if that was what it would take to ensure that he would fall in love with her.

Georgiana looked across the coach at him, seated with his Aunt Edwina's knitting basket across his thighs and chatting with his eager aunties about who had been absent from Parliament. She'd never imagined him this way; domesticity and Tristan Carroway had always seemed polar opposites. Something about it was enticing, especially with the memory of his kiss warm on her lips.

"I meant to tell you, my dear," Edwina said, catching her attention, "I've never seen you in that dress before. It's lovely."

She glanced down at the silver-and-green muslin. "I saw the material at Willoughby's at the beginning of the Season, and practically had to wrestle it out of Lady Dunston's hand. Madame Perisse works wonders, doesn't she?"

"I don't know whether it's the dressmaker or the dress wearer," Milly said. "Don't you agree, Tristan?"

He nodded, a slow smile curving his mouth. "It brings out your eyes."

"I've been longing for a dress from Madame Perisse." Edwina sighed. "Something in blue, I think."

Georgiana locked gazes with Tristan, who leaned forward. "Blue? Did you say 'blue,' Aunt Edwina?"

"Well, dear Tigress has been gone for a year, now. And Georgiana always looks so stunning. I'm inspired."

" 'Tigress'?" Georgiana mouthed.

"Her cat," Tristan murmured back at her.

She nodded. "You know, Edwina, Lucinda Barrett's black cat just had kittens. It's up to you, of course, but if you'd like, I could inquire if any are available."

Edwina was silent for a long moment. "I will think about it," she finally said.

The coach bumped to a stop. "Are you ready, Aunt Milly?" Tristan asked, handing the sewing basket to Georgiana so he could rise.

"Oh, dear. Is it very crowded out there?"

The footman, Niles, opened the door and flipped the step down. Tristan exited, then helped Edwina to the ground. "I told Gimble to pick an isolated spot," he said, leaning back inside. "Just a few horsemen across the pond and a governess with some infants throwing bread to the ducks."

"Then I suppose I'm ready."

With Georgiana steadying her from behind, and Tristan and the footman on either arm, Milly descended to the grass. "Hold there, my butterfly, and I'll get Georgiana and your cane," Dare said, giving her hand over to Edwina.

Georgiana handed out the basket and Milly's cane. As she took Tristan's hand and stepped down from the coach, he grinned at her. Before she could stop herself, she smiled back at him. "I hope this goes well." Lud, she wasn't supposed to be smiling at him accidentally. "I don't want Milly to be discouraged."

"She's difficult to discourage," he said, keeping his light grip on her fingers.

"And I'm sorry to take you from your engagement today," she added, slipping her hand free.

"I'm not. Not with such lovely company."

Heat rose in her cheeks. A week or two ago she would have had a witty, biting response for him. Now she had no idea what to say to him at all.

They'd been at odds for so long that when he said something nice or complimentary, she felt as though he knew what she was thinking and plotting, and that he was only humoring her until the moment he laughed at her and said that he could never fall in love with her, and that she was worse than foolish to think he might do so.

"Georgie?"

She shook herself. "What?"

He wore an alarming look of quiet speculation she'd never seen before. "Where did you go?" he asked.

She shrugged, moving away from him. "I was just remembering that I try not to repeat my mistakes."

"So do I, Georgiana." Before she could decipher that, he turned to his aunt. "Shall we, my dear?"

With her cane in one hand and a firm grip on Tristan's arm with the other, Milly took a single wobbling step across the grass. Georgiana and Edwina, along with Niles and Gimble, cheered, and she took a second and a third step.

"I knew you could do it!" Georgiana laughed.

"I'm so glad you suggested this, Georgie," Edwina said, beaming. "It's a miracle."

Tristan sent her a sharp look, then went back to maneuvering his aunt in a wide circle around the coach. When Milly claimed exhaustion, they pulled down the wheeled chair and set it beneath a tree for her. Niles laid out the blankets and the basket of food while Georgiana attended to her charge.

"Luncheon is served, my lord," Niles said, bowing.

They seated themselves in a semicircle around Milly while the footman offered them Madeira and sandwiches. Gimble had indeed managed to find a quiet spot in one corner of the park. It was very nice, Georgiana decided, to be able to sit and laugh and chat without three or four dozen men all trying to make eye contact or ride their horses by in the most daring fashion possible to catch her attention.

"So with whom will you dance first after your recovery?" she asked, accepting an orange from Edwina.

"I think I shall ask the Duke of Wellington. I considered Prince George, but I don't wish him to become infatuated with me."

"I should like a kitten, if one is still available," Edwina announced.

"I'll send a note over to Lucinda this afternoon," Georgiana promised her.

While Niles cleared the luncheon and Milly and Edwina brought out their embroidery, Tristan climbed to his feet. "If you ladies are comfortable, I thought I might stretch my legs a little," he said, brushing a stray leaf from his gray trousers. "Georgiana, would you care to join me?"

She hadn't thought to bring any sewing or a book, dash it all, so she would look

128

like an idiot and a coward if she declined and had to sit there in the grass, staring at her hands. "That would be nice," she said, and allowed him to help her to her feet.

Dare offered her his arm, and with a slight hesitation she wrapped her fingers around his sleeve. "We won't go far," he said to his aunts, and headed toward the path by the pond.

"I hope you didn't mind my mentioning the kitten to Edwina," she said, before he could ask her which mistake she wasn't repeating, or why she had really bullied him into a picnic. "Since you'd already had a cat in residence, I didn't think you would mind another."

"With four younger brothers, cats are the least of my worries. Why did you suggest the outing today?" he asked, undeterred. "Is it because you want me to apologize for last night?"

Heat crept along her veins. "I scarcely remember last night. It was late, and we were both tired."

"I wasn't tired. I wanted to kiss you. And I think you do remember it." He pulled a box from his pocket and presented it to her. "Which is why I thought you might have need of this today."

She opened it. The fan was even lovelier

than the last one, white with small yellow flowers sprinkled amongst the ivory ribs. Georgiana wondered whether he'd realized that the fans she'd cracked over his knuckles were never the ones that he'd given her. Those stayed in a drawer, where she could pretend to ignore them. "Tristan, this is very confusing for me," she said, glad that for once she could speak the truth.

She belatedly realized they were hidden from the aunties by a small stand of elm trees. No one else was in sight at all. "It doesn't have to be," he murmured, and tilted her chin up with his fingers.

Panic rising fast enough to choke her, Georgiana backed away. The first kiss she could blame on Tristan; a second kiss would be equally her own fault. "Please don't."

Tristan froze, then closed the space between them again with one slow step. "If you remembered the way I waltz, you must remember other things, too."

That was the problem. "Are you certain you want to remind m—"

He leaned down, and feather-light touched his lips to hers, tasting her as though they'd never kissed before. Georgiana sighed and twined her fingers through his wavy dark hair. Lord, she had missed this. She had missed him, the feel of his strong arms around her, and his seeking, beckoning mouth. He deepened the kiss, a small sound coming from deep in his chest.

What was she doing? Georgiana pulled away again. "Stop it! Stop it, Dare."

He let her go. "There's no one to see, Georgiana. It's just us."

"That's what you said before," she panted, straightening her shawl and glaring at him. Pretty as her new fan was, she was tempted to put it across his skull.

"And you gave in then, too," he said with a slight grin. "You can't blame me, alone. It does take two to do it properly, and as I recall —"

An outraged growl spilling from her chest, Georgiana stepped forward and shoved against his chest.

"Bloody damnation!" He lost his balance and went backward into the pond.

As he shot to his feet, waist deep in water and with a lily pad sliding from one shoulder, he looked angry enough to spit fire. Georgiana gathered her skirt in her fists and ran.

"Niles!" she yelled as she reached their party. "Gimble! His Lordship has fallen into the pond. Please help him!"

As Tristan slogged out of the water onto the muddy bank, his servants came pounding down the path. "Are you all right, my lord?" Gimble called, skidding to a halt and nearly toppling the three of them back into the water. "Lady Georgiana said you had fallen."

Still swearing under his breath, Tristan shrugged out of the servants' grip. "I'm fine," he growled. "Leave be."

She'd certainly drowned his lust, damn her. Niles and Gimble at his heels, he stalked back to the coach. Georgiana stood there, apparently explaining his clumsiness to the aunties. As she caught sight of him, she paled.

His first thought was to drag her back to the edge of the pond and toss her in, just so they'd be even. "Put everything back into the coach," he ordered. "We're leaving."

Edwina asked, "Tristan, are you all —"

"I'm fine." He glared at Georgiana. "I fell."

Surprise showed in her green eyes as she rolled Milly to the coach. He didn't know what she expected; he certainly wasn't going to start bellowing to all and sundry that he'd kissed her and she'd shoved him into the pond.

Tristan paused. Any other female would have enjoyed his embrace. So he supposed that in a sense, what *she'd* done was . . . comforting. If she'd been planning something underhanded, she certainly wouldn't have risked his anger by dousing him. Given their past, he wouldn't have been surprised by a knee aimed at his nether regions. Being pushed into the duck pond was probably the mildest reaction he could have hoped for. She *was* warming to him, by God.

"Back to Carroway House," he said with less heat, helping Milly into the coach. Georgiana pulled herself up the steps while he settled his aunt. He sat back, wringing water out of his gray jacket.

"Are you certain you're all right?" Edwina asked, patting his wet knee.

"Yes. I deserved it, I suppose, for teasing the ducks." He wiped water from his eyes. "Silly things didn't realize I meant them no harm."

It wasn't subtle, but his reassurance seemed to work; Georgiana relaxed her clenched fists, though she kept a wary eye on him all the way home and back inside the house.

Once Milly was settled, he left the morning room to go change. Georgiana stood in the doorway, and he slowed as he passed her. "I do respond to verbal communication," he murmured into her ear. "Next time, I'll ask."

She turned, following him. "Next time," she said to his back, surprising him into a halt, "perhaps you'll remember that you're courting someone else. Amelia Johns, I believe?"

He faced her. "Is *that* your only quarrel? I haven't declared anything to Amelia. I'm still trying out the length of my patience with the debutante flock."

"What does *she* expect, though? Have you even thought of that, Tristan? Do you ever think of anyone but yourself?"

"I think of you, all the time."

Despite the opening, she said nothing as he continued up the stairs to his bed chamber. Interesting, that. And he'd given her something more to reflect, anyway.

Tristan chuckled as he shrugged out of his jacket and his valet burst into the room, weeping at the destruction to his wardrobe. Who would have thought that being thrown in a duck pond could be a good thing?

Milly stalked back and forth in the morning room. "You see? And you said it

134

was romantic when they went off walking together."

Her wary gaze on the door, Edwina gestured at her sister to sit again. "They both said it was an accident. Besides, they *did* have some sort of quarrel all those years ago," she reminded Milly. "You have to expect a bump or two in the road."

"Things did seem to be progressing. This, however, is definitely a setback, Wina."

"A small one. Give them some time."

"Humph. I'm getting tired of sitting about all day."

"Milly, if you don't stay in that chair, Georgie will have no reason to remain with us."

Milly sighed and clumped back to her overstuffed nest. "I know, I know. I just hope I don't get gout again before this is over with. And what about those anonymous letters she's been getting?"

"Well, we'll just have to find out about them, won't we?"

Milly brightened. "I suppose we will."

Chapter 8

You draw me, you hard-hearted adamant.
— A Midsummer Night's Dream,
Act II, Scene i

So Tristan thought of her. Good. That was what she'd intended. But she doubted he had anything good in mind for her, and if anyone knew better than to fall for the charms of this particular rake, she did.

He might think he hadn't made a declaration to Amelia Johns, but Miss Johns thought he very nearly had. And whether he was lying about the seriousness of his commitment or not, the girl's heart would surely be the next one he broke. So despite the shivers that ran down her arms at the thought of being kissed by the too-experienced viscount, Georgiana would not forget why she had come to Carroway House. Her heart would never again rule her head where any man was concerned.

The day's excitement over, she settled

back into the morning room with Edwina and Milly. If she'd still been at Hawthorne House with Aunt Frederica, the afternoon would have been occupied with taking care of the dowager duchess's correspondence and replying to the dozens of invitations that flooded in daily. Taking an hour or two to read seemed delightfully sinful.

"You know you don't need to waste your entire day here," Milly said into the silence.

Georgiana looked up. "Beg pardon?"

"What I mean to say is, I love having you here, and your company is a joy, but you must find us two old fossils terribly dull compared with your friends."

"Nonsense! I enjoy being here. Believe me, one can only spend so much time shopping and dancing without finding that very dull, indeed." She straightened as an alarming thought occurred to her. If they'd somehow realized that she'd been responsible for Dare's swim, they might be looking for a polite reason to send her on her way. "Unless you're trying to get rid of me, of course," she said, trying to sound amused.

Edwina shot to her feet and hurried over to grab Georgiana's hand. "Oh, never! It's just that . . ." She looked at her sister.

"It's just that what?" Georgiana asked, her heart sinking even further.

"Well, Tristan said that you've received correspondence from a gentleman. With all of the males here, we thought . . . perhaps your letter-writer might be intimidated."

"You mean he might be afraid to call on me here?" Georgiana asked, relieved. "If he were serious, I'm sure he would do so, regardless."

"Just a flirtation then, is it?" Milly suggested.

For a moment Georgiana wondered whether it was the aunties or Tristan who was trying to discover the identity of her mystery suitor. Best to play it safe until she knew for certain. She sighed. "Yes, I'm afraid so."

"Who is he, dear? Perhaps we can talk some sense into him."

She looked from one to the other. She could never tell them her true plan for Tristan; besides breaking their hearts, the news would make them hate her, when she was truly quite fond of them. "I really prefer not to discuss it, if you don't mind."

"Oh, of course. It's just that . . ." Edwina paused.

"What?" Georgiana asked, her curiosity deepening.

"Nothing. Nothing at all, dear. Just a flirtation. We all like a good flirtation now and then."

Abruptly Georgiana realized what the aunties were up to. They thought they were matchmaking — between her and Tristan, of all people! "A flirtation, of course, is only the beginning," she offered as she sipped her tea. "Who knows what might come of it later?"

They both looked downcast. "Yes, who knows?"

Georgiana suppressed a pang of guilt. At least she could blame all of the subterfuge on Dare; he'd started it. All of this was his fault.

Even the way she almost liked him, sometimes.

She liked him a little less as the extended Carroway family sat down for dinner. Despite his soaking in the duck pond, the look in his eyes was unmistakably superior. As he held her chair for her, Georgiana was tempted to ask him just what he was smirking about, but it probably had something to do with their kiss. If that was it, a little silent gloating was certainly better than his boasting about it aloud.

"You should have seen me, Tristan," Edward chortled, as Dawkins and the footmen passed around the roast chicken and potatoes. "I made Storm Cloud jump over a huge log! We were magnificent, weren't we, Shaw?"

Bradshaw swallowed a mouthful. "It was a sad little twig they jumped, but other than that, the Runt has the tale right."

"It was not a twig! It was a . . . a . . ." He sent Andrew a pleading look.

"A healthy-sized branch," the second-youngest Carroway brother supplied, grinning, "with broken bits sticking up into the air."

"Like a porcupine," Edward finished, his chest jutting out.

"That's stupendous, Edward!" Georgiana said, smiling as the boy beamed. "And you know, speaking of porcupines, Tristan had his own adventure with wildlife this afternoon."

"He did?"

"Do tell," Bradshaw entreated.

"Georgi—"

"Well, we were strolling along in Hyde Park," she began, ignoring the black look Dare sent at her, "and I spied a duckling caught in some reeds at the edge of a pond.

Your brother rescued the poor thing —"

"— but he fell into the water during the attempt!" Aunt Milly finished.

With the exception of Robert, the entire family burst into laughter.

"You fell in a duck pond?" Edward asked through a fit of giggles.

Lord Dare slid his gaze from Georgiana. "Yes, I did. And you know what else?"

"What?"

"Georgie gets smelly, perfumed love letters from secret admirers."

Her jaw dropped. "Don't make it sound so . . . torrid," she demanded.

Tristan shoved a forkful of potato into his mouth and chewed. "It *is* torrid. And *very* stinky."

"It is not!"

"Then tell us who they're from, Georgiana."

Color and heat suffused her cheeks. All five Carroway brothers were looking at her, four with a mix of humor and curiosity. The expression in the gaze of the fifth one, though, was what kept her attention. Her heart sped.

"Tristan Michael Carroway," Aunt Edwina said, looking as though she wished he was still small enough for a spanking, "you apologize."

141

The viscount's lips curved upward, his gaze still on Georgiana. "And why should I?"

"Lady Georgiana's correspondence is none of your affair."

The few-second delay gave Georgiana enough time to rally her thoughts. "Perhaps we should discuss *your* correspondence," she ventured. "Or do you feel left out, perhaps, because you haven't received any love letters?"

"*I* feel left out," Bradshaw commented, reaching for a biscuit.

"Me too," Edward added, though from his expression he had no idea what everyone was talking about.

"Perhaps it's that I manage to keep my personal matters private," Tristan mused, his expression growing harder.

"And yet you feel the need to gossip about mine," she returned, then blanched.

Dare only lifted an eyebrow. "Tell me a secret worth keeping, and I will do so." With a glance at their rapt audience, he motioned for Dawkins to refill his glass of claret. "Until then, I will settle for discussing your odorific correspondence."

Was he again trying to reassure her that he could be trusted, or was he attempting to draw her out? Georgiana didn't feel ready to press her luck any further. Instead, she turned the conversation to the Devonshire ball at the end of the week, considered to be the event of the Season. "Do you attend?" she asked Milly and Edwina.

"Heavens, no. With the crush the duke's likely to have, I'll be flattening everyone's toes with my wheeled chair."

"I'm staying home with Milly," Edwina said firmly.

"You're going, aren't you?" Tristan asked, the devilry fading from his expression.

"I will stay with your aunts."

"Nonsense, Georgiana," Milly cooed. "Edwina and I will probably be in bed long before the dancing even begins. You must go."

"Well, I'm going," Bradshaw said. "Rear Admiral Penrose is supposed to be there, and I want to press —"

"— him about getting your own ship," Andrew and Edward finished in a chorus.

Georgiana saw the pull of Tristan's jaw as it tightened, but the expression was gone before anyone else noticed. Whether Bradshaw earned a captaincy or bought one, it was an expensive proposition. She knew the Carroways had dire money troubles; everyone knew that. But the burden of it, and of the solution, rested on Tristan's shoulders.

She shook herself. He might very well need to marry a wealthy female like Amelia Johns, but he could still be nicer about it. Making the poor girl feel like a necessary pariah was cruel, even if he held no genuine affection for her.

"It's settled, then," he said. "Bradshaw, Georgiana, and I will be attending the Devonshire ball." He glanced at his quiet brother, seated at the far end of the table. "And you, Bit? You're invited as well, you know."

With what might have been a shudder of his broad shoulders, Robert shook his head. "I'm busy." He pushed away from the table and, giving a slight bow, left the room.

"Damn," Tristan murmured, in so quiet a voice that Georgiana almost didn't hear him. His gaze was on the doorway through which his brother had vanished.

"What happened to him?" she whispered, as the rest of the table began discussing the upcoming soiree.

Blue eyes slid in her direction. "Other than his being nearly shot to death? I don't know. He won't tell me."

"Oh."

He gestured at the biscuit remaining on her plate. "Are you going to eat that?"

"No. Why —"

Tristan reached over and took it. "I'm glad you're going to the ball." He tore off a piece of the rich bread and popped it into his mouth.

"I don't know why you should be," she returned, glancing sideways to make sure they weren't being overheard. "I'll only use the occasion to torment you."

"I like being tormented by you." He, too, looked down the length of the table before returning his attention to her. "And I like having you here."

So, her plan was beginning to work. Georgiana put the speeding of her heartbeat to satisfaction. "I sometimes like being here," she said slowly. If she melted too quickly, he would be suspicious, and she'd have to start all over again.

"Sometimes?" he repeated, taking another bite of her biscuit.

"When you're not making silly announcements about my correspondence, or about how willing you are to keep secrets."

"But you and I do have secrets, don't we?" he murmured.

Georgiana lowered her eyes. "You'd do better to stop reminding me."

"Why should I? It was exceptionally memorable, and you refuse to forget it yourself. It's your excuse for not marrying."

Georgiana narrowed her eyes. "No, *you're* my excuse for not marrying. What in the world makes you think I'd wish to marry any man, after the poor example you've set?" she snapped. "What makes you think I'd give any man the power to . . ." She stopped, flushing.

He pounced on the words. "The power to —"

She shoved to her feet. "Excuse me. I need some air."

While the remaining Carroways gazed at her, startled, she hurried from the room. Dawkins didn't have time to reach the front door before she yanked it open and ran down the shallow stone steps. She knew better than to wander about London alone in the dark, even in Mayfair, so she turned for the small rose garden on the east side of the house.

Cursing under her breath, she plunked herself down on the small stone bench beneath a bending elm tree. "Stupid, stupid, stupid!"

"What do you tell people, when they ask why we seem to hate each other so much?"

Tristan's quiet voice came from the

shadows at the front of the garden. He approached slowly, stopping beside the tree to lean against the worn trunk.

"What do *you* tell them?" she countered.

"That I only got as far as a kiss when you found out I was after your stocking for a wager, and that you weren't happy about being the object of any kind of wagering."

"That's close to what I tell them, except I add the part about me punching you in the face when you tried to lie to me about it."

He nodded, his gaze wandering the garden in the moonlit darkness. "That was six years ago, Georgiana. What are the odds you'll ever forgive me?"

"Very low, if you keep mentioning odds and wagering in my presence," she returned, her voice sharp. "I just don't understand, Tristan, how you could be that . . . unfeeling. To anyone. Not just to me."

His eyes met hers for a moment, dark and unreadable. Then he straightened. "Come inside. It's cold out tonight."

She swallowed. The air did bite at her flesh through her thin evening gown, but something had happened this evening. Something aside from the first civil, honest discussion she and Tristan had shared in six years. Something that made her look at his lean profile as he stepped closer and offered her his arm.

Folding her hands in front of her so she wouldn't be tempted to touch him, she stood and led the way back to the house. This absence of anger unsettled her, and she wasn't certain what to say next.

"Would it make any difference," he said quietly from behind her, "if I apologized again?"

Georgiana faced him. "Apologized for what? For making me think you cared for me, or for getting caught at lying?"

Anger touched his gaze for a moment. Good. He was easier to deal with when he wasn't being sensitive and considerate.

"I'll take that as a no, then," he said, motioning her to continue along the walkway. "If it makes a difference, though, on that night . . . hurting you was the furthest thing from my mind. I didn't mean to do that, and that's what I'm sorry for."

"That's a good start," she said, her voice not quite steady as she climbed the steps to the front door. "Or it would be, if I believed you."

Another letter arrived for Georgiana the next day. Tristan took a reluctant sniff, but whoever perfumed them had apparently used the entire bottle of cologne on the first few missives.

Glancing up at the door, he slit the wax seal and opened it. " 'My dear lady,' " he read, " 'I have debated the contents of this letter for several days now. Despite your —' "

"My lord?"

Tristan jumped. "What is it, Dawkins?" he asked, lowering the letter to his lap.

"The picnic basket is ready, my lord, and the curricle is in the drive just as you requested."

"I'll be out in a moment. Close the door, please."

"Yes, my lord."

Lifting the letter again, he skipped his eyes to the bottom. Westbrook — so she *was* receiving correspondence from male acquaintances. He'd half thought she'd been sending letters to herself. Well, he'd opened it, so he might as well finish reading it. " 'Despite your kind acceptance of my apology for my poor behavior at Regent's Park, I feel I owe you a further explanation. I have long known of your animosity toward Lord Dare, and I fear I sprang too quickly to your defense when I overheard his cutting remarks to you.' "

Tristan narrowed his eyes at the letter. "Cutting remarks? I was being nice, you swine," he muttered. " 'Please know that I only interceded because I hold you in the highest regard, and will continue to do so. Your servant, John Blair, Lord Westbrook.' "

So Georgiana had a suitor who wasn't interested in her money. Tristan didn't know the marquis well, though he'd seen him at White's and the Society a few times. Westbrook's wagering was far more conservative than his own, and other than a passing encounter or two, their paths rarely crossed. Neither did they share the same politics. They did seem to have one thing in common, however.

Tristan looked at the letter for a long moment, then folded it again. Rising, he put one corner against his desk lamp, under the glass. The missive smoked and curled into flame. Once it was well engulfed he tossed it into his trash and dumped the contents of the nearest vase in after it.

Tristan gave a grim smile. Whatever was going on, he wasn't about to let Georgie win. All was fair in love and war — and this was definitely one or the other.

Tristan stood at the near wheel of his curricle as he handed Amelia Johns to the ground. It had taken better than a week of halfhearted attempts, and some unexpected maneuvering around Georgiana, but he'd managed to make it to Johns House and arranged for a picnic with Amelia.

"Oh, it's so lovely here," Amelia cooed, swishing her yellow muslin skirt over the ankle-high grass. "Did you choose this spot in particular for us?"

He lifted the basket down from the back of the vehicle while his groom led the curricle and the horses a short distance away. "Of course I did. I know you like daisies."

She looked at the patches of flowers grouped at the edges of the small clearing. "Yes, they're lovely. And they match my dress, don't they?" Amelia giggled. "I'm so glad I didn't wear my pink gown, because then the effect would have been less."

"I would have taken you to a rose garden, then," Tristan answered, snapping the blanket out flat and letting it settle onto the grass. "Have a seat."

Gracefully she sank down, her skirt billowing out around her so artfully he wondered whether she practiced the motion. Probably. He hadn't noticed that she did anything poorly.

"I hope you like roast pheasant and

peaches," he said, opening the basket and pulling out glasses and Madeira.

"I would like anything you chose, Tristan."

She agreed with everything he said, which was a nice change from Georgiana. He could say the sky was blue and Georgie would inform him that the color was some sort of illusion caused by refracted sunlight. Yes, an afternoon with Amelia was a definite change for the better.

"Mama let me arrange all of the flowers downstairs today," she said, accepting a napkin and a glass from him. "She says I have quite the talent for flower arranging."

"I'm sure you do."

"Who arranges your flowers?"

"My flowers?" He thought about it for a moment. "I have no idea. One of the maids, I suppose, or Mrs. Goodwin, the housekeeper."

She looked dismayed. "Oh, you should always have someone very skilled do your arranging. It's very important."

Tristan took a sip of wine. "And why is that?"

"A well-done flower arrangement is the sign of a well-managed household. Mama always says that."

"That makes sense." It also explained

why he really didn't care who arranged his posies, and why he didn't think twice about dumping them into wastebaskets to put out fires he'd started. "Well-managed" and "Carroway" weren't precisely synonyms.

"Do you use roses, or irises, or daisies as your main theme?"

Blinking, Tristan took another swallow, then realized that he'd emptied his glass. "Lilies," he said absently, refilling it. Georgiana had once told him she preferred lilies over any other bloom. Her taste and sense of fashion were impeccable, so it seemed a safe answer.

Amelia pouted, probably to bring his attention to her mouth. He'd learned about that trick during his trip to Emma Brakenridge's girls' school last year, and he had no difficulty deciphering what she was up to.

"Not daisies?" she said, fluttering her lashes at him.

Another trick, well-done, but obvious. "Well, you did ask."

"Do you want to kiss me?"

That caught his attention. "Beg pardon?" he asked, trying not to choke. Another glassful of the sweet wine had vanished.

"I would let you, if you wanted to kiss me."

Surprisingly enough, he hadn't ever thought about kissing her. Once they were married, he would have to do it on occasion, he supposed, along with other, more intimate acts, but . . . He looked at her for a long moment. Sex had always been a pleasurable act, with whomever he chose to indulge. Lately, however, he'd been craving a particular, rare dish — one he'd tasted only once before. And it wasn't Amelia. "Kissing you wouldn't be proper."

"But I want you to like me, Tristan."

"I do like you, Amelia. Kissing isn't necessary. Just enjoy your pheasant."

"But I would if you wanted me to. You're very handsome, you know, and a viscount."

Good God, Georgiana had never been this naive, even at eighteen. If he wanted to secure a marriage with Amelia, he could probably topple her over and lift her skirts right there in the middle of Regent's Park, and she wouldn't even complain. Georgiana would gut him with the carving knife and pitch his remains into the duck pond.

He chuckled, then cleared his throat when Amelia looked at him. "Apologies. And thank you. You're exceptionally lovely, my dear."

"I always try to look my best."

"And why is that?"

"To attract a husband, of course. That's what women are for. The ones who take the most care to look their best are the ones who make a match."

That was interesting, in a horrifying sort of way. "So the women who aren't married are . . ."

"Not trying hard enough, or are of inferior quality."

"What if a female chooses not to marry?" Despite the insult to his happily spinstered aunties, he was actually thinking of Georgiana. She certainly wasn't of inferior quality, and the idea that she would attempt to attract a husband because that's what women were for — well, that was laughable.

"*Chooses* not to marry? That's absurd."

"My aunts are unmarried, you know."

"Well, they are very old," she said, biting into her peach.

"I suppose they are," he agreed, mostly because the idea of attempting an argument with her was absurd. He would have more luck disagreeing with a turnip.

He hadn't used to find her this dull and simpering. And the reason for the change was obvious. Georgiana. He hadn't been able to get her out of his thoughts in days, and now he was comparing every bit of inane conversation he had with poor Amelia to the stimulating tête-à-têtes he engaged in with Georgie.

The problem, though, remained the same. He needed to marry an heiress, before fall harvest. If he didn't, he would have to begin selling off unentailed bits of his land, and he refused to finance his present with his descendants' futures. Georgiana was an heiress, and definitely more interesting than any of the other wealthy chits he'd cultivated. She, however, hated him.

The idea remained intriguing, nonetheless. He didn't hate *her;* in fact, the heated desire that ran through him every time he set eyes on her was becoming difficult to hide. She had softened a little toward him, but he couldn't afford to wait more than another three or four months.

"Tristan?"

He shook himself. "Yes?"

"I didn't mean to say that your aunts are inferior. I'm sure they're very nice."

"Yes, they are."

"Sometimes, I think that maybe I should be cross with you, you know."

"Cross with me?" That seemed an odd thing to say, since he'd gone to the trouble

156

of taking her out on a picnic.

"Yes, because you always pay so little attention to me. But you seem nicer today. I think you're learning your lesson."

Tristan looked at her, his mind pulling free of the dullness she inspired in him. She was certainly saying interesting things, all of a sudden. Lessons for him? She seemed to have used the word deliberately. And Amelia thought he was learning not *a* lesson, but *his* lesson. Did she have reason to think that someone was teaching him some sort of lesson? Not her; she was in his company to get married, and nothing besides.

He could guess who it might be, but had no idea why Amelia would be aware of Georgiana's machinations when he hadn't been able to discover anything himself. Perhaps she did mean a lesson in general and had worded it poorly, and he was merely being suspicious.

On the other hand, being suspicious had saved him from serious trouble on more than one occasion. "I'm trying very hard," he offered slowly, trying to draw her out further, "to learn my lesson."

She nodded. "I can tell. I think you're listening to me today, when you almost never do."

"Is there anything else you've noticed my doing better today?"

"Well, it's too soon to tell, but I have high hopes for you. If we are to marry, I would like you to be at least a little pleasant."

He suppressed a shudder. Now was the perfect time to inform her that he meant to speak to her father about that prospect. It was what he needed to do, for his family. In the back of his mind, though, one thought kept repeating itself: he still had three months. Three months, and a woman sleeping under his roof who didn't annoy him nearly as much as Amelia did, though she aroused and aggravated him considerably more.

"I shall continue to work on being pleasant, then," he hedged. Best not to let the issue fall on one side or the other; talking about marriage could be as binding as promising it, and in three months, if she was still his best prospect, he would have to do so.

"I still think your kissing me would be pleasant."

Good God. Tristan wondered if she had any idea what sort of reputation he'd had in his younger days, or what it would mean if someone caught them kissing. Of course, that might have been what she had in mind.

"I have too much respect for our friendship to risk ruining it, Amelia." He dug into the basket again. "Apple tart?"

"Yes, please." She took it in dainty fingers and nibbled at one corner. "Do you attend the Devonshire ball tomorrow night?"

"I do."

"I know it's forward of me to ask, but will you dance with me there? The first waltz, perhaps?"

"It would be my pleasure."

He'd scheduled two hours for their outing, and it seemed like their time must nearly be up. He pulled out his pocket watch and snapped it open. Thirty-five minutes had passed since he'd collected her at her father's door. Tristan stifled a sigh. He wasn't certain he could stand another hour and a half. He hoped his family would appreciate it. And he hoped that Georgiana was having an equally dull time somewhere, and that she was wondering what he might be up to.

Chapter 9

The world's a huge thing; it is a great price
For a small vice
— *Othello*, Act IV, Scene iii

"I have a question, then." Lucinda curled up on Georgiana's bed, her chin propped on her hand. She looked supremely at ease.

Georgiana envied her poise, though she'd never seen Lucinda the least bit out of sorts about anything. It probably came from having a brilliant, highly disciplined general for a father, who after his wife's death had decided to give his daughter the full benefit of his own education and wealth.

As for herself, every nerve ending felt like it was on fire. Every sound made her jump, and even the softest silk against her skin felt rough and scratchy. Of course, changing into her fifth gown in twenty minutes might have had something to do with that.

"What's your question?" she asked, turning to see her back in the dressing mirror. The blue was nice, but she'd worn it before. *He'd* seen her in it before.

"How far are you going to take this, Georgie?"

Another flutter of nervousness ran through her, and she motioned at Mary to unbutton the back of her gown. "Let's try the new one."

"The green one, my lady?"

"Yes."

"But I thought you said that one was too . . ."

"Immodest. I know. But the rest of them just aren't . . . right."

"Georgie?"

"I heard you, Luce." She glanced in the mirror at her maid, occupied with unfastening the back of her dress. She trusted Mary, but her reputation was her entire future. "Mary, would you mind seeing if Mrs. Goodwin has any peppermint tea?"

"Of course, my lady."

As the maid closed the door behind her, Lucinda rose and finished helping Georgiana strip off the gown. "This is serious, isn't it?"

"If the lesson isn't learned, all of this will be for nothing. He hurt me, Luce. I won't let him do that to anyone else."

"That's the most you've ever said about it," her friend said, studying her expression. "But teaching him a lesson doesn't mean you have to risk being hurt again."

Georgiana forced a laugh. "What makes you think I'm going to be hurt? I've learned my lesson where Tristan Carroway is concerned."

"You just don't look like someone brimming with anger and determination."

"What do I look like, then?"

"You look . . . excited."

"Excited? Don't be ridiculous. This is the sixth year I've been to the Devonshire ball. The festivities are always splendid fun, and you know I like dancing."

"Are you riding with the Carroways, or is your aunt sending a coach for you?"

"Aunt Frederica. Milly and Edwina aren't attending, and I can't very well make an appearance in the company of Tristan and Bradshaw."

"A few weeks ago, you only referred to him as Dare. He has a Christian name again."

"I'm pretending to woo him, remember? Or to let him woo me. I have to be nice."

"What's Tristan's favorite color?"

"Green. Why does that . . ." Georgiana

looked down at her new gown as Lucinda buttoned the back. The silk shimmered in emerald washed with lighter shades of green, the skirt and sleeves covered with a fine green gauze. The neckline was lower cut than she'd worn in some time, but as she twirled before the mirror, she felt beautiful. And her new yellow and white fan would be perfect with it. "I like green."

"Mm hm."

Georgiana stopped twirling. "I know what I'm doing, Luce. You may have thought our lists were just a silly way to pass an afternoon, but every time I think of poor Amelia Johns and how much Dare could hurt her with his stupid insensitivity, believe me, I am very serious."

Lucinda stepped back, taking in Georgiana and the gown. "I believe you. But this is to teach him, Georgie, not to ruin *you*."

"I won't let that happen. Once burned, twice shy." She smiled, twirling again. "I think this is the one."

"You'll catch his attention, that's for certain."

Positive as Lucinda was, Georgiana paced and fretted in her bedchamber for half an hour after her friend left. Alone, it was more difficult to tell herself that she remained unaffected by Tristan. When she'd been eighteen, his attention, charm, and good looks had overwhelmed her. Thanks a great deal to him, she wasn't that same girl any longer.

Even so, the less logical part of her still felt drawn to him. Six years later, he seemed more . . . thoughtful, more conscious of those around him, and more mature than before. And she'd never expected the open warmth and affection he showed for his family. In perhaps the most telling change of all, he'd apologized to her. Twice now, and almost as though he understood how much damage he'd done and genuinely regretted it — or, at least, as if he wanted her to think that.

At half past eight a footman scratched at her door. "My lady, your coach is here."

"Thank you." With a deep breath, she exited her room and made her way downstairs.

Bradshaw, dressed in his naval finest of deep, rich blue and white, stood in the foyer shrugging into his greatcoat. He looked up as she entered, and froze. "Sweet . . . Georgie, please don't let Admiral Penrose see you before I speak with him. He'll never pay me any notice once he catches sight of you."

Feeling slightly reassured, she smiled. "I'll do my best. You look very fine yourself, though."

He grinned back at her, sketching a salute. "It's not quite the same thing, but thank you."

The air stirred behind her. Resisting the urge to smooth her skirt, Georgiana turned around. Dare had donned a charcoal gray jacket, his trousers black as midnight and his cravat frothing white at the neck over a buff waistcoat. He wore no ornamentation at all, but he didn't need any. Dark hair curled at his collar, and his light blue eyes glittered like sapphires as he took her in from head to toe and back again.

Warmth crept up the backs of her legs to her scalp. She hadn't expected to react to him physically. Yes, she still enjoyed his kisses, but she'd thought herself immune to his compelling masculinity. To cover her discomfiture, she curtsied. "Good evening."

Tristan wanted to wet his lips. Instead, he nodded, unable to keep from running his gaze down her slender figure once more. She shimmered, the gauze picking up the dim lamplight and turning it to emeralds. In the well-lighted ballroom, he could only imagine the effect. The low-cut neckline heaved with her deep breath, the round, creamy curve of her breasts beckoning and tantalizing him.

A blush swept up her cheeks, and he shook himself. Idiot. He needed to say something. "You look stunning."

Georgiana inclined her head. "Thank you."

Dawkins cleared his throat, offering Georgiana an ivory lace shawl. Tristan swept in, snatching the garment from the butler's surprised fingers. "Allow me." Her eyes followed him as he moved closer, and Tristan took a slow breath. "Turn around," he murmured.

With a start, as though waking from a dream, Georgiana did so. The gown left her shoulders and most of her shoulder blades bare. Tristan wanted to run his hands along her skin, to know if she was as warm and smooth as he remembered. Instead, he draped the shawl across her shoulders, stepping back hastily as she took the ends from him to clasp over her breast. A curl of soft golden hair brushed his cheek as she faced him again.

"My coach is here," she said unnecessarily.

"I'll see you out."

He offered his arm as Dawkins pulled open the front door. Georgiana wrapped her fingers around his sleeve, and even through the heavy superfine of his jacket, he could feel her trembling as he led her down the shallow steps to the waiting coach.

"Georgiana, Lord Dare," a female voice said from the depths of the vehicle. "I was beginning to think you'd murdered one another."

He bowed. "Your Grace, my apologies. I hadn't realized you were waiting out here."

"I hadn't either, Aunt Frederica," Georgiana chimed in, flushing as she freed her hand and stepped up into the coach. "I would never have kept you waiting."

"I know, my dear. I shall blame Dare."

"Please do." He managed to catch Georgiana's eye as she sat opposite the dowager duchess. "I'll see you shortly."

He watched the coach down the drive and then went back inside to collect his coat and gloves. Bradshaw handed him his hat and settled his own navy tricorn on his dark hair.

"What was that all about?" his brother said in a quiet voice.

"What was what about?"

"You two. The hairs on my arms were prickling."

Tristan shrugged. "Maybe it was the weather."

"I wouldn't want to be caught in that storm, then."

His own coach pulled up, and he and Bradshaw climbed in. He'd tried to talk Edwina, at least, into joining them, but his aunt had refused. Georgie's friend, Lucinda Barrett, had brought by the new kitten that afternoon, effectively fore-stalling his plan to enable Georgiana to share his coach.

It annoyed him, but neither could he argue with the happy light in Aunt Edwina's eyes as she took possession of Dragon, which for some reason she'd be-come set on as the name of her new black cat. Tristan thought the little thing looked more like a rat, but he wasn't about to say that aloud. Not when Georgiana had cud-dled the ball of fur beneath her chin and cooed at it.

"The Runt said you went on a picnic yesterday."

Tristan blinked. "Yes."

"With Amelia Johns."

"Yes."

Bradshaw scowled at him. "You sound like Bit. How was your luncheon? In more than two words, please."

"Very pleasant, thank you."

"Bastard."

"If I am, then you get to be the viscount and marry Miss Johns. That would be interesting."

"Horrifying, more like." Bradshaw crossed his ankles. "So you've settled on Miss Johns, then? Definitely?"

Tristan sighed. "She's the most likely candidate. Wealthy, pretty, and obsessed with gaining a title."

"A pity you and Georgiana don't get on well. Or do you, now? All the inclement weather confuses me."

"And why is that such a pity?" Tristan asked, mostly to hear what his brother would say. "She's too tall, headstrong, and has a tongue like a rapier." Of course, those were three of the things he liked most about her.

"Well, you're looking for wealthy and pretty, and she certainly is that. Of course, her father's a marquis, so she's probably not hunting a title — though I can't imagine her pursuing something like that, regardless." He fiddled with his watch fob. "If Westbrook wasn't after her, along with the money-starved horde, I might consider pursuing her myself. With her funding and influence, I'd make admiral by the time I was thirty-five."

Westbrook, again. And no doubt he was

already waiting for her at the ball, damn him. "You think it's that easy, then? You decide, she says yes because, well, that's what women are for, and you live happily ever after?"

Bradshaw looked at him. "Amelia turned you down?"

"I haven't asked her, yet. I keep hoping . . . I don't know. For a miracle, I suppose."

"Don't look for one where money's concerned. Father was very thorough about spending every penny he could beg, borrow, or steal."

Tristan sighed. "One must keep up appearances, you know." That was the trickiest part — spending money he didn't have to spare, so the family would look as though they *did* have some money.

"Don't tell me you sympathize with him. Not after what his mess has put you through over the last four years. Is still putting you through."

"I didn't exactly help things while he was alive. I might have taken more of an interest in the properties."

"You made your own way. And I had no idea we were that close to ruin until it was too late. I don't know how you could have seen it coming," Shaw said.

"I knew I was the heir. I didn't take that very seriously."

"And now you are. That's more than he did. If his creditors hadn't spread the rumors all over the *ton* when he died, I don't imagine anyone would even suspect the mess he made of everything."

"He was careful," Tristan said.

"No, he wasn't. *You* were careful. You still are."

Tristan smiled. "So full of compliments tonight. You want me to have a word with Penrose, don't you?"

Bradshaw chuckled. "No. Just the opposite. I want you to stay as far away from him as possible. He still remembers that two hundred quid you won from him at faro. I can't tell you how many times he's reminded me of that 'damned lucky brother of mine.' "

"Luck had nothing to do with it, my boy."

Sighing, Shaw patted his brother on the knee. "And I suppose I wanted you to know that I understand how little you like the idea of marrying for wealth, and that I appreciate it."

"I was actually thinking that you look so splendid tonight, *you* might snag an heiress and *I* could go back to pursuing actresses and opera singers."

"Not likely," Shaw scoffed.

"Me with the opera singers, or you getting married?"

"Either one."

Bradshaw was probably correct, and on both counts. Without the lure of a title, Shaw's prospects were even less promising than his own.

It wasn't that Tristan had lacked for partners, but he'd become more circumspect about the process. Mistresses didn't want him for his money, though they did still seem to want him. At times, however, he felt like a prime stag with his antlers missing. Women were more than willing to share his bed, but he didn't get shown off much. He understood it, but he didn't like it, all the same.

For that reason he'd almost come to dread gatherings like the one at the Devonshire ball. This evening, though, anticipation ran hot under his skin. It had nothing to do with his promised dance with Amelia, however, and everything to do with seeing and holding Georgiana in that emerald gown. If she said her dance card was full, someone was going to get hurt.

He saw her as soon as he and Shaw

strolled into the ballroom. He had been right about the gown; in the chandelier's glow she seemed to have an ethereal light that drew his, and every other male's, attention. Even if she'd been in rags, though, he would have noticed her.

"Your Amelia is fluttering at you," Bradshaw muttered.

"She's not my —"

"And there's Penrose. You're on your own, brother."

Tristan was used to seeing a crowd of single men around Georgiana at every soiree, and he'd never attempted to make himself part of it. The two of them together had been simply too volatile. Catching her for a swift exchange of insults or a knuckle-bashing late in the evening had been the best he'd hoped for, and it was enough, barely, to satisfy his masochistic desire to see her up close. Tonight, though, he needed to join the throng. Tonight, he wanted to dance with her.

"Tristan, I've saved the first waltz for you," Amelia said, sweeping up to him, angelic in pink and white.

"And when is the first waltz?"

"As soon as they end this quadrille. Doesn't everyone look magnificent tonight?"

"Yes, magnificent." He glanced at the orchestra. In two or three minutes he would be out on the floor with Amelia, and by the time the waltz ended, Georgiana's dance card would be full with a dozen alternates waiting in the wings for slips or falls on the part of primary partners. Damnation. "Will you excuse me for just a moment?"

Her pretty face fell into a heartbroken frown. "I thought you might want to chat with me."

Tears would be next; he'd seen the progression before. "Of course I do. And I'll chat with you after the waltz, as well. But Lady Georgiana is looking after my aunts, and I had a message from them for her."

"Oh. That's all right, then. Hurry back, though."

"I will." Sweet Lucifer. He hadn't even asked for her hand, and she was already trying to dictate with whom he could socialize. Whatever the outcome of the next few weeks, that particular irritation was not going to continue.

Without a backward glance, he strode across the edge of the ballroom floor up to the cluster of males surrounding Georgiana. He was taller than most of them, and she caught sight of him immediately. To his surprise and suspicion, she smiled.

"Lord Dare, there you are. I was about to give your spot away."

She'd saved a dance for him. "My apologies."

The Marquis of Halford stepped into the tiny clear space around them. "Are you playing favorites, Lady Georgie?"

"Careful, my lord, or your spot will open up, as well," she said, regarding the marquis evenly. "We're all friendly tonight."

The broad-shouldered Halford glared at Tristan for a brief moment, then sketched a bow in Georgiana's direction. "I have learned never to argue with a beautiful woman."

"What a ridiculous thing to say," Tristan scoffed. "Now you can't argue with any woman, or she'll think you believe her to be ugly."

A stifled laugh sounded in the crowd. Halford's face turned red, but before he could respond, Georgiana grabbed Tristan's arm and steered him toward the refreshment table.

"Stop that."

"No. It was a half-witted thing to say, and you know it."

"I hear half-witted things from men all the time," she returned, her voice low.

The quadrille ended, and Tristan

glanced over his shoulder to see Amelia looking at him hopefully. He would rather have spent the waltz talking with Georgiana, but he'd given his word.

"Are you ready?" Georgiana asked, holding out her hand.

"Ready for what?"

"Our waltz."

Tristan uttered a low curse. "Georgie, I . . ." He took a breath as the waltz began. "I can't."

Her mouth opened and then closed again. "Oh."

"I promised this waltz to Miss Johns yesterday."

She glanced past his shoulder, her expression unreadable, before she nodded. "Then go dance with her."

Before she could turn around, Tristan seized her arm. "Don't be angry," he murmured. "This is not a slight to you."

Surprise crossed her emerald eyes. "I'm not angry. But I wanted . . ."

"You wanted to dance with me," he finished, with a slow smile. "And you will."

She scowled. "What makes you think —"

"I have to go."

He released her to lead Amelia onto the dance floor, and Georgiana watched them begin. Amelia was skilled at the waltz, and

Tristan had always been one of the most athletic, graceful men she'd ever known. They made an attractive couple, swaying across the floor and keeping just the proper distance between themselves.

Tristan had kept a commitment to Amelia. Georgiana should have felt elated; instead, she felt frustrated.

Lord Westbrook strolled up to her. "Lady Georgiana, I can't believe you decided to forgo the evening's first waltz."

"I've just been waiting for you, my lord," she said, holding out her hand and smiling.

"You accept my apology, then," the tawny-haired marquis said, taking her hand to kiss her knuckles.

Georgiana blinked. "Your apology? Oh, for that silly exchange in the park. Of course I do. I blame Dare entirely."

"I wonder, then, why you continue to tolerate his presence."

She couldn't begin to explain that, herself. "He's my cousin's closest friend," she said, giving her standard answer, "and his aunts are delightful."

"No, Georgiana, *you* are delightful."

Accustomed as she was to meaningless flattery and compliments, Lord Westbrook didn't give them lightly. He was also one of the few gentlemen of her acquaintance, aside from Tristan Carroway, who had never proposed to her. Yet, anyway. "You are very kind, my lord."

"You called me John, a few days ago."

"John, then." She smiled into his serene brown eyes. "How is it that you have no partner for the waltz?" With his wealth and title, he was as closely pursued as she was.

"I hadn't intended to dance, tonight."

"Oh. I'm sorry, then. I —"

"Because I thought your card would be full. I'm happy to be mistaken."

Across the floor she caught a glimpse of Tristan looking at them as he turned Amelia in his arms. The dark expression in his eyes startled her. He was dancing with the woman he was supposed to marry, for heaven's sake, yet he looked as though he would rather be brawling with Lord Westbrook over her.

Jealousy from him was new, if that was what this was. He'd made a point of arguing with the marquis in the park, but she'd ascribed that to his general contrariness.

Then again, perhaps her plan was working, and even better than she'd expected — which both thrilled and horrified her.

Chapter 10

I am glad 'tis night, you do not look on me,
For I am much ashamed of my exchange.
— The Merchant of Venice, Act II, Scene vi

It was past two o'clock in the morning when the Dowager Duchess of Wycliffe's coach stopped in front of Carroway House. Georgiana rubbed her tired toes one last time and stood as the liveried tiger pulled open the door for her.

"I'm glad Milly's doing better," Frederica said. "Do tell her I said so."

"I will." Georgiana kissed her aunt on the cheek. "Good night."

"Come and visit me more often, my dear."

She stopped, looking over her shoulder at the duchess. "I won't be here forever. Milly's nearly able to get about on her own, and then you'll be able to get tired of me all over again."

"Never, child."

Dawkins couldn't seem to remain awake

during the day, much less after one in the morning, so Georgiana let herself in. Tristan and Bradshaw had vanished fairly early in the evening, undoubtedly to one of the half dozen gaming rooms the Duke of Devonshire had set up. She'd hoped Tristan might come by the ballroom again to at least see with whom she might be dancing, but he hadn't. She wondered whether Amelia had looked for him as well, but swiftly dismissed the thought. At least Amelia had gotten to waltz with him.

One lamp still burned in the foyer and she saw another at the top of the stairs, enough to light the way to her bedchamber. She'd told Mary not to wait up for her, so she would have to find a way to unfasten the back of her dress on her own, or she would have to sleep in it. She wasn't eager to take it off, anyway.

The way Tristan had looked at her, practically devouring her with his eyes, had started that once-familiar warmth in the pit of her stomach. Six years ago it had thrilled her, knowing *she* had been the one to catch his attention, and that Dare had eyes for no one but her. Good Lord, she had been stupid and naive. What did it say about her, that a compliment and a hungry look from him could still make her feel that way?

"Georgiana."

The whisper, coming from the dark drawing room, made her gasp. "Tristan? What —"

"Come here."

Frowning, she crossed the hallway to where he stood just inside the doorway, all dark planes of shadows but for his eyes. Thank goodness he couldn't read minds.

He took her hand, pulling her into the room and closing the door behind them. "Don't move," he murmured, his breath warm on her temple. "I'll get the light."

In a moment the table lamp flared, bathing the room in golden, flickering light. Tristan still wore his formal clothes, though he'd shed his gloves and his great-coat. He straightened from the lamp, his eyes dark and glittering in the dimness.

"It's very late, Tristan," she said in the same low voice. "Tell me whatever you want to tell me, because I want to go to bed."

He smiled, a slow, delicious curving of his lips that made her mouth go dry. "Where did you get that gown?"

"Madame Perisse. Is that why you wanted to see me?"

"It looks like something faeries would weave from spiderwebs and dewdrops."

She'd been complimented all night, and none of the words touched her as much as those did. "That's what I thought when I first saw it. Thank you."

He took a step toward her. "Dance with me. I promised you a waltz."

"And music?"

"I'll sing if you want, but I wouldn't recommend it."

She chuckled. "I think I can count the time, if necessary."

He was in a very good mood. For a moment she wondered whether he'd proposed to Amelia and she'd accepted, but Georgie didn't think that would make him smile. The two of them danced with too much precision to be in love — yet.

The thought of him with Amelia made a sensation very like panic rise. She took a deep breath. This was ridiculous. Nothing had happened; he wasn't ready to marry yet. She hadn't prepared him for it yet. Not even to herself would she admit that she hadn't prepared herself for his marrying someone else, either.

"Come here," he repeated, holding out his hand.

"How did your waltz with Miss Johns

go?" she asked instead, folding her hands behind her back. She'd grown more wise over the years; she knew that. Why, then, couldn't she seem to resist him?

"I would rather have danced with you," he answered in his low voice. "Are you going to take my hand, Georgiana? I promised you a waltz."

"You've made me promises before that you haven't kept."

His eyes narrowed. "That was a long time ago. I keep my promises now. Or I try to, anyway. You're making it a little difficult."

"I —"

"I want to waltz with you."

He took another step closer, smooth and sure as a panther. Oh, this was a mistake. She needed to leave before she ruined everything she'd been planning, because she couldn't seem to hate him any longer. "I have a question for you," she said, trying to make her brain work again. "I want to know —"

"Why?" he finished. The question didn't seem to surprise him at all.

"No lies or flowery explanations, Tristan," she said flatly. "Just tell me."

Slowly, he nodded. "For one thing, I was twenty-four, and very stupid. When I heard someone at White's propose the wager to win a kiss and one of Lady Georgie's stockings, I jumped at it." He gazed at her, the confident arrogance for once missing from his expression. "Not because of the wager, though. That just gave me an excuse."

"An excuse for what?"

He reached out, running the back of one finger along her cheek. "For this."

Georgiana trembled. "There was a time I would have given you my stocking. You didn't need to . . ."

"And that's all I meant to do — ask you for your stocking. But once I touched you, I wanted more than that. I was used to getting what I wanted. And what I wanted was you, Georgiana."

She knew what he meant. When he had kissed her — when he kissed her even now — lightning swirled up her spine. "All right, I'll accept that. But when I heard about the wager, why didn't you explain anything?"

Tristan gave a brief frown, looking down at his boots like a guilty schoolboy. "I was wrong to do what I did," he said, catching her gaze again, "whatever my reasons for participating. You had every right to be angry with me."

Her mouth was dry. "Then where's my stocking?"

For some reason that made him smile. "I'll show you, if you like."

He still had possession of it, then. Somewhere in the back of her mind she'd hoped that he'd kept it. It had always worried her, that he might have given the stocking to someone else or discarded it where someone could find it, and because of the wager they would realize whose it was. She'd lived with the fear of being ruined in everyone's eyes for years, never knowing when it might happen. "Show me."

Lifting the lamp in one hand, Tristan motioned her to follow him. He headed down the hallway toward the west wing of the house, and she hesitated. His private rooms and his bedchamber lay in that direction. But if he thought she might forgive him, then perhaps he could fall in love with her in time to help Amelia. She followed his quiet footsteps as if this midnight escapade didn't unsettle her in the least.

They stopped before a closed door. With a backward glance at her, as though to make certain she was still there, he opened it and stepped inside. Squaring her shoulders, she entered behind him.

"This is your bedchamber," she said, swallowing as he closed and latched the door behind them.

Without answering her, he walked to the chest of drawers at one end of the large, dark room and opened the top drawer. "Here," he said, facing her again.

He held a small wooden box in his hand, nearly the same size as her fan boxes. Frowning, she crossed to him and lifted the engraved mahogany lid. Her stocking, neatly folded, lay inside. She knew it was hers, because she had embroidered the flowers along the top of it herself.

She looked up to find his gaze steadily on her face, assessing her expression. "You did lose the wager, then," she whispered.

"I lost more than that." Setting the box back in the drawer, he gently took her face in his hands. "I'm sorry, Georgiana," he murmured. "Not for what I did that night, because I still wouldn't change that, but for everything it's done to you since then. I'd make it right, if I could."

Before she could answer, he touched his lips to hers. Heat seared through her, but he didn't deepen the kiss as she'd expected, and wanted. Instead, his hand swept down her back to her waist, while his other slid down her arm to her fingers.

"And now," he said, smiling again, "I owe you a waltz."

Tightening his grip around her waist, he

swept her in a slow circle around his bed and in front of the glowing fireplace at its foot. Georgiana had never thought she would be dancing in the half dark silence of any man's bedchamber, much less his. As a giddy breathlessness filled her, she knew that with no man but Tristan would she dare be so bold.

He turned her again, moving to a silent waltz she seemed to feel beating in her heart. Her skirt rustled around his legs while he held her far too closely for propriety. In here, though, they could do as they liked. No one would know.

"Wait," she whispered.

He slowed and stopped, not questioning, as she leaned against him and twisted sideways. Slipping out of one slipper, and then the other, she nudged them toward the fireplace.

"Much better."

His low chuckle started warmth deep between her legs. "When was the last time you waltzed barefoot?" he asked.

"When I was ten, in the drawing room at Harkley. Grey was teaching me the steps, and he insisted that I take off my shoes if I was going to trample him like an elephant. Mother was appalled." She leaned her cheek against his chest as they moved in a slow circle again. His heart beat hard and fast, in time with hers. "I think at the time she fancied the idea of Grey marrying me. As if I would ever marry someone so mean."

"He used to talk about you, at Oxford," Tristan's low drawl mused as they danced.

She closed her eyes, listening to his heart and to the rhythm of his voice. "Nothing nice, I suppose."

"He mentioned tossing you in the Wycliffe duck pond when you wouldn't stop following him about the estate."

"Yes, headfirst. I surfaced with a leech attached to my nose. For days after that, he insisted that it had sucked out my brains. I was six, and he was fourteen, and for a while I believed him, until Aunt Frederica made him stick a leech on his head to prove he was lying."

His laugh deepened. "He always spoke of you very affectionately, mostly tales about how stubborn and bright and self-assured you were. I had always imagined you striding about in breeches with a cheroot clamped between your teeth, for some reason. When I first set eyes on you . . ." He was silent for a long moment as they slowly twirled about the room. "You took my breath away."

188

He had done the same to her. Georgiana leaned back, letting her hips sway to the beckoning silence of the waltz. Tristan leaned in, running his lips down the base of her jaw to her throat. With her hips against his, she became aware of his arousal as they stepped and turned. It should have made her angry to think he would dare try to convince her to join him in bed again, after what had happened the last time.

In her deep excitement, though, she didn't have room to be angry. It had been so long since she'd been in his arms, and she had missed his touch so much it nearly brought tears to her eyes.

"Let your hair down, why don't you?" he suggested in a controlled, husky voice. "You'll be even more comfortable."

If she had any sense remaining, she would flee as fast as her stockinged feet could carry her. But then he would have to stop kissing her, and she didn't want him to stop. She freed her hands and lifted them to her head, pulling pins and clips and dropping them to the floor. Her hair cascaded down her back, golden and curling in the candlelight.

The waltz slowed and then stopped before the fireplace. "My God, Georgiana. My God."

His hand shaking a little, he curled his fingers into her hair, drawing it forward over her shoulder. Before she could lose her nerve she wove her hands through his hair and pulled his face forward to kiss him. "Just promise me one thing," she said, her own voice unsteady as she buried her face in his neck. He smelled faintly of soap and cigar smoke. The combination was intoxicating.

"What?" he asked, his sure hands trailing and tugging down her back. Her gown slipped to the floor almost before she was aware of what he was doing.

She swallowed. *My goodness.* She was remembering other things about that night. About how good it had felt to be in his embrace. "Promise me that you won't promise me anything."

His mouth sought hers again. "I promise."

The air felt cool in the room as she stood in just her shift and her stockings, cool except for where his hands touched her. Plans, lessons — nothing but Tristan and how he made her feel mattered, as burning memory and sensation filled her.

He shrugged out of his jacket, dropping it on the floor beside the puddle of her dress. His mouth still on hers, he unbuttoned his waistcoat and pulled it off, as well. "I missed you," he murmured.

The deep sound resonated inside her. She had his cravat unknotted in only a moment. "You see me all the time," she said breathlessly, as his hands swept up her waist, tugging her against him for another kiss.

"Not like this."

His mouth trailed along the neckline of her shift, his warm, skillful lips and tongue making her tremble. His passion frightened her a little; until tonight she'd been dictating how close they became, how far they went. Tonight he felt like a summer storm, wild and powerful and ready to break over her in a torrent she couldn't resist.

She pulled his shirt free from his trousers and ran her hands up the warm skin of his stomach. His hard muscles jumped beneath her touch. "Do I feel the same?" he murmured.

"Yes, and no. I know you, this time."

He raised his arms and she lifted the shirt over his head, dropping it with the rest of their clothes. Tristan kissed her again, pressing her back against the tall bedpost. "Georgiana," he murmured, nudging her chin up and running his mouth along her throat.

A moan broke from her, and she closed her eyes, drinking in the sensation of his mouth and his hands caressing her. His head dipped, and his mouth touched her breast through the thin fabric of her shift. Her nipples grew taut, pushing at the fine silk. Unable to help herself, she groaned again, tangling her fingers through his coal black hair and pulling him to her.

Tristan sank to his knees before her. Long fingers slid with slow purpose up her legs, drawing her shift up with them. For a moment, she panicked. Not again. She wasn't going to let herself be hurt like that again.

"Tristan."

He looked up at her. "I promised no promises, Georgiana," he said in a low voice, "but —"

"No. It's all right." She didn't want to hear him say he cared for her, or that he would be there when she awoke in the morning, or that she wouldn't regret what she was doing. She wanted him tonight. She would worry about what came next when tonight was over.

"Are you certain?"

His words resonated into her, and she trembled. "Yes."

His hands resumed their trail up her

right leg, caressing and kneading. High up on her thigh he slipped his fingers beneath the top edge of her stocking, rolling it slowly down her leg, then lifted her foot and pulled it from her toes. He offered it to her wordlessly. With a shaking breath she took it from his fingers, clenching it in her fist until he offered her the second one in the same way.

He wanted the gesture to mean something, but she refused to let it. Tonight was tonight. Neither yesterday nor tomorrow mattered. Holding his gaze, she dropped both stockings into the pile their clothes were making. "Now it's your turn," she said unsteadily. "Off with your boots."

Rising, he leaned against the footboard and yanked one gleaming black Hessian and then the other off his feet, and flung them into a dark corner. "Anything else you wish me to remove?"

He was letting her take the lead again, which steadied her a little. At the same time, it would be more difficult later, when she tried to justify her actions to herself. That, though, was later. She stepped forward and unfastened the top button of his breeches. "Oh, yes."

With that small motion, the storm broke over her. Tristan took her face in his hands, kissing her again, deep and rough, his tongue plundering her mouth and leaving her panting and breathless. She undid the remaining two buttons and shoved his trousers down.

She felt him come free. Unable to resist, she broke the kiss and looked down. A light dusting of dark, curling hair across his chest narrowed in a line down his flat, muscled stomach, drawing her eyes lower. "This, I remember."

At twenty-four he had been handsome. At thirty, he was breathtaking — more muscular, all man in the angular planes of his face and the knowing expression in his eyes.

Georgiana touched the warm smoothness of his manhood, and his muscles jumped. Emboldened by the fact that he was completely naked and she still wore her silk shift, she curled her fingers around him. Slowly she stroked the length of his shaft while he stood absolutely motionless before her, beautiful as a marble sculpture, but warm and alive and strong.

"Tristan," she whispered, looking up to meet the glittering blue of his gaze, "I still seem to be partially dressed."

"Not for long." He slipped the straps of her shift off her shoulders and gently tugged the garment down. She had to release him as the material flowed down past her arms and her waist, pooling at her feet.

His hands traced her collarbones, then teased downward to circle her breasts, then her nipples, before cupping and releasing them. "I remember you, too," he murmured, bending down to take her left breast in his mouth.

She gasped, grateful for the support of bedpost behind her, the only thing keeping her from sliding to the floor. He suckled, biting down gently on her nipple, and with another gasp her legs did give way.

Tristan caught her up in his arms, kissing her hard and openmouthed as he lifted her and brought her over to the middle of the bed. She couldn't seem to let go of him and kept her arms around his neck, kissing him as he had kissed her. He yanked the sheets down one-handed, and laid her in the middle of the soft dishevelment.

Slipping onto the bed beside her, he captured her breast again. Her body hummed with excited tension; she knew what was to come. He continued laving her nipple, sliding his hands in languorous circles down her stomach, then lower. His finger dipped inside her, and she bucked.

"You want me," he murmured, kissing her again. "You want me inside you."

His finger moved again, and she moaned. "Yes, I want you."

Satisfaction and desire mingled in his eyes. "I didn't think you would."

She ran restless hands down his back. "I shouldn't, but I do."

Tristan parted her legs and settled himself along her body. "There hasn't been anyone besides me, has there?" he murmured, raising up a little on his arms and kissing her again.

"No one."

Last time he had been patient and careful. Tonight he didn't need to be, and she lifted her hips to meet him as he pushed inside her. She cried out, not with pain but with satisfaction. He muffled her cry against his mouth, moaning as he began to move inside her. The bed rocked with his rhythmic thrusts, another dance just for the two of them.

The tension inside her built until she thought she would die from it. Georgiana dug her fingers into his shoulders, holding herself as close to him as she could, wanting to be part of him, part of the fire sweeping them along.

"Say my name," he murmured breathlessly, kissing her ear.

"Tristan. Oh, Tristan." Like a gate opening, she shattered, trembling and pulsing around him. All she could feel was him, inside her and around her, holding her and loving her.

"Georgiana." With another groan he sank hard into her again, holding himself tightly against her before he relaxed and lowered his head against her neck.

She loved the warm weight of him lying on top of her. It seemed like forever since she had felt this, that she was part of two rather than someone alone. Then she had awakened to find him gone from her bed-chamber and her stocking missing. A memento, she'd thought, until she'd heard about the wager.

He ran his hands beneath her bottom and rolled, still inside her as he turned onto his back with her lying along his chest. For a long time they lay quietly like that, his fingers gently twining in her hair. As her breathing slowly returned to normal, she lifted her head enough to look down at him.

"Am I the same as I was?"

"No. You're curvier." With a slow, wicked smile he ran his hands over her bottom again.

She sighed. Reality was still on the other side of his dark bed curtains, and she would be very happy if it stayed there for a while longer. Her caressing hands moved up his chest, pausing at a small indentation along his left collarbone. "This is new," she said. "What did this?"

"A horse threw me about three years ago and I landed on a rock. Hurt like the devil." He brushed hair from her eyes, tilting his head a little to meet her gaze. "You remember that well, to notice a scar?"

I remember everything, she started to say, but didn't. "I thought maybe it was one I had given you."

He chuckled, warm and quiet. "Not for lack of trying, Georgie. My toes are still bruised, and my knuckles let me know when the weather's changing."

"You exaggerate."

"Maybe a little." He kissed her forehead. "Are you cold?"

"I'm starting to be."

"Here."

Sliding out from under her, he pulled the blankets up around them. He lay back again and she tucked her head against his shoulder, her hand curled across his chest.

She felt relaxed, ready to sleep for weeks

tucked beside him, with his arm around her shoulder keeping her close. Still — "What about Amelia Johns?"

"I'll deal with her later. Talk about something else, my sweet one."

She meant to question him further, but her eyes drooped shut, and she fell asleep to the soft sound of his breathing and the steady beat of his heart. When she awoke, gray dawn was peeking around the edge of his blue curtains. She lay still, feeling the slow rise and fall of his chest beneath her cheek.

She didn't want to leave. Neither, though, could she stay. Carefully shifting his arm from her shoulder, she sat up. He stirred, turning his face toward her but not waking. She wanted to kiss his cheek, but steeled herself against it.

He'd finally let her in, had decided she'd forgiven him. Well, she had — and she hadn't. But that didn't matter, because she could never trust him with her heart. What had happened last night was merely lust, the pent-up frustration of six years of antagonism.

Moving cautiously, she slipped off the bed and pulled her shift back on. A stocking tumbled to the floor, and she looked at it for a moment. It would serve him right. And it would ensure that he understood he'd been taught not to trifle with her, or with the heart of any female.

His writing desk was open, and she dipped his pen and wrote a quick note, laying it and her stocking on the pillow beside him. That done, she retrieved the box from his drawer and opened it, leaving that beside the note, as well.

He deserved it, she reminded herself fiercely, refusing to look at his face. He'd done it to her, and he deserved it.

Making no sound, she gathered her dress and her shoes and slipped out of the room, closing the door behind her. With luck, she would be out of the house before he woke up. With more luck, she'd be able to go home to Shropshire before he decided to retaliate. With immense luck, she'd be able to get out of Carroway House without crying.

Georgiana wiped at the tears on her face. She didn't have that much luck.

Chapter 11

Puck.
— *A Midsummer Night's Dream,*
Act II, Scene i

The light scent of lavender clung to the bedsheets and the pillow on which his cheek rested. Eyes closed, Tristan breathed deeply of her, of Georgiana.

Six years was a damned long time to wait for her, but he would have waited longer. As he came more awake, he still couldn't quite believe that he'd been forgiven. He wanted to thank her again — several more times, in fact — before the household rose and she had to leave his room.

But even then he wouldn't let her escape from him or his bed for long. Now that he had earned another chance with Georgiana, he wasn't going to ruin it. Thank God he hadn't proposed yet to Amelia; at least in Georgie he'd found a wife with whom he enjoyed sex.

He stretched carefully, not wanting to wake her, then opened his eyes. Her side of the bed was empty. Tristan scowled, sitting up. "Georgiana?"

Silence answered him.

As he shifted, something slid against his bare backside. He reached back and lifted it. The box. For a long moment he looked at it, willing his sated brain to begin working again. Swiping his hand through his disheveled hair, he turned his attention to the pillow where the box had been. A stocking lay neatly across it, a folded paper beneath.

With all his being, he didn't want to look at that note. Neither could he sit naked in bed all morning staring at it, though, so with a deep breath he picked it up and opened it. In Georgiana's neat hand it said, "Now you have a pair of my stockings. I hope you will enjoy them, for you won't have me again. Georgiana."

She'd planned it all along. And he'd fallen for it with all the ardor of a schoolboy suffering his first crush. Anger ripped through him, and he crushed the note in his fist, hurling it into the fireplace. A single curse tore from his chest, quiet and vehement.

He shot out of bed, grabbing for trousers

and a clean shirt. *No* one played him for a fool. He'd been planning proposals and entwined bodies, and she'd been waiting for him to wake up, laughing about how she'd waited six years to do it, but she'd finally gotten even.

Deeper than the anger, a knot of solid hurt wound tighter and tighter inside him, as though someone had kicked him in the gut. He tried to push it aside, but it remained, keeping him from breathing. This was unacceptable. He did not like feeling this way.

He slowed, yanking on his boots. When he'd bedded her six years earlier, it hadn't been to win the damned wager. It had been because he'd wanted her. He hadn't been thinking any further than finding pleasure in her body; he hadn't expected to spend the next six years remembering and wanting her again.

Tristan strode to the wardrobe, grabbing a waistcoat and a jacket, pulling them on with cold, black anger. Last night had been different, even better than before. He'd been thinking beyond the moment this time.

He scowled, reaching for a clean, starched cravat and knotting it around his neck. Georgiana had been thinking beyond the moment, too. She'd been thinking about how she planned on getting even.

Even. They were even. The word was somehow significant, but he was too furious to dwell on it. Tristan stalked to his door, slamming it open and striding down the hallway to the east wing of the house. He didn't bother to knock on her door, but shoved it open. "Georgi—"

She wasn't there. Clothes lay strewn across the coverlet and the floor, but the bed hadn't been slept in. Drawers hung half-open, clothes dripping from them to the floor in multicolored falls of silk and satin, and half the toilette items on her dressing table were gone.

He assessed the chaos. She had gathered some things together quickly, not bothering to hide the fact. That meant she hadn't packed yesterday, in advance of her little *coup de grâce.*

Turning on his heel, he went back to his bedchamber. The note lay just inside the fireplace, and he picked it up, smoothing it out and brushing off smudges of charred coal. Her writing wasn't as precise as usual, the ink smeared a little because she'd folded the missive before it was dry. She'd been in a hurry.

The question was, why? Had she wanted

to finish before he awoke, or before she lost her nerve? Shoving the note in the drawer of his nightstand with both stockings, he returned through the hallway and down the stairs. Dawkins stood in the foyer, yawning.

"Why are you up already?" Tristan demanded, the frayed rein on his anger threatening to pull loose and run rampant over the next person he came across.

The butler straightened. "Lady Georgiana summoned me nearly half an hour ago."

"Why?"

"She requested that I call a hack, my lord, for herself and her maid."

She'd taken her maid. That meant she didn't plan on returning. Tristan's muscles were wound so tightly with fury and tension that he shook. "Did she say where she was going?"

"She did, my lord. I —"

"Where?" Tristan growled, taking a step closer.

The butler took a quick step backward, stumbling into the hat stand. "To Hawthorne House, my lord."

Tristan reached around him and snatched his greatcoat. "I'm going out."

"Shall I have Gimble saddle Charlemagne for you?"

"I'll do it myself. Move aside."

Swallowing, Dawkins sidestepped, and Tristan then yanked open the front door. He took the steps two at a time, shrugging into his coat as he went. The stable was dark and quiet, since it was barely dawn. He was surprised to see Sheba still in the stall beside his gelding. She wouldn't have left her horse if she'd been thinking ahead. She wouldn't have brought her horse here in the first place, if she'd meant to leave as she had.

He paused as he tightened the girth of Charlemagne's saddle. Last night had not been a game. He'd felt her heat and her passion, and she'd been as moved as he had been. Whatever lesson she'd decided to teach him, then, had been an afterthought. Or at least the method had been.

Or maybe that was wishful thinking, trying to justify why he'd once again been utterly unable to resist the lure of her body, damn all the consequences. Tristan swung into the saddle and urged Charlemagne out of the stable, bending low against the bay's neck as they passed under the low doors and out to the street.

Even this early, Mayfair was filling with vendors and wagons delivering milk and ice and fresh vegetables. He wove through them to Grosvenor Square, where the Dowager Duchess of Wycliffe's manor stood amid the abodes of the oldest and wealthiest families in England. No groom appeared as he jumped down from the gelding; the duchess's household was probably still abed.

But someone would have had to let Georgiana into the house. He pounded on the door. A few long seconds passed with no response from inside, and he knocked again, louder.

A bolt slid and the door opened. The butler, looking much more composed than Dawkins, stepped into the doorway. "The servants' entrance is — Lord Dare. My apologies, my lord. How may I help you?"

"I need to speak with Lady Georgiana."

"I'm sorry, my lord, but Lady Georgiana isn't here."

Tristan waited a heartbeat, trying to draw his raw temper back under control. "I know she's here," he said, very quietly, "and I need to speak with her. Now."

"The . . . please . . ." The butler stepped back into the foyer. "If you will please wait in the morning room, I shall inquire."

"Thank you." Tristan strode into the house. He was tempted to continue up the stairs and straight to Georgiana's bedchamber, but he wasn't certain if she still slept in the same one she'd kept six years ago — and angry as he was, he knew questions would arise if others realized that he knew precisely which bedchamber out of twenty was hers.

Too angry to sit, he paced back and forth across the morning room, hands clenched into fists at his sides. His skin still smelled faintly of lavender. Damnation. He should have taken the time to scrub her scent off himself, before it drove him mad.

According to the clock on the mantel, it was forty-eight minutes past five. If she'd left Carroway House half an hour before he awoke, in a hired hack, she'd probably been there for perhaps fifteen minutes. He'd taken less than ten to cross through Mayfair, since he'd been on horseback and furious.

Another curse broke from him. If she didn't come down soon, he was going to go and find her. Escape was *not* going to be that easy. Not after what he'd felt between them last night. Not after the plans he'd made.

"Lord Dare."

"What in hell . . ." He trailed off as he faced the doorway. "Your Grace," he said, sketching a bow.

"You're here early," the dowager duchess said, cool green eyes assessing him from the doorway. "Would you care to finish your sentence?"

He swallowed down a retort. She was dressed and her hair put up; she'd likely awoken the moment Georgiana returned. Had Georgie expected him to come by and ruin everything? To make this little escapade of hers into his fault? "No, Your Grace, I would not. I am here to see Lady Georgiana."

"So Pascoe informed me. You appear to be highly agitated, my lord. I suggest that you return home, shave, get control of yourself, and return at a decent hour for visitors."

"With all respect, Your Grace," he snapped, as he stalked back and forth, "I need to speak with Georgiana. I am not playing games."

She lifted an eyebrow. "No, I can see that you're not. I have already inquired of Georgiana, however, and she does not wish to speak with *you*."

Tristan took a deep breath. Everything meant something, he reminded himself. His days as a gambler had taught him that much, and he had learned it well. "Is she . . . all right?" he forced out.

"She is in a state nearly identical to your own. I will not speculate, but you need to leave, Lord Dare. If you do not do so voluntarily, I will call my footmen to see you out."

He nodded stiffly, his muscles beginning to ache from being held so tightly. Pushing through a wall of her aunt's footmen might be satisfying for a moment or two, but it wouldn't serve his cause. "Very well. Please inform Georgiana that her message was . . . received and understood."

The curiosity in the duchess's eyes deepened. "I will do so."

"Good morning, Your Grace. I won't be returning today."

"Good day then, Lord Dare."

She vanished from the doorway, and Tristan returned outside to Charlemagne. This wasn't over. And if his growing suspicions were correct, the way Georgiana had left things might be the best news he'd received in six years. All he needed to do was keep himself from killing her for long enough to find out.

"He's gone, my dear." Aunt Frederica's quiet voice came from the hallway.

Georgiana pulled in her breath with a gasping sob. "Thank you."

"May I come in?"

The last thing she wanted was to face her aunt, but she was acting like a mad-woman, and the duchess deserved some sort of explanation. Wiping her tears, Georgiana stumbled to the door, slid the latch off, and opened it. "If you wish."

Frederica took one look at her face and brushed past her. "Pascoe! Send up some herb tea!"

"Yes, Your Grace."

The duchess shut the door behind her and leaned back against it. "Did he hurt you?" she asked, very quietly.

"No! No, of course not. We . . . argued, is all, and I just . . . didn't want to be there any longer." She drew a shaky breath, retreating to the reading chair by the window. Curling into it, she drew her knees up to her chin and wished with all her might that she could become invisible. "What did he want?"

"To speak with you. That's all he would say to me." Her aunt stayed by the door, no doubt to intercept a maid before she could barge into the room with the tea and witness the duchess's niece looking like an escapee from Bedlam. "Except for one thing he asked me to tell you."

Oh, no. If he was angry enough, he would be quite capable of ruining her. "What . . . what was that?"

"He said to tell you that he'd received and understood your message."

She straightened a little from her fetal curl in the chair, nearly ill with relief. "That was it?"

"That was it."

The tea arrived, and the duchess went into the hallway to get it herself. Georgiana took a deep, sniffling breath. He hadn't ruined her. He hadn't brought her stockings back and flung them to the ground and shouted that he'd bedded Lady Georgiana Halley twice now and that she was a hoyden and a lightskirt.

"Oh, and he said he wouldn't be returning here today. He emphasized 'today,' which I took to mean that he would be calling at a future date."

Georgiana tried to pull her thoughts together, still too relieved with the present to let the future frighten her. "Thank you for seeing him."

The duchess poured a cup of tea, dropped two lumps of sugar and a large measure of cream into it, and brought it over to her. "Drink."

It smelled bitter, but the cream and sugar smoothed the taste, and Georgiana took two large swallows. Warmth spread from her stomach out to her fingers and toes, and she took another drink.

"Better?"

"Better."

Her aunt sat in the deep windowsill, far enough back that Georgiana didn't have to look at her if she didn't want to. If Frederica Brakenridge was one thing, it was intuitive.

"I must say, I haven't seen you in hysterics for . . . six years, it must be. Dare had something to do with that, as well, if I recall correctly."

"He just upsets me."

"I can see that. Why associate with him, then?"

Georgiana looked into the tea, at the slow swirls of cream in the delicate china cup. "I . . . I was teaching him a lesson."

"He seems to have understood it."

Georgiana managed to summon a degree of indignation. "Well, I should hope so."

"So why are you crying, my sweet?"

Because I'm not sure he deserved it, and because I really don't hate him, and now he hates me. "I'm just tired. And mad at him, of course."

"Of course." The duchess stood. "I'm going to send my Danielle in to get you into your nightgown. Finish your tea, and get some sleep."

"But it's morning."

"Just barely. And you have nothing to do today, no obligations, no appointments — nothing to do but sleep."

"But —"

"Sleep."

The herb tea was definitely doing something, because her eyes were drooping shut. "Yes, Aunt Frederica."

Frederica Brakenridge sat in her office, addressing her correspondence, when the door opened.

"What the devil is going on?" a deep voice snapped.

She finished the letter and lifted a paper to begin her next missive. "Good afternoon, Greydon."

She felt her son's large form hesitate, and then cross the room to her. Tawny hair entered the corner of her vision as he leaned down to kiss her cheek. "Good afternoon. What's going on?"

"What have you heard?"

With a sigh he dropped into the overstuffed chair behind her. "I ran across Bradshaw Carroway at Gentleman Jackson's. When I inquired about Georgiana, Shaw told me she'd left to return here, and that Tristan was rabid about it — or about something, anyway."

"Bradshaw didn't say?"

"He said he couldn't say, because Tristan wouldn't say."

Frederica continued with her letter. "That's just about all I know, as well."

"It's the 'just about' I want to hear from you, Mother."

"No."

"Fine." Material rustled as he stood. "I'll ask Tristan."

Hiding a frown, Frederica turned in her chair to face him. "No, you won't."

"And why is that?"

"Stay out of it. Whatever it is, it's between them. Not us."

Grey didn't bother hiding his scowl. "Where's Georgie, then?"

The duchess hesitated. She disliked not knowing all the facts; it made treading through the mess all the more difficult — and delicate. "Sleeping."

"It's nearly two in the afternoon."

"She was upset."

Greydon met her gaze. "How upset?"

"Very."

The duke turned for the door. "That's it. I'm going to beat the answers out of Dare."

"You aren't going to do any such thing. From what I saw of him this morning, he's itching to beat something, himself. You will lose his friendship over this, if you interfere."

"Bloody . . . Then what am I supp—"

"Don't do anything. Be patient. That's what I'm doing."

He tilted his head at her. "You really aren't certain what's going on, are you? You're not just keeping it from me on principle."

"No, I don't know everything, despite my reputation to the contrary. Go home. Emma will probably have heard the rumors by now, too, and I don't want to have to go through this again."

"I don't like it, but all right. For now."

"That's all I ever ask."

"Like hell it is." With a brief, concerned smile, he left the room.

Frederica bent her head over her letter again, then sat back, sighing. Whatever was going on, it was serious. She'd thought that Georgiana had begun to forgive Tristan for the equally mysterious misstep he'd made before. Now, she wasn't certain. She would have allowed Greydon to interfere if Georgiana had been the only one hurt this time. She would have insisted on it, in fact. But Dare had been in pain, himself. Deep and obvious pain. And so she would wait and see what happened next.

"I really don't want to go out tonight," Georgiana said, as her aunt reached the first floor.

"I know you don't. That's why we're going to dinner with Lydia and James. It'll be a small gathering, and an early evening."

Frowning, Georgiana joined the duchess at the front door. "It's not that I'm afraid to see him or anything."

"That's none of my affair," her aunt answered. "I'm just glad you're back home."

That was the problem, Georgie reflected. She *wasn't* back home. She really didn't have a home. Her parents were in Shropshire with her sisters, her brother was in Scotland, Helen and her husband Geoffrey were in York, and she was welcome to stay with Frederica or even with Grey and Emma, if she wished it. Where she had most enjoyed staying, however, had been at Carroway House, spending afternoons chatting with the aunts and playing Commerce with Edward and talking about faraway lands with Bradshaw. And, of course, seeing Tristan.

"Georgiana, are you coming?"

"Yes."

Despite her aunt's assurances, she was on edge all night. If Tristan had been as angry as Frederica had intimated, he wouldn't just let this go. *She* hadn't, when he'd hurt her before. She had been awful, saying things to him that other people probably found amusing, but that he had to know meant she hated and despised him. Would he do the same thing to her?

For the next two days she stayed close to the house, and he didn't come calling or send her a note. She wondered whether he'd gone to call on Amelia Johns, but quickly pushed the thought away. If he had, then good. That had been the reason for all this mess, anyway.

She was supposed to attend the Glenview soiree with Lucinda and Evelyn, and while she didn't want to go, neither did she want to become a hermit. The wisest thing to do would have been to return to Shropshire, as she'd initially planned. That would mean that she was a complete coward, though. Besides, she had nothing to run from. He hadn't retaliated, and she hadn't done anything wrong, anyway. Well, she had, but no one but Tristan knew that, and he deserved what had happened.

"Georgie," Lucinda said, hurrying across the room and grasping her hands. "I heard you'd returned to your aunt's. Is everything all right?"

Georgie kissed her friend on the cheek. "Yes. Fine."

"You did it, didn't you? You delivered your lesson."

Swallowing, her gaze on the crowd beyond Lucinda's shoulder, she nodded. "I did. How did you know?"

"You wouldn't have left Carroway House, otherwise. You were very determined."

"I suppose I was."

Evelyn approached them from the music room. "Everyone's saying that you and Dare fought again."

"Yes, I would have to say that we did." Though since she hadn't set eyes on him in three days, she didn't know how anyone could know they were fighting. Possibly because they were *always* fighting.

"Well, then you should probably know th—"

"Good evening, ladies."

"That he's here," Evie finished in a whisper.

Georgiana froze. With all of her being, she didn't want to turn around. Yet she couldn't keep herself from doing so. Tristan was just a few feet away, close enough to touch. She couldn't read his expression, but his face was pale, and his eyes glittered.

"Lord Dare," she said, her voice not quite steady.

"I was wondering if you would speak with my aunts for a moment, Lady Georgiana," he said, his voice curt and his spine stiff. "They're worried about you."

"Of course." Squaring her shoulders and pretending not to notice the concerned looks from her friends, she walked off with him.

He didn't offer his arm, and she kept her hands folded behind her. She wanted to run, but then everyone would know that something had happened between them. Rumors were one thing, but if she or Tristan did anything to confirm them, she would have no choice about going back to Shropshire.

She sneaked a sideways glance at him. His jaw was clenched, but other than that he gave no outward sign of agitation. She was fairly shaking with it, but he didn't round on her as she expected. Rather, he did as he'd said he would, and stopped beside his aunts.

"Oh, dear Georgie," Edwina said, grabbing her arm and hugging her. "We were so worried about you! Just leaving like that without saying anything."

"I'm so sorry," she answered, squeezing the older woman's hand. "I . . . had to leave, but I shouldn't have done it without saying something first. I didn't mean to worry you."

"Is your aunt all right?" Milly asked, coming forward.

"Yes, she's . . ." Georgiana looked at her for a moment, belatedly realizing that she didn't have to look down at Tristan's aunt. "You're walking!"

"With the help of my cane, but yes. Now, what's happened to you? Did Tristan say something to make you angry again?"

She felt his gaze on her face, but refused to look at him. "No. I just needed to go. And look at you! You don't need me any longer."

"We still enjoy your company, my dear."

"And I enjoy yours. I'll come to visit very soon. I promise."

Tristan stirred. "Come, Georgiana, I'll get you a glass of punch."

"I really don't —"

"Come with me," he repeated, his voice lower.

This time he did offer his arm, and with his aunts watching, she didn't dare refuse it. The muscles were tight as iron, and her fingers trembled on his sleeve.

"My lord, I —"

"Are you afraid of me?" he asked in the same quiet voice.

"Afraid? N . . . no. Of course not."

He looked down at her. "Why not? You should be. I could ruin you in less than a second."

"I'm not afraid, because you deserved it."

Tristan leaned closer, a sneer pulling at his mouth. "What, exactly, did I deserve?"

Across the room Aunt Frederica was looking at them, her expression concerned. Grey stood beside her, his stance aggressive. Georgiana looked back up at Tristan. "We shouldn't do this here."

"You wouldn't see me elsewhere. Answer the damned question. Was this just revenge?"

"Revenge? No. It . . . I . . ."

"You know what I think?" he said, still more quietly, his hand covering hers.

To their audience it no doubt looked like a gesture of affection; they couldn't know his grip was steel, and that she couldn't have broken away from him if she tried. "Tristan . . ."

"I think you *are* afraid," he whispered, "because you enjoyed being with me."

Oh, no. "That is *not* it. Let me go."

He did so immediately. "You decided to hurt me before I could hurt you again."

"Nonsense. I'm walking away now. Don't follow me."

"I won't — if you'll save a waltz for me."

She stopped. This wasn't supposed to happen. He was supposed to go crawling off to Amelia Johns and be a good husband. She needed to be sure he understood that the lesson she'd dealt him wasn't just about revenge. If that meant dancing with him tonight, so be it. "Fine."

"Good."

Chapter 12

Troilus You have bereft me
of all words, lady.
Pandarus Words pay no debts,
give her deeds.
— *Troilus and Cressida*, Act III, Scene ii

He'd expected gloating, or smugness, or aloof arrogance. Instead Georgiana had trembled. Beyond his anger at her presumption — she'd actually thought she could teach him a *lesson* — Tristan had to admit that the more entangled their lives became, the more interesting he found it all.

He watched as she rejoined her friends, studying her gestures, the way she held herself. She was hurt, which didn't make sense, since he hadn't left her and hadn't asked her to leave. He'd been verging on asking her to marry him. It had seemed perfect: all of his money problems gone, and a woman he desired, in his bed. Obviously he'd missed something, and

Georgie held all the answers.

He'd studied her short missive until he had every smudge, every swirl memorized. It all meant something, and he would figure out what.

"You look like you want to eat her," Bradshaw muttered from behind him, "and not in a good way. For God's sake, look at someone else."

Tristan blinked. "Did I ask for your opinion? Go annoy an admiral or something."

"You're not helping anything."

The viscount turned and looked at his younger brother. "What, precisely, am I supposed to be helping?" he snapped.

Bradshaw raised his hands. "Never mind. But if this explodes in your face, just remember that I warned you. Be more subtle, Dare."

Before Tristan could reply, Shaw vanished toward the staircase. He took a deep breath, trying to relax the tense muscles across his back. His brother was right; six years ago he'd nearly killed himself keeping the rumors under control, and tonight he was stomping around like a bull in heat.

"Good evening, Tristan."

He looked over his shoulder. "Amelia. Good evening."

She curtsied, dainty and delicate in a blue gauze gown. "I have decided to be forward and ask you for a dance," she said, dimpling.

"And I thank you, but I don't intend to stay tonight. I have some . . . business to attend to."

The excuse sounded pitiful but he wasn't in the mood to come up with a better one, or to listen to her inane chatter. Instead he offered her a stiff bow and stalked off to shadow Georgiana.

She seemed to be making every effort to stay away from him, huddling with her friends at the far end of the room and now and then giving a nervous laugh as though to convince everyone that she was enjoying herself. He knew better.

Finally, Lady Hortensia called for the orchestra, and the scattered pockets of conversation migrated toward the dance floor. Tristan didn't know whether anyone else had asked a dance of Georgiana, though he would assume so. He didn't care, except that the first waltz was his.

He had to wait through two quadrilles and a country dance, watching her twirl about the room with Lord Luxley — apparently forgiven for his accident with the orange cart — and Francis Henning and then Grey. The only positive note was that Westbrook had yet to make an appearance.

When the orchestra launched into a waltz she was standing with her cousin and his bride, Emma. Tristan made himself stroll at a normal pace to her side.

"This is our dance, I believe," he drawled, holding his hand out to her and trying not to look as though he was contemplating dragging her off and demanding an explanation.

Grey scowled. "Georgiana's tired. You don't mind if —"

"Yes, I do mind." He kept his gaze on Georgiana, though he sensed the duke looming beside him. If Grey wanted a fight, he was definitely in the mood to accommodate him. "Georgiana?"

"It's all right, Grey. I promised him."

"That doesn't matter, if you don't want —"

"I appreciate your chivalry, cousin," she interrupted, her voice sharper, "but please allow me to speak for myself."

With a curt nod, Greydon took his wife's hand to lead her to the dance floor. "As if I could stop you," he muttered.

Tristan ignored their departure; all of his attention was on Georgiana. "Shall we?"

Georgiana took his hand. Keenly reminded of their half-naked waltz in his bedchamber, Tristan slid his arm around her waist and stepped into the dance.

She did everything she could to avoid his gaze, looking at his cravat, the other dancers, the orchestra, and the decorations along the far wall. He kept his silence, trying to decide how best to broach his questions without losing any more ground, and angry enough to be satisfied at her discomfiture.

Finally, she gave a heavy sigh and looked up at him. She seemed tired, fine lines around her eyes dimming their sparkle. "This was supposed to make you leave me alone."

"You encouraged me, and then you insulted me. What made you think I wouldn't want an explanation?"

"You told my aunt you'd understood the message. I don't think you did. Otherwise, you wouldn't be dancing with me."

"Explain it to me, then." He lowered his head, brushing his cheek against her ear. The lavender scent of her made him swallow. Angry or not, he wanted her again. Badly. "I felt passion, Georgiana. And so did you. So please, explain to me why you left the way you did."

A slow blush crept up her cheeks. "Fine.

You were supposed to be courting Amelia Johns; you said so yourself. And yet you couldn't wait to seduce me. I wanted you to know how it felt to expect something from someone and then have them snatch it away. To teach you that you can't go about breaking hearts just because it suits you to do so."

"You did as much seducing as I did, my dear."

"Yes, to teach you a lesson." She paused, glancing at the nearest dancers, too far away to hear their quiet conversation. "It just so happened that this lesson had the added bonus of making us even."

"Even," he repeated, anger and desire creeping intermingled along his veins.

"Yes — you hurt me, and I hurt you. The lesson is over. Go back to Amelia and behave like a gentleman, if you can."

For a long moment he looked down at her. They *were* even now, except for one thing. "You're right."

"So go get married and be a good husband."

"I meant that you're right about us being even — with one small difference."

She eyed him warily. "What difference?"

"You ran last time, and I let you go. I have no intention of doing so, this time."

"What . . . what are you talking about? What about Amelia? She expects a proposal."

"If we're even," he returned, ignoring her interruption, "then there's no reason we can't begin again. A clean slate between us, as it were."

Her jaw fell open. "You can't be serious!"

"I am perfectly serious. You interest me much more than Amelia Johns ever could. To be blunt, and because you'll throw it in my face anyway, you also happen to be an heiress, and everyone knows that I need to marry an heiress."

"I don't believe you," she snapped, jerking her hand free from his. "You can't stand losing, so you're embarking on another game you think you can win, and at my expense. I will not participate."

"It's no game, Georgiana," he growled, grabbing her hand again.

She pulled backward, freeing herself from his grip and nearly causing the Earl of Montrose and his partner to fall over both of them. "Then prove it, Dare."

Tristan smiled grimly. He loved a challenge, and the higher the stakes, the better. "I will." Before she could stomp away, he took her hand once more, placing a kiss on her knuckles. "Believe you me, I will."

★ ★ ★

The next day Georgiana sat with her aunt in the morning room, halfheartedly working on some embroidery. She was contemplating how nice it would be to escape the house and the quiet, incessant ticking of the mantel clock when Pascoe scratched on the door.

"You have a caller. Lady Georgiana."

"Who is it?"

"Lord Dare, my lady."

Her heart jumped into her throat, and with effort she swallowed it down again, "I'm not receiving callers this morning, Pascoe."

"Very good, my lady." The butler vanished.

"Greydon has offered to speak to Dare, if you want this settled," Aunt Frederica said in the careful voice she'd been using since Georgiana's return, as if she were afraid her niece would become hysterical again if she said the wrong thing.

"Grey is Dare's friend. That shouldn't change just because of this."

"My lady?" Pascoe reappeared in the doorway.

"Yes, Pascoe?"

"Lord Dare has returned your horse. He wishes to know if you would care to go riding, and to discuss the return of the re-

231

mainder of your personal items to Hawthorne House."

If Tristan had said that, he was making a great effort to be diplomatic. "Please thank Lord Dare, but —"

"Ah, I'm also to inform you that the . . . Runt is here as well, and would like to ride with you."

"Pascoe, she has said no. Please do not —"

That devious blackguard. Georgiana set aside her embroidery and stood. "I should at least say hello to Edward. I'm certain he has no idea why I vanished as I did."

"Neither do I," her aunt muttered, but Georgiana pretended not to hear that as she left the room.

"Georgie!" Edward shrieked, hurling himself at her as soon as she entered the sitting room.

"Edward," Tristan said sharply, and the boy skidded to a halt. "Decorum."

With a frown, the lad nodded and swept a bow. "Good morning, Lady Georgiana. I've missed you very much, and so has Storm Cloud."

"I've missed you, too. I'm so pleased you've come by."

"Are you going riding with us? It'll be smashing. No one has to hold the reins for me any longer."

She looked into the boy's eager gray eyes and smiled. "I would love to go riding with you."

"Hurray!"

"I will have to change, first."

"We'll wait," Tristan drawled, lifting an eyebrow when she glared over his brother's head at him.

When she returned downstairs a few minutes later, both the Carroway brothers were out on the front drive, waiting for her. As she appeared, Tristan lifted Edward onto Storm Cloud's back, then strolled over to help her up onto Sheba.

"You are a cheat," she hissed, standing her foot harder than she needed to in his cupped hands. "And a sneak."

"Yes, I am. And clever, too. The Runt's an excuse and a chaperone, all in one." Grasping her ankle, he slid her foot into the single stirrup.

"What about our appearance? Man, woman, and child. Wasn't that your objection to Bradshaw's escorting me anywhere?"

"My objections to Bradshaw are many and varied. If one works to keep him somewhere else and me here, I will use it."

"What do you think you're doing here, anyway?" she asked. She'd have to be careful about what she said with Edward present, blast it all.

"I'm calling on you." He stepped back. "Is Hyde Park acceptable?"

"Yes, I suppose that's fine."

He swung into Charlemagne's saddle, and the three of them trotted toward the nearby park. She watched as he leaned sideways, correcting his brother's hold on the reins. Tristan was a born horseman, and even when she'd hated him, she'd enjoyed watching him ride. Now, though, it wasn't his horsemanship as much as his seat that she was admiring.

"Just so you know," he said as he returned to her side, "I don't intend to do or say anything the least bit unpleasant today. I'm beginning a courtship. But I'll only behave for as long as you do."

She kept her gaze between Sheba's ears as they entered the park. "I don't understand, Tristan," she said slowly, unsure of how much she should be saying aloud. "Why take the risk? You have an heiress already in your pocket."

"I have never made anything even resembling a promise of marriage to Amelia Johns," he said, sounding annoyed. "Put her out of your mind; this is about us, and about how much I want you again."

"So are you courting me, or seducing me?" She couldn't keep the tremor from her voice.

"I'm courting you. The next night we share, neither of us will be fleeing."

Georgiana blushed. She'd supposedly just broken his heart, and he was already planning their next naked rendezvous. Perhaps he *didn't* have a heart. "You're very sure of yourself."

"It's one of my better traits."

Obviously she'd miscalculated somewhere. Now he thought he could dictate when and how they met, and what it should mean. She narrowed her eyes. If they were even, then she had an equal right to decide just how much she would let him get away with. And whom she wished to see.

"Please take me back now," she said, turning Sheba as she spoke.

"We only just got here."

"I know, but I'm to go on a picnic with Lord Westbrook in an hour, and I need to change and freshen up."

His expression darkened. "You don't have any such thing planned. You just made that up."

"I did not. Wait until he arrives, if you wish, but you'll look even more foolish than you do now, paying attention to a woman who is known to despise you."

Tristan's lips compressed into a hard, thin line. "That is not how this is going to proceed."

"Yes, it is. I'm not needed by your aunts, any longer, and I have therefore accepted invitations from several gentlemen. You're only one of them."

He urged Charlemagne closer. "You said you had no intention of ever marrying," he said, in so low a voice it was almost a growl.

"Yes, and I've been thinking about that. It was you, as I recall, who pointed out that I could marry anyone who needed my dowry. And given how much money that is, I could marry just about anyone."

"Reconsider. Westbrook's a bore, and he doesn't need your money."

"And because he doesn't, I presume that he likes my company and my conversation. You said if a man loved me, he would forgive that he wasn't my . . . first. You give sound advice, Tristan."

"Reconsider. Spend the day with me."

It annoyed her that for a bare moment she was tempted. "No. We are even, Dare, and therefore you have no more right to my time than anyone else in the world."

"I think I do. I could make you spend time with me, Georgiana. I could even make you marry me."

She met his hard, glittering eyes. "If you wish to press your suit in that manner, I will hate you, I will be ruined, and I will return home to Shropshire — as an unmarried woman."

After a long moment he blew out his breath. "Damnation. You knew I was bluffing."

Her heart resumed beating. "Yes, I did." Thank goodness she *could* lie to him, apparently.

"Doesn't that count for something?"

"I'm here riding with you," she said, gesturing between them, "so yes, I suppose it does. But your keeping your poor behavior a secret can only go so far in gaining my good graces."

To her surprise he laughed, the sound rolling out warm and deep from his chest. Edward looked back at them, grinning in response. Georgiana found herself wanting to smile as well, and sternly resisted the temptation.

"What is so funny?" she demanded.

"A few weeks ago all my poor behavior got me was a smashed toe and cracked knuckles," he said, still chuckling. "I

237

seem to be making progress."

She sniffed. "Not much. Now take me back."

Tristan sighed. "Yes, my lady. Runt, we're going back."

"But why?"

"Georgie has other men waiting to see her."

"But we're still seeing her."

"We didn't have an appointment."

She scowled at him, but he pretended not to notice. This was going to be a problem. Part of her wanted to melt every time he looked at her, and the other part wanted to shriek and throw things. He might have the advantage at the moment, but she would figure him out. She knew better than to trust him, especially when he was supposedly being honest. Perhaps she couldn't help that she lusted after him, but she would never — ever — fall for him again.

One of the grooms helped her dismount before Tristan could do so, and she favored the servant with such a warm smile that the poor man flushed and practically ran away, towing Sheba behind him. Drat. Looking like an idiot wouldn't help her against Lord Dare, either. "Thank you for a pleasant outing," she said to Edward.

"You're welcome."

"Do you attend the fireworks at Vauxhall on Thursday?" Tristan asked, dismounting to walk her to the door.

He could find out easily enough, she supposed, and she wouldn't be dancing at the Gardens, anyway. "Yes, my aunt and I will be there."

"Might I send my carriage and offer both of you my escort, then?"

Damnation, he was sneaky. "I . . . can't answer for Aunt Frederica, of course."

Tristan nodded. "If you would please inform her of my request, and that my aunts will be along as well, I would appreciate it. Milly's been looking forward to the fireworks all Season. She couldn't go while she was off her feet, so this will be her first opportunity to go."

Georgiana clenched her jaw. "You don't play fair."

"I'm not playing, remember? And I'm in this to win."

"Very well. I'm certain Aunt Frederica would love the opportunity to chat with your aunts. I'll inform her of your request. But I'm not happy about it."

Bending down, he took her hand in his. "Have a lovely picnic, Georgiana," he murmured, and released her.

As she climbed the steps, it wasn't the upcoming picnic she was thinking of. It was his long-lashed blue eyes and the promises — or lies — they held for her deep inside them.

"Tristan," Edward said, as they rode back to Carroway House, "why did you make me come all the way over here? I told you I already went riding with Andrew and Shaw."

"Because I wanted to see Georgiana, and I knew she would want to see you."

"Why wouldn't she want to see you? Is she mad at you?"

Tristan gave a small, grim smile. "Yes, she is."

"Then you should send her flowers. That's what Bradshaw does, and he says all the chits like him."

"Flowers, eh?" The more he thought about it, the better it sounded. "What else does Bradshaw send the chits to make them like him?"

"Chocolate. Lots of chocolate. He said that Melinda Wendell would roll with an ox for a good box of chocolates."

He and Bradshaw were going to have a talk about what got said in front of Edward; this was getting out of hand. "Did

Shaw say that to you, specifically?"

Looking sheepish, Edward grinned. "No, he said it to Andrew, when Andrew was trying to get Barbara Jamison to roll with him. I'd like to go rolling. It sounds fun."

"When you're older. And *never* mention rolling to Georgiana, all right?"

"Doesn't she like rolling?"

Given her response the other night, she liked it very much. "Rolling, Runt, is something only men discuss, and only with other men. In fact, only with your brothers. Understood?"

"Yes, Dare. Not even with the aunties?"

"Good God, no."

"All right."

"Thank you for the idea about the flowers, though. I may try that."

"I think you should. I like Georgiana."

"So do I." When he didn't want to strangle her.

Arguing with her had practically become foreplay now. Yes, she made him furious, and frustrated. Mostly, though, he just wanted to roll with her. A lot.

Chapter 13

Author's Note: There will be no chapter thirteen. It is my feeling that Tristan and Georgiana have enough work cut out for them without adding unlucky numbers into the mix.

Chapter 14

Once more unto the breach,
dear friends, once more;
Or close the wall up
with our English dead.
— *Henry the Fifth*, Act III, Scene i

Georgiana Halley was intelligent and suspicious — especially of him — so the way to defeat her was to keep her off-balance. Tristan sat opposite her in his coach, newly washed and sprung, and gazed out the window into the darkness. This was a war, no doubt about it, and it was one he intended to win.

Of course a complete victory would mean no less than marrying her: She'd set the stakes that high when she'd climaxed in his arms and then left him with a gift, as though he were some sort of cock-bawd. Making her his would leave him the ultimate winner and keep her from escaping him and his bed again.

The only question was how to go about it. He enjoyed her company, and he desired her body. She desired him, but he wasn't certain that she actually liked him. Whatever his machinations, he had to convince her to say yes. At least she'd agreed to join him tonight.

"I wasn't aware that any boxes were still available for rent at Vauxhall this far into the Season."

The Dowager Duchess of Wycliffe, looking even more aloof than Georgiana, had been glaring at him since he arrived to escort them, as if she expected him to expire under her close scrutiny. He needed her there to ensure Georgie's presence. Other than that, he barely noted her glassy, disapproving gaze.

Even her underlying implication that she had no idea where he might have gotten the money to rent a box left him annoyed only for a moment. "The Marquis of St. Aubyn had to leave London for the week," he improvised. "He loaned me his box."

"You associate with St. Aubyn?"

Uh-oh. "I know him."

She didn't seem to count that as a point in his favor. "And so he simply offered?"

"Yes." After Tristan had won fifty quid off him at faro. "And of course my first thought was of you and Georgiana."

"But I was under the impression that your aunts would be accompanying us," the duchess said, her tone becoming even more accusing.

"They are. My brothers are escorting them."

Georgiana had refused to meet his eyes since he'd arrived, but he couldn't help gazing at her. She wore dark blue, with a shimmering silver shawl draped across her shoulders and silver-and-blue clips in her golden hair.

When he'd helped her into the coach, just taking her hand had made his mouth go dry. He wanted to run his fingers over her skin again, wanted to feel her hands on him and feel her writhing beneath him.

"Georgiana," her aunt said, making him jump, "tell me about your picnic with Lord Westbrook."

"I really don't think Lord Dare wishes to hear —"

"Probably not, but *I* do. Tell me."

Tristan didn't need to be reminded that she had other suitors. He'd been tempted to trail her on her luncheon, just to make certain she wasn't lying about it or enjoying herself too much. If he hadn't had to track down St. Aubyn for his box,

245

he would have done it.

"It was very nice. He brought roast duck."

"And what did you discuss?"

"Nothing important. The weather, the entertainments of the Season."

"Has he offered for you yet?"

This time her gaze met Tristan's, then slid away again. "You know he hasn't. Please stop interrogating me."

"I'm only anxious for your happiness."

"That doesn't sound like what —"

Tristan's jaw clenched. "You expect him to offer for you?"

"Oh, look, we're here."

The coach turned into Vauxhall Gardens, joining the crush of vehicles already there. His groom pulled open the door and flipped down the steps, and Tristan stepped down to help the ladies out. The duchess came first, still eyeing him as though he had contracted the plague.

"Why are we here with you?" she asked.

"Aunt Frederica," Georgiana warned from within the coach.

Tristan met the duchess's eyes. "Because I'm courting your niece," he answered. "And because I'm very charming and intriguing, and you couldn't resist my invitation."

To his surprise, she let out a short laugh.

"Perhaps that's what it was."

"Georgiana," he said, as the duchess made her way to the path, "are you coming down, or should I join you in there?"

Her hand extended from the coach, and he gripped her fingers. Even through their gloves, he could feel the pulse of lightning between them. She stepped down beside him, but he kept hold of her hand. "Do you let Westbrook kiss you?" he murmured.

"That is none of your affair. Let go."

He released her reluctantly. "I want to taste you again," he continued in the same low tone, offering his arm.

"That's *not* going to happen." She turned her face away, which exposed the graceful curve of her neck to his gaze.

Tristan went hard. Thankful for his caped greatcoat, he leaned closer to her. "Does Westbrook make you tremble?" he whispered. It took all of his self-control to keep from kissing her ear.

"Stop it. At once. One more word in that vein and I will kick you so hard you'll be able to join the boys' choir at Westminster."

"Say my name."

She sighed. "Fine. Tristan."

He stopped, making her do so, as well.

"No, look me in the eye and say my name."

"This is ridiculous."

"Humor me."

With a deep breath that made her bosom heave, she lifted her face to meet his gaze, her eyes soft and moss green in the moonlight. "Tristan," she breathed, a tremble on her breath.

He could drown in those eyes. The problem was, she undoubtedly still wanted him to. "That's better."

"Is there anything else you want me to say? The name of your horse, or the multiplication tables?"

His lips twitched. "My name will do. Thank you."

They continued on, hurrying to catch up with the dowager duchess. "I don't know why you persist," she said, her voice still pitched low enough that no one in the crowd would be able to overhear. It was a tone they'd perfected over the years. "I told you I would never trust you."

"You already trust me, sweet one."

"And what in the world makes you think that?"

"You've left several very personal items in my possession, and whatever you pretend to think of me, you know I would never use them against you." He caught her arm, turning her to face him again. "Never."

She blushed. "So you have one redeeming quality. Amid all the poor ones, it's hardly something to brag about."

"I'm beginning to think I should have brought you a fan."

"I—"

"There you are," the duchess said, taking Georgiana's other arm and snagging her away from Tristan. "You must rescue me from Lord Phindlin."

"You're an attractive woman, and a widow," Georgiana told her aunt, all charm again now that she wasn't conversing with him. "You can hardly blame him."

"I think it's my money he wants," the duchess commented, glancing over her shoulder at Tristan.

Bloody wonderful. Now he was just another of the greedy, grasping male multitude.

"It could be, Your Grace," he drawled, "that he just has very good taste. If it was only money he wanted, he might have set his cap toward a more . . . amenable woman."

Both of the duchess's eyebrows lifted. "Indeed."

The aunts, Bradshaw, Andrew, and, surprisingly, Bit, had already commandeered the box when they arrived. Georgiana greeted everyone, favoring Milly and Edwina with kisses on the cheek, then sat amid the trio of aunties. Frederica settled in for a chat, ignoring the fireworks and the orchestra in the nearby square. Tristan watched the lot of them with increasing frustration. He knew he affected Georgie; if he didn't, she wouldn't bother hiding. As long as she was keeping the duchess between the two of them, though, he couldn't do much in the way of wooing.

Tristan gave a brief smile. He'd never thought to put "wooing" and "Georgiana" together in the same sentence. He couldn't keep his eyes off her, and as she glanced back at him, heat soaked into his veins. She'd been so angry at him six years ago that all of this might be the beginning of another game; she'd as much as said that he hadn't learned his lesson. But he'd been playing games of chance for longer than she had. However high the stakes, he would play this one to its end.

"Wasn't it the marquis, Georgiana?"

Georgiana shook herself, tearing her gaze from Tristan and looking at her aunt. "I'm sorry, what were you saying?"

Frederica's brow furrowed, then smoothed again. "Milly was asking about your suitors."

"Oh. Yes, it was the marquis, then. Of course."

That was at least the third time since Tristan had picked them up that her aunt had mentioned suitors, Georgiana thought, and she didn't like it.

She wasn't going to marry Lord Luxley or any of the others who proposed almost weekly. Even if she had no particular reason for refusing them, she wouldn't have been interested. Most of them bored her. And the idea that Tristan could be pursuing her with the idea of marriage was simply . . . absurd. She'd humiliated and angered him, and now he was trying to do the same to her. He expected her to fall for him all over again, just so he could laugh at her and walk away the victor. She could walk across the Thames on the multitude of hearts he'd broken, yet he simply couldn't stand taking his own medicine.

The way he kept finding excuses to take her hand or brush her arm might make her hot and shivery, but that was just lust. Her body craved his, but her mind was her own. And only where her mind went would her heart follow.

"Georgiana, stop daydreaming."

She jumped again. "I'm sorry, what is it?"

"Where are you this evening?" her aunt asked, while Milly and Edwina gazed at her.

"Just thinking. What did I miss?"

"Lord Westbrook's prospects."

"Oh, for heaven's sake, Aunt Frederica," she said, standing and pulling her shawl closer around her shoulders. "Please don't do that."

"It's a compliment, to be pursued by so many men."

"I feel like a worm on a hook, hounded by trout. Is it my pretty wriggling that entices them, or the fact that I'm nice and plump?"

Bradshaw broke into a laugh. "I always thought of myself as a flounder, rather than a trout." He glanced at his brothers. "What kind of fish are you?"

"A minnow," Andrew said, grinning.

"Shark," Bit muttered, his attention still apparently on the fireworks.

Tristan's gaze shifted to his brother, and Georgiana couldn't help admiring him for his patience and understanding. He was simply there, if and when Robert needed him.

"Would anyone care for an ice?" Tristan rose, facing his aunts.

"I haven't had a lemon ice in ages," Milly said, smiling.

"One for me, too," Edwina added.

Everyone wanted an ice, and Tristan stepped down from the box. "Might I have a volunteer to help me carry them?" he asked, his gaze again on Georgiana.

Andrew started to stand, then sat abruptly when Robert wordlessly clamped a hand on his coattail and yanked him back down. Bradshaw seemed to understand that he wasn't invited, and of course Milly and the duchess wouldn't go. Before Edwina could offer, Georgiana stepped around her chair and down the steps. Damnation. Apparently her body and her heart were forming a conspiracy.

"We'll be right back," Tristan said, offering his arm.

She shook her head, willing her mind back into control. "Not without a chaperone."

He said something under his breath that might have been a curse, then looked at his brothers. Andrew would have stood again, but Robert brushed past him. He glanced at Georgiana, and she thought she saw a touch of humor in his dark blue eyes. "Let's go."

Robert kept walking, and she and Tristan had to hurry to keep up with him.

"That wasn't a very subtle attempt at privacy," she said. "Especially when Bit tackled Andrew."

"I didn't know he was going to do that. I'll thank him later. He's a prime chaperone, as well." He glanced ahead at Robert, a good dozen yards in front of them. "We'll lose sight of him completely in a matter of seconds."

Georgiana chuckled, her hand on Tristan's sleeve. She wished she didn't like touching him so much, but she seemed helpless to resist it. "Isn't it a bit chilly to be getting ices?" she said, when her mind began to wander toward how much she liked touching his naked skin.

"I couldn't think of anything else that sounded innocent enough to lure you away from your guard."

She felt her face warm. "*You* invited Aunt Frederica."

"Because you wouldn't have come without her."

The paths through the Gardens, running between the boxes and the main gazebo, were dark and sheltered, with trees and bushes and flowers creeping up to the edge of the stone and leaning over it. Robert slowed, facing them.

"I'm going back to Carroway House,"

he said. "Good night."

"Bit," she called after him, abruptly realizing that without him, she and Tristan would be completely, totally, alone. "Are you all right?"

He paused, glancing over his shoulder at them. "Yes. Just too many people."

In a moment, he had vanished. Though she could hear laughter and conversation from the other nearby boxes, no one was in sight.

She swallowed, glancing up at Tristan's profile as they continued strolling toward the center of the complex. "Will he be all right?"

"As ever. I told you he was a sterling escort."

Georgiana blew out her breath. Why couldn't she feel this rush under her skin with Luxley, or Westbrook, or any of the other trout swimming after her? Why only Tristan, the most unsuitable of her supposed suitors?

"What do you see?" he murmured, still looking straight ahead.

"I wish I knew," she said, belatedly looking away from him.

"Not a trout, I hope."

"That depends. Would we still be playing this game if I were a pauper?"

Tristan stopped, tightening his arm against his side to bring her to a halt beside him. To her surprise he didn't look angry, but very serious. "I don't know. I would want to be. I . . . don't want to see you with another man. Ever."

"So it's just jealousy? Preventive courting, to keep everyone else at arm's length?"

"No." He frowned, running a hand through his black hair. "I am in a certain situation. I won't complain about it, but it is reality. And I won't shirk my duty to my family. What I wish, though, is only for me to know." He leaned closer, tilting her chin up so she had to look him in the eye. "Would you choose to be a pauper? Would you be any less suspicious of a suitor's motives if you were poor and pretty?"

He'd never spoken with her like this before, and the honest curiosity in his voice was almost painful. "I . . . don't know."

"Then we won't speculate on circumstances that aren't real. Agreed?"

He was right. "Agreed."

"Good." With a quick glance down the path, he touched his mouth to hers.

Raw desire flooded her. Georgiana dug her fingers into his arm to keep from flinging her arms around his neck and pulling herself into him. She made herself stand rigid, frozen as a statue, but she couldn't help molding her mouth to his, saying with her lips what she refused to say with her body.

Someone laughed, very close by. Tristan broke the kiss, moving her back to his side again, as a small party of men and ladies came into view ahead of them.

They continued down the path, passing through the other group with nods and greetings she could scarcely remember uttering. A few of them looked at her curiously, but she imagined it was only amazement at seeing her and Dare walking together without blood being spilled rather than speculation that something further might be going on.

He would have slowed again as soon as they were alone, but she refused, giving him the choice of keeping up with her brisk pace or being left behind. They were *not* going to end up naked in a clump of rhododendron. And if he kissed her like that again tonight that was absolutely what would happen.

"Why are we running?" he asked after a moment, laughter in his voice.

At least one of them was amused. "Because if you're running, you can't be putting your tongue into my mouth."

"I probably could, if I put my mind to it."

"It's not your mind that concerns me." She glanced up at him. "And quit laughing."

"It's funny."

Well, he didn't have to point it out, for heaven's sake. "And you shouldn't be kissing me, anyway."

"Because you've taught me my lesson already?"

That stopped her in her tracks. "You *needed* to be taught a lesson, Dare, before you hurt someone else."

"I've learned my lesson. And now I want to be inside you again."

Good Lord. She hurried into a walk again. "If you'd learned your lesson," she said as the vendor carts came into view, "you would have been escorting Amelia Johns here."

"For the hundredth damned time, I don't want Amelia Johns," he whispered, running his cheek against her hair. "I want you. Everyone else be hanged."

"That is *not* what was supposed —"

"You don't get to dictate everything, Georgie. We're even now, remember?"

He was *not* supposed to be using her own logic against her. She'd been so stupid to try to use her own weakness for him to try to teach him a lesson. And now it was too late, and she needed to figure out what he was planning before a worse disaster occurred. Until then, she needed to stall.

"Get the ices, why don't you?"

With a slow, wicked smile at her, he ordered the ices. Handing half of them to Georgiana, he picked up the rest and they returned to the path. This was better. He couldn't touch her or kiss her with his hands full. Not without the ice melting all over his handsome hunter green jacket and his crisp white cravat.

They returned to the box without incident, and though Frederica looked at her a little closely, Georgiana didn't think anyone knew she'd let Dare kiss her. She really needed to stop doing that, however intoxicating his embraces were — both for Amelia's sake and for her own. Because no matter what Tristan said, he couldn't seriously be courting her.

"Where's Robert?" Milly asked, looking past them.

"He uttered a complete sentence and retreated to recuperate," Tristan drawled as he passed out the treats. "He nearly said two sentences. I think Georgie inspired him." He dropped onto the seat beside her as she carved out the center of her lemon ice. "Enjoying yourself, I hope?" he asked.

"Yes, very much," she answered, relieved to be able to give a straight answer. "Were you teasing about Bit being inspired by me?"

His expression darkened a little. "Why?"

"Jealous?"

"That depends on what you're asking me."

Georgiana grimaced. "Never mind. I thought I might be able to help, but if it means you beating your chest, forget it."

Tristan tilted his head, eyeing her. "My apologies. I forget sometimes that you're not as cynical as you pretend."

"Tris—"

"If you can get him to talk, please do so. But be careful. He . . ."

"He's been through a great deal," she supplied.

"Yes." Light blue eyes watched as she took another bite of the cold, bittersweet ice. "I'm glad you decided to come."

"It doesn't mean anything."

He grinned. "Everything means something."

Georgiana blushed. As soon as the conversation returned to themselves, her sensibilities turned to mush. "Well, how about 'I still don't trust you'? What does that mean?"

"You said 'still,' instead of 'will never.' Which means you could, one day." He brushed a finger across the corner of her mouth, then put it to his lips. "Lemon."

Aunt Frederica appeared, taking the seat beside her. From the look in her eyes, she had seen Tristan's gesture. Georgiana sighed.

Her feelings were so tangled. She should hate him, or at the least be angry with him for thinking his pursuit might lead somewhere. Instead, every time she looked at him her pulse raced, and everything, including her resolve, seemed hopelessly muddled. If this had been the first time he'd pursued her rather than the second, she would have ended up in his bed by now.

Georgiana frowned. She *had* ended up in his bed — again. Something was definitely wrong with her.

"Why the dour face?" he asked.

"I was thinking about you," she answered, though if she'd had any sense she would have just shrugged. If there was one good thing about Dare, however, it was that she rarely needed to watch her tongue in his presence — except when it was trying to end up in his mouth.

"What were you thinking about me?"

"About how you never seem to realize when you're not wanted."

"I think it's *your* skills at realization that should be called into question," he said, licking the last bit of cherry ice off his thumb. "Not mine."

"Hm. Well, you're wrong."

His answering chuckle made her pulse flutter. "I have always wondered why you —"

"Georgiana," the duchess interrupted, standing, "I'm feeling quite fatigued this evening. Lord Dare, do you think you might have someone see us home?"

"I'll be happy to do so myself, Your Grace." He stood, offering Georgiana his hand.

She took it, feeling disappointed. They had been getting into their first good argument in several days, and she'd finally begun to relax a little.

"That's not necessary, my lord. I'm sure you wish to remain here with your family. If you'll just lend us your coach, that will suffice."

He nodded, his expression unreadable. "I'll walk you to the carriages, then."

They walked to the edge of the gardens, Tristan in the middle, and Aunt Frederica keeping up a stream of polished small talk.

Clever and amusing though it was, it kept Tristan from even looking in Georgiana's direction, much less from speaking with her. Whatever the duchess had seen, she obviously hadn't liked it.

At Tristan's whistle, his coach rolled out from the mass milling across the street and came to a stop before them. He helped Frederica in, then finally turned his attention back to Georgiana.

"I wish you could stay," he murmured, taking her hand and bending over it.

"My aunt is tired."

With a slight grimace, he straightened. "Yes, I know." He handed her up into the coach, keeping hold of her fingers a moment longer than he needed to. "Have a good evening, Georgiana. And pleasant dreams."

Humph. She'd be lucky if she slept a wink. Georgiana sat back as the coach rolled off again. "What was that about?" she asked her aunt. "You're never fatigued this early in the evening."

The duchess was pulling off her elbow-length gloves. "I shall summon Greydon in the morning and have him inform Lord Dare that his pursuit is unwanted, and that it will cease immediately."

Georgiana's blood went cold. "Please don't," she bit out.

"And why shouldn't I? Dare obviously wants your money, and you've said all along how little you enjoy his company. We might as well end this unpleasantness without any further delay."

"I don't want to ruin Grey and Dare's friendship," she replied, trying to gather her thoughts enough to make a logical argument — a difficult prospect, when logic told her that Aunt Frederica was absolutely correct.

"I, for one, wouldn't mind seeing it ruined. Dare is a poor influence. I pity his aunts."

"He cares for his aunts a great deal — and for his brothers." Now she sounded as though she was defending him, blast it. "Just let me take care of this myself. I won't have anyone else fighting my battles for me. You know that."

The duchess sighed. "Yes, I do. But Tristan Carroway is a rake and a gambler, and he's been known to be very wicked. He may say he's courting you, but I doubt he has any idea how even to go about it in the proper manner. For heaven's sake, he was practically drooling on you. Anyone who passed by would know that he's in pursuit. Hardly the way to conduct a proper courtship."

"You knew about his supposed courtship before tonight," she returned, suspicious. "Why are you suddenly so adamant?"

"Because you were blushing, Georgiana. And smiling."

"What? I was being polite!"

"To Dare?"

"His aunts were present. And I . . . will take care of this myself," she said, shoving aside her own growing doubts. "Please promise me that you won't involve Grey."

Frederica was silent for a long moment. "You and I are going to have to have a serious chat very soon."

"Is that an agreement?"

"Yes. For now."

Her aunt had offered to dispose of Tristan in a way that meant she wouldn't have to say anything at all to him, and she'd declined. She needed to have a serious chat with *herself.*

When she came downstairs in the morning after another night of Tristan-scented dreams, half the staff stood gathered around the hallway table, chattering to wake the dead. "What's happened?" she asked.

The crowd parted. A bouquet of a dozen yellow lilies, wrapped with delicate yellow and blue ribbons, occupied the center of the table. For a moment all she could do was stand and look at it. *Lilies.*

"It's lovely," she said finally, before the servants could begin their muttering speculation again.

"There's a card for you," Mary said, dimpling.

She knew who they were from without looking. Only one man had ever asked her what her favorite flower was, and that had been a long time ago. Her heart raced as she lifted the card out of the leaves and ribbons.

Her name was scrawled on the outside, in a hand she recognized. Trying to keep her fingers steady, she unfolded the small card. "Entwined," was all it said, with a 'T' written beneath it.

"Oh, my," she breathed. This was becoming very complicated, indeed.

Chapter 15

The web of our life is of a mingled yarn,
good and ill together; our virtues would be
proud if our faults whipped them not;
and our crimes would despair if they were not
cherished by our virtues.
— *All's Well That Ends Well*, Act IV, Scene iii

Georgiana liked to ride early on Mondays. With that in mind, Tristan dragged himself out of bed at half past five, threw on his riding clothes, and went downstairs to have Charlemagne saddled.

If nothing else, his pursuit of Georgie was keeping him out of the clubs and gaming hells he used to haunt. He'd also received several notes, as annoyingly perfumed as the ones to her had been, from ladies expressing their displeasure at his recent absence from their bed chambers. Still, he had no desire to find relief from his frustration elsewhere.

Six years ago, he hadn't taken a single

step out of his way to woo her. She'd come, wide-eyed and practically panting, to him. It wasn't until after he'd taken her that his life had become irreversibly and permanently knotted.

The look in her eyes the next night when he'd approached her at the Ashton ball was something he would never forget. And it was something for which he would never forgive himself. She had known then that he'd only been amusing himself; and what had been an act of desire and pleasure instantly became base and deceitful. Whatever she thought to do to him, whatever lesson she thought he deserved, they would *never* be even.

But for the first time, he thought he might be able to gain her forgiveness. He wanted that from her, and for the first time, he wanted more. He wasn't certain what, but when he gazed at her, and even more when he held her in his arms, something felt right.

He caught up to her halfway down the Ladies' Mile in Hyde Park. She wore his favorite riding dress — a deep, brushed green that made her eyes look like emeralds. Her breath and Sheba's clouded in the chilly dawn air as they galloped down the path, her groom falling farther back with each step. She was glorious.

With a kick to Charlemagne's ribs, he went pounding after her. Leaning low to duck the wind, he and the bay slowly began to gain ground. Sheba was fast, but Charlemagne was bigger. She could probably beat him in the turns, but on a straight track and flat ground, the mare didn't have a chance. Georgiana glanced over her shoulder, obviously hearing their approach, and urged her mare on. It wasn't enough.

"Good morning," he said, as they drew even.

She grinned at him, the mare's mane whipping up into her face and tangling dark hair with her golden curls. "I'll race you to the bridge and back," she said breathlessly.

"I'll win."

"Maybe." With a snap of her reins, she sent Sheba into a dead run.

Racing was forbidden in Hyde Park; they would be fined if they were caught. Hearing her throaty laugh floating back to him as she pulled ahead, he didn't care how much it might cost.

He kicked the impatient bay in the ribs again, and they lunged forward. By the time they reached the bridge that spanned one of the park's narrow streams they'd caught up again, and she tried to crowd Sheba into them. Tristan had no intention of ending up in the water a second time, and he sent Charlemagne into a wide turn, avoiding her.

Obviously seeing her chance to pull ahead once more, she used her crop to send Sheba into an even tighter turn back toward the track. Tristan saw the stone just as the mare's foot caught the edge of it, and his heart stopped. *"Georgiana!"*

Sheba's foot rolled, and the mare went down headfirst, pulling the reins from Georgiana's hands and throwing her to the damp ground. Swearing, Tristan yanked the gelding to a halt and jumped from the saddle. He ran to Georgie as she lay in a tumbled heap on the ground, the mare thrashing and whinnying a few feet away.

He flung himself down beside her. "Georgiana? Can you hear me?" Her hat had come off, her golden hair splayed across her face. His fingers shaking, Tristan gently brushed the curls aside. "Georgiana?"

With a great gasp, she opened her eyes and sat up. "Sheba!"

Tristan grabbed her shoulder. "Sit still

and make sure nothing's broken," he ordered.

"But —"

"Are you all right?" he demanded again.

She blinked, then sagged back against his chest. "Ouch."

"What hurts?"

"My bottom. And my hip. Is Sheba all right?"

The groom pounded up, hurrying to the mare. "I'll see to 'er, my lady."

Tristan kept his attention on Georgiana. "You'll be lucky if you didn't crack your tailbone."

She gasped again. "Fix my dress. For heaven's sake, it's practically up to my neck."

Stifling a grin of relief, he reached across her and flipped her riding gown back down past her knees. "Can you sit up straight?"

She flinched, but did so. "Yes."

"And your legs, and arms? Bend them. Make fists."

"I'm all right. Is Sheba hurt? John?"

"Just tangled in the reins, Lady Georgie. My lord, I'd be grateful for a hand with her."

His heartbeat beginning to return to normal, Tristan kept his hand on Georgiana's shoulder. He didn't want to let go of her. "Just a moment. Georgiana, if you get up from this spot before I tell you to, I will make it my business to —"

"I understand. I'll stay right here."

Tristan stood, brushing dirt from his knees, then lay across Sheba's neck to hold her steady so John could cut the tangled reins. That done, the mare plunged to her feet and stomped, shaking her head. He grabbed her bridle to keep her from taking off, and crouched to examine the foreleg that had rolled on the stone.

Georgiana sat where he'd left her, her sleeve ripped and hair falling across her face. Dare turned the mare back over to John, then helped Georgie to her feet.

"She's got a strained knee," he said, "but nothing's broken. Both of you were damned lucky."

Limping, Georgiana made her way over to Sheba and rubbed the mare's nose. "I'm sorry, my sweet one."

She stumbled, wincing, and Tristan caught her arm. "I'm taking you home," he stated, and turned to the groom. "Follow with Sheba."

"I am not leaving my horse."

"You can't ride her, and you're not walking all the way back. John will walk her home. It'll be good for her knee, anyway."

"But —"

"For once, you're going to do as I say. John, will you hand Lady Georgiana up?"

"Yes, my lord."

Reluctantly releasing her again, Tristan swung back up onto Charlemagne. Leaning down, he lifted Georgiana under her arms as John boosted her from below. In a moment she was seated across his legs, one arm around his neck for balance. Things were looking up, after all.

She kept her gaze trained over his shoulder, watching her horse, until they entered the trees. "That was so stupid," she muttered. "I should have known better."

"I bring out the worst in you, Georgie. It's not your fault."

With a sigh, she leaned her head against his shoulder. "Thank you."

He resisted the urge to lower his face to her hair. "You scared me, chit."

She looked up at him. "Did I?"

Hardly daring to breathe, he bent down a little and kissed her. "I'm sorry you hurt your bottom, my lady. I'll rub it for you, if you like."

"Stop it," she protested, squirming. "Someone will see."

"No one's awake but the milkmaids."

Georgiana settled back again. "What are you doing out here, anyway? Heaven knows you're not a milkmaid."

"I felt like taking the morning air."

"At the Ladies' Mile."

"Yes."

"You were looking for me, weren't you?"

"I like seeing you in the morning. It doesn't happen as often as I would wish."

She shifted sideways, her warm, lithe body against his making it very difficult to concentrate. With almost no one in the park, any secluded glade would give them all the privacy they would need.

"Ouch," she muttered, shifting again.

Shaking himself out of his lust, he tugged her a little closer against his chest, taking more of her weight on his shoulders. "When we get you home, take a long, hot bath. As long and as hot as you can stand it."

"So you're an expert in horse-related injuries?" she asked, her voice softer.

"I've been thrown a few times myself."

Her free hand touched his jacket just below his shoulder, where the scar was. "I remember." Slowly her hand traveled up along his face and tangled into his hair. "You looked so worried," she murmured,

274

and pulled his face down to kiss him.

She must have been delirious. He hadn't checked her for head injuries. Even so, Tristan couldn't resist kissing her back, uttering a soft moan as her tongue flicked along his teeth. Charlemagne came to a halt, swinging his head around to look at them as Tristan relaxed the reins and enfolded Georgiana in his arms, deepening the embrace of their mouths.

"My lord, is Lady Georgiana all right?"

His spine stiffened, and he whipped his head around as John came up behind them, Sheba in tow. "Yes, she's fine now. She lost consciousness for a moment, and I was worried she'd stopped breathing."

Georgiana buried her face in his chest, her shoulders shaking with suppressed laughter.

The groom looked alarmed. "Should I ride ahead for help?"

"Yes, I think you should. I'll take Sheba."

"That isn't necess—" Georgie began.

"Be quiet," he murmured, keeping her face close to his chest. The groom handed over Sheba's cut reins and pounded off in the direction of Hawthorne House.

"He'll frighten my aunt half to death," Georgiana complained as he released her.

"Yes, but *I* will look very impressive, my dear."

She chuckled again. Perhaps her brains *were* addled. He urged Charlemagne into a walk again, Sheba limping behind them.

"Is she really all right? I feel like such an idiot."

"Don't. I promise I'll take a look at her again when we get back, and make up a compress. She's not complaining, though, and it doesn't look badly swollen. She'll be fine, my love."

"I hope so."

"I'm more concerned about you. Did you know your elbow is bleeding?"

She looked down. "No, I didn't. Oh, you've blood all over your jacket. I'm sorr—"

"Stop that, Georgiana. I urged you into a race, and you fell. Hush and kiss me again."

To his surprise, she did so. By the time he lifted his head to take a breath, he was ready to begin looking for a secluded glade. It didn't help that she'd noticed his discomfiture and was wriggling again.

"You're doing that on purpose," he muttered.

"Of course I am."

"Well, stop it. Your groom's back."

John galloped back up the path, three of his fellows behind him. Tristan didn't know what four servants intended to do with one horse, but whatever they had in mind, he wasn't relinquishing Georgiana to any of them.

"My lord," John said, panting, "Bradley here is to fetch a physician, if one is necessary."

Tristan looked down at Georgiana again. She was in all likelihood fine, but if she wouldn't let him look at her bottom, someone needed to. He nodded. "Do so."

"Tris—"

"You may have cracked something. Don't argue."

That left three grooms hovering around them. Charlemagne began tossing his head and stomping, and Tristan wrenched him back under control. The last thing he wanted was for Georgie to be thrown to the ground again.

"See to Sheba," he ordered, handing the mare's reins back to John. "The rest of you, keep back, for Lucifer's sake."

With a chorus of "yes, my lords," they did so. By the time they reached Hawthorne House, Tristan felt like the drum major of a parade. The dowager duchess hurried out to the front portico as they arrived, and he had the feeling that things were going to get worse again.

"What in the world happened?" she demanded, coming down the steps to grip one of Georgiana's feet. "Are you all right?"

"I'm fine," Georgiana said, turning so Tristan could hand her down. "There's no need for hysterics."

Her knees buckled as she touched the ground, and she grabbed the stirrup to keep from falling. Tristan jumped down and caught her up in his arms once more. "Allow me."

"This way," the duchess instructed, clearing the hallway of gawking servants.

He was fairly certain that he knew which bedchamber to enter, but allowed Frederica to lead the way. No sense ruining things now, just when they were beginning to look mendable. Carefully, he set Georgiana on the bed, noting her wince as her backside contacted the soft coverlet.

"Thank you, Lord Dare," the duchess said. "Now, if you will kindly leave so I can tend to my niece?"

As he nodded, Georgiana reached out and grabbed his hand.

"You promised you'd look after Sheba," she said.

Tristan smiled. "And I will."

Georgiana watched him as he slipped out her door, closing it softly behind him. He'd never promised her anything before, and something about that seemed significant. So did the way he'd looked so worried, and the way his hands had shaken when he first held her after her fall.

"Let's get you out of that dress," her aunt said, pulling her out of her daydream.

"It's really not that bad. I just landed rather hard."

"Your elbow's bleeding."

"Yes, I know. It stings. Serves me right, though, for racing against Dare. No one ever beats him."

Her aunt stopped moving. "You were racing Lord Dare? Why is that?"

"Because I wanted to. No one else was about, and I thought it would be fun." And it had been fun — exhilarating fun — until Sheba threw her.

"Was this 'fun' his idea?"

"No, it was mine." Georgiana slid to the edge of the bed, wincing again and trying to keep her weight on her left haunch, so she could shed her shoes. "And I think I nearly scared him to death when I fell, so don't go yelling at him for it."

"I don't understand you," Frederica

said, going to work on the buttons of her riding dress. "You hate him, and then you go to live in his house. You run from there, and then you go riding with him."

"Ouch. I don't understand it myself, Aunt."

"Where are you hurt?"

"Mostly my bottom. Tristan thinks I might have cracked my tailbone."

Her aunt's fingers paused again. "You told Lord Dare that you hurt your bottom?" she asked, very slowly.

A blush crept up Georgie's cheeks. "It was fairly obvious."

"Oh, heavens. I hope he doesn't go telling everyone about this, Georgiana. Really, you used to know better."

"He won't tell anyone."

Frederica continued to gaze at her with a quizzical expression, but Georgiana feigned light-headedness so she wouldn't have to talk until the physician arrived.

One thing seemed certain: Tristan truly did bear her some affection. And she was beginning to care for him more than she felt comfortable admitting. If she knew anything for certain, though, it was that caring for Tristan Carroway was a sure way to a broken heart.

Thankfully, the physician decided that

having her take a hot bath and lie on her stomach for the next day would take care of the worst of her injuries. She didn't know how he could be so certain, considering that he wouldn't even lift her shift to take a look at her injured bottom, but Tristan had said the same thing.

Once the physician had gone she took her bath, letting the hot water relax the sore muscles and clean the scraped skin of her backside and elbow. Then with Mary's help she climbed into bed and propped her chin on her folded arms.

Her aunt entered the room again. "He's still here, and he wants to see you."

"Please have him come up, then, if you don't mind."

"Only to the doorway."

Drat. She was going to ruin herself, if she wasn't more careful. "Of course only to the doorway."

"I'll tell him," Frederica muttered, leaving again.

A moment later another knock sounded at her door. "Georgiana?" Tristan's deep voice came. He pushed open the door, but stopped before she could order him to do so. Evidently, he'd already been warned. "I really don't think your aunt likes me at all," he drawled, leaning against the doorframe.

She chuckled. "How's Sheba?"

"As I thought, it's a muscle strain. John and I put a compress on it, and he's to walk her twice a day for a week. After that you might try riding her, but no galloping for a month or so."

"I won't be ready to gallop for at least that long," she said ruefully.

He glanced at Mary, hovering unobtrusively to one side of the room. "I'm just thankful you didn't break any bones."

"So am I."

Light blue eyes studied her face for a long moment before he stirred. "I need to go," he said, pushing upright. "I was supposed to be in Parliament an hour ago." He stood there, still looking at her, then visibly shook himself. "I'll come see you this evening."

There he went, dictating again. "If you're courting me, you must ask my permission to come calling."

He lifted an eyebrow. "Very well. May I come by to see you this evening?"

"Yes." She smiled, trying to cover the low flutter in her stomach. "By then I'll be grateful even for your company, I imagine."

"One can only hope."

She actually had more visitors than she'd expected. Before noon, Lucinda and Evelyn came to call. "Heavens," Lucinda said, closing the door as Mary exited, "I half expected to see you covered in bandages from head to toe."

Georgiana frowned. "It was just a little fall. And how did you know about it, anyway?"

"Mrs. Grawtham's maid was at the milliner's at the same time as Dr. Barlow's daughter."

"Oh, no." Georgiana buried her face in her pillow. "Mrs. Grawtham couldn't keep a secret about herself."

"Anyway," Evie said, sitting on the edge of the bed, "everyone's talking about how your horse threw you and Lord Dare carried you home."

That wasn't too awful. "Well, I suppose it's true," she said, emerging from the soft pillow so she could breathe.

"And about how Dare was so worried that he wouldn't leave your bedside until Dr. Barlow swore that you would be all right and the duchess said she would send word to him if anything at all changed."

"That didn't —"

"Everyone's saying that he's in love with you," Lucinda took up, her dark brown eyes serious. "Georgiana, I thought you were teaching him a lesson. Now it's gotten you injured. If you're still intent on leading Dare on, this could be very dangerous."

"I'm not leading him on, and he's most certainly *not* in love with me. We don't even like each other, remember?"

"That's why everyone thinks it's romantic." Evelyn looked rather worried herself. "You swore never to wed, and never, ever to Dare, and now he's courting you, and you're bound to change your mind."

"Oh, good heavens!" She kicked her feet under the blankets, which only made her backside ache again. "I never swore anything, and I'm not changing my mind, and — damnation!"

Lucinda and Evelyn looked at one another. "I'm not choosing anyone to teach a lesson to, if this is what's going to happen," Evelyn said.

"Nothing is going to happen," Georgiana stated, beginning to wonder whom she was trying to convince.

"What about Dare's escorting you to Vauxhall Gardens, the other night?" Lucinda leaned her chin in one hand. "And you must have been riding with him, if he carried you home."

"He says he's courting me, but he doesn't mean it," she protested. "For heaven's sake, he's only trying to get even for my getting even."

Evelyn looked even more confused, but Lucinda's expression darkened. "Wait just a moment," she said, leaning forward. "He *says* he's courting you? You mean he *is* courting you, Georgie. And everyone already knows it."

Georgiana buried her face again. "Go away. I don't know what I mean."

Lucinda patted her on the arm. "Well, you'd better figure it out soon, my dear. Because we aren't the only ones asking the questions, and we're the nice ones."

Less than an hour after they left, someone scratched on the door. When Mary opened it, Josephine, a downstairs maid, curtsied.

"Lady Georgiana, I'm to tell you that Lord Westbrook is downstairs, come to call on you."

"My goodness, I forgot. We were to go walking. Please have Pascoe explain that I've been injured, and have him give the marquis my apologies."

Josephine curtsied again, "Yes, my lady."

A few minutes later the maid returned. "Lord Westbrook expresses distress at hearing of your injury, and says that he will write you a letter."

"Thank you, Josephine."

Afterward Georgie lay on her bed for a long time, thinking. The world at large thought Tristan was courting her, and that she welcomed his attentions. The problem was, she did. She couldn't help looking forward to each and every encounter; and her entire being reacted to his voice and to his touch.

What if this wasn't part of a game? What if he was sincere? And what if he actually did ask her to marry him?

Georgiana groaned, wishing she could stand up and stalk about the room. She always thought better when she could pace. This was a disaster, and the worst part of it all was that it was entirely of her own making.

"Oh, I give up," Edwina said, leaning down to capture Dragon and cuddle him in her lap. "I have to admit, you were right about their combustibility."

Milly wished she could find some satisfaction in Edwina finally admitting she was right about something. "It's such a pity. For a few moments they actually seemed to want to patch things up."

Her sister sighed. "Do you suppose it'll be Miss Johns, then?"

"Probably, dash it all. She's wealthy enough, but she seems far too stiff to be Carroway material. And once they're married, it'll be back to Essex for us. We may as well say good-bye to the boys now; I doubt we'll see them except at Christmas, once we're banished back to the cottage."

Dragon leapt off Edwina's lap to attack the nearest curtain. "Oh, why couldn't it have been Georgiana?" she grumbled.

Milly patted her on the knee. "He's not married yet. I won't say good-bye until the new Lady Dare throws me out the front door. So for now we'll just have to hope for the best."

"And pray that no one breaks their neck," Edwina added, summoning a smile.

"That's the spirit."

Chapter 16

Cudgel thy brains no more about it . . .
— *Hamlet*, Act V, Scene i

"And then she fainted, and he carried her in his arms all the way home to her aunt's. He was so worried, he wouldn't leave her bedside." Cynthia Prentiss popped another chocolate into her mouth.

Amelia Johns picked through the dessert tables' delicacies, though with less enthusiasm than she'd had a few moments earlier. "Their families are very close. I should imagine he wished to make certain she was well. What's so surprising about that?"

"Hm," Felicity mused from her other side, "when was the last time *you* went riding with Lord Dare, Amelia?"

"We went out on a picnic just last week," she reminded them, settling on the sugared orange peels. "And he was quite attentive." He'd been so attentive, in fact, that she'd returned home ready to choose the material for her wedding gown. Since then, though, she hadn't even seen him, much less received a letter or a bouquet.

"They say he sent her a huge bouquet of flowers, too," Cynthia said, confirming what Amelia had heard. "And that was before the riding incident."

Amelia forced a careless laugh. "You two will gossip about anything. Everyone knows Tristan and Lady Georgiana don't even like one another. I'm sure he was just being kind, for the sake of her cousin, the Duke of Wycliffe."

It was true that the last few days hadn't unfolded as she'd expected, but she knew how her viscount and Lady Georgiana felt about one another — he'd even made a few comments in her presence about the stubborn, tart nature of his adversary. Tristan was simply being taught a lesson that would make him fall madly in love with her, and she would be a viscountess before the end of the summer.

"Well, I suppose you could be right," Felicity said. "I mean, Lord Dare is handsome enough, of course, but everyone knows he has no money. All he has is his title, and Lady Georgiana is already a marquis's daughter, and cousin to a duke. Why would she want to become a viscountess?"

"Exactly. And everyone knows I receive three thousand a year, so I don't see any further need to discuss this nonsense."

Tristan Carroway *was* going to marry her. He had begun courting her because of her money and because he found her charming, and he would marry her for the same reasons.

"There he is," Cynthia whispered. "Maybe you should remind *him* about your income."

Taking a breath, Amelia turned. Lord Dare had just strolled into the main room at Almack's. He was alone, wearing a black, long-tailed evening jacket that looked molded to his broad shoulders. For a moment she just looked at him, admiring.

With his tall, dark looks and her pretty, petite form, they would make a striking couple. Of course they belonged together — and her father had just last week offered her an additional fifty pounds a month pin money upon the announcement of their engagement. Lady Dare . . . yes, she would make a perfect viscountess.

He seemed preoccupied with something, and so with a backward glance at her cynical friends, she strolled in the general direction of the orchestra, on a course that would bring her straight into his path. She was glad she'd worn her yellow satin gown with the white lace sleeves this evening; everyone said it made her eyes look the perfect blue of a china doll's.

At the last moment she turned to offer Cynthia a wave, and stepped backward straight into him. "Oh, my goodness," she breathed, stumbling so that he would catch her under the arms.

"Amelia, my apologies," he drawled, smiling at her as he lifted her back upright. "I generally keep my eyes open when I walk. I seem to be rather distracted this evening."

"No apology is necessary, Tristan," she said, smoothing the front of her gown so he would be certain to notice the low-cut bodice.

His light blue gaze drifted down, and then back up to her face. "You look quite fetching this evening."

"Thank you." Smiling, she offered a shallow curtsy which exposed even more of her bosom to his gaze. For all of Lady Georgiana's talk of elaborate lessons, sometimes men were very easy to figure out. "If you continue talking so sweetly, I shall have to save you a waltz tonight."

"If you keep being so generous, I shall ask you for one." With a slight bow, he took a step away from her. "If you'll excuse me, I see someone I need to speak to."

"Of course. We can chat later."

His smile deepened. "Or sooner."

Ah, success. He never used to be so polite. The smile of triumph she sent back to her silly friends faded though as she turned to see with whom he'd gone to converse. Lady Georgiana Halley stood between the Duke of Wycliffe, and his wife. She had to admire Emma Brakenridge, though in going from a girls' school headmistress to a duchess, she had perhaps reached a little high.

Amelia sighed. She only wanted to move up from being an earl's brother's grand-daughter to a viscountess — and now even that didn't appear to be as promising as it once had. The look Tristan gave Lady Georgiana was one he'd never had for her.

It was best to face facts as they were. Lady Georgiana might think she was helping, or she might only be saying that when she intended something else, but it was obviously going to be up to Amelia to set Tristan in the right direction. And given what she knew of men, she had a very good idea just how to do it.

Grey didn't look very happy to see him, but Tristan was more concerned with the presence of Luxley, Paltridge, and to a lesser degree, Francis Henning, hovering about Georgiana. After the fright she'd given him yesterday, he didn't like even the idea of another man looking in her direction.

"Georgiana," he said, elbowing Henning aside to take her hand, then bringing it to his lips. "The sparkle is back in your eye. Are you feeling better?"

"Much," she said, smiling, "though I'm not quite up for dancing."

He thought that comment was probably aimed at her other suitors, but none of them took the hint and wandered off. Instead, they favored her with a squawking chorus of sympathy and compliments that made him scowl. If her warning was for his benefit, well, he wasn't going anywhere. Before he could encourage the buffoons to go hunting elsewhere, Emma took his arm.

"You very nearly sounded like a hero, yesterday," she said, her warm hazel eyes dancing.

With an irritated glance at the pack, he left the circle of Georgiana's admirers. "Yes, I suppose I reacted before my wiser nature could take hold and shake me out of it."

The duchess chuckled. "I don't believe

that," she said in a lower voice. "I've seen your good heart, Tristan."

"I would appreciate if you didn't bandy that about. A good heart and empty pockets make Dare a very lonely lad." He glanced in Georgie's direction. "Especially when certain other females don't believe that 'good heart' bit."

"Well, you'll have to convince her. I, for one, am on your side."

He lifted an eyebrow. "And how does the mighty Wycliffe feel about that?"

"He's more protective of Georgiana. I advise being patient yet utterly relentless."

"Your advice, dear Em, will probably get me killed." Tristan kissed her on the cheek to soften the words. "But I do appreciate it."

"How many times do I have to tell you," Grey rumbled, approaching with Georgiana on his arm, thank God, "to keep your lips off my wife?"

"You won't let me kiss you," Tristan drawled, "so I have no other options."

"How about escorting me to the refreshment table, instead?" Georgiana held out her hand to him.

That had been good of Wycliffe, to separate her from the wolf pack. "With pleasure. Your Graces, if you'll pardon us?"

"Oh, bugger off," Grey said. "But keep an eye on her. She nearly fell coming down from the coach."

"I tripped on my dress," Georgie protested, flushing.

"I shall guard her with my life."

She looked up at him, and despite the obvious skepticism in her expression, he was surprised to realize that he meant it. Letting someone else have Georgiana was out of the question. Whatever it took, he would make her his. Permanently.

"So how did I win out over your other suitors?" Tristan asked, guiding her around the less crowded side of the room.

"I can't tell them to go to the devil if they annoy me," she answered easily. "You, I don't mind saying it to."

"I suppose I have built up a tolerance for your insults, over the years," he agreed. "How is your bottom?"

Her blush deepened. "Black-and-blue, but better. Thankfully most everyone seems to think I merely wrenched my knee, and my bottom has remained out of the conversation."

Tristan nodded. In the past he might have claimed the credit he deserved for encouraging the wrong rumor to spread, but he felt so bad about her being hurt that he didn't want any thanks. "I'm glad you came this evening," he said, to have something to say.

She searched his eyes for a moment. "So am I. Tristan —"

"There you are," Lucinda Barrett said, hurrying up to grasp Georgie's free hand. "I was hoping you felt well enough to attend tonight."

Stifling his annoyance, Tristan nodded a greeting to the auburn-haired chit. "I myself would have faked illness to *avoid* Almack's."

Georgiana looked at him in obvious disbelief. "Then why didn't you?"

"Because you're here."

"Hush," she ordered. "You'll have everyone talking about us."

"Everyone already is," Lucinda said, grinning. "The two of you are the talk of London."

For the first time, Tristan looked around the room. They did seem to be the object of conversation. Well, so be it. She wasn't going to escape him again, either because of his folly or her stubbornness. And this kind of rumor could only help his chances.

"Don't be silly, Luce. He only wants my money."

Lucinda paled, her eyes darting in his direction. "Georgie, you shouldn't say such things."

Tristan clamped down his sudden anger. He'd heard such talk before, of course; once he'd even overheard several ladies discussing whether his services in the bed-chamber could be bought. That had been quite the evening.

But Georgiana had never mentioned his finances to anyone, that he knew of — and even if she was joking, he didn't appreciate it one damned bit.

Carefully he extracted his arm from her grip. "Miss Barrett, if you would tend to Lady Georgiana, I've promised a dance to Miss Johns." He sketched a shallow bow. "Ladies."

Before he could move away, Georgie gripped his sleeve again. "Dare."

He stopped, looking down at her coolly. "Yes?"

"Luce, go away," Georgiana murmured.

Miss Barrett complied, looking relieved to escape unscathed. The mutterings around them grew louder, but he didn't give a damn about that. People would talk; the only thing he could do was to make certain they had nothing more serious than an argument to speculate over. He and Georgiana argued all the time, anyway.

"I'm sorry," she whispered. "I wasn't serious, and it was mean."

He forced a careless shrug. "It was true — partly. But money's not all I want from you, Georgiana, and you know it."

"I know what you tell me, but I don't know what I believe. You've tricked me before."

"And you've tricked me, haven't you?" he returned in a low voice. "So how shall I prove it to you?"

As he spoke, he realized that this may have been just what she was waiting for: to force him to declare his intentions toward and affection for her before the world, so she could laugh at him and humiliate him in public. And because he couldn't resist being near her, touching her, he'd fallen right into her trap.

She sighed. "I don't know what to think, sometimes."

Tristan made his shoulders relax. "Don't think so much. I never do."

She gave a short laugh. "Drat, I don't have a fan. If my bottom felt better, I would kick you."

A slow smile tugged at the corners of his mouth. "If your bottom felt better, I would suggest several far more pleasant things for us to do together." Looking down at her, he just barely resisted running a finger along her cheek. "I want you," he murmured. "Badly."

Georgiana swallowed. "You're just trying to make me blush. It won't work, so stop it."

"I don't want you to blush," he continued in the same low voice. "I want you to call out my name, and come for me."

"Shut up," she enunciated unsteadily. "You're obviously mad."

His smile deepened. This seemed to be working well, though he was becoming rather uncomfortable. "Say you'll go for a walk with me tomorrow in Covent Garden, and I'll stop."

"I'm having tea with Lu—"

"And I want to feel your warm skin under my fingers, and your body beneath mine, my Georgi—"

"All right!" Blushing deep red, she yanked him toward the refreshment table. "Be by at ten sharp, or I *will* kick you the next time I set eyes on you."

He nodded. "Fair enough."

The night had actually gone rather well, considering. He'd found a strategy that seemed to work. She *did* want him, which made the next step that much easier.

★ ★ ★

Would he have walked away, if she hadn't grabbed his arm? Georgiana hadn't meant to stop him, but the moment he had released her, she hadn't been able to keep from reaching out for him. And he hadn't left, and now she'd agreed to go walking with him. She still kept him close by, supposedly in case she fell, but in truth because she craved the heat and the wanting he caused in her. Just hearing him say those things aloud left her hot and trembling for him.

Even worse, the entire assembly at Almack's had seen them deep in conversation for an extended time. They had seen her smile and his smile and the way she'd blushed like a complete nodcock. If she hadn't agreed to go walking with him, though, she had the distinct feeling that he would have dragged her off to the nearest empty alcove, pulled her gown off, and ravished her — and even with her sore bottom, she would have enjoyed that far too much for her own good.

Twelve men had proposed to her over the last two years, and she reacted to none of them as she reacted to him. Since their second foolish night together, she'd even tried to imagine herself naked and impassioned with any of her other suitors. After all, if she married one of them, she would be required to share his bed on occasion.

But all those imaginings had given her was a faint feeling of disgust. Some of the gentlemen were pleasant enough to look at and several, like Luxley and Westbrook, were quite handsome. However, nothing she tried worked. She couldn't tolerate even the idea of one of them touching her and kissing her, much less putting their —

"My lady," the Earl of Drasten said, striding up to her, "I beg you to give me this dance."

Beside her, Tristan stiffened, the muscles in his arm tensing. She forced a polite smile. No one was going to brawl over her, and certainly not at Almack's. She'd be banned for life. "I'm not dancing this evening, my lord."

"That's simply too cruel," the dark-haired earl protested, favoring Dare with an unfriendly glance. "You cannot deprive us of your company in favor of this rake."

She could feel the force of Tristan's sudden, dark anger flowing around her. "Are you deaf, Dr—"

"Lord Drasten," she interrupted, before Tristan could challenge the idiot earl to a duel, "I was injured in a riding accident the day before yesterday, and I am not up to dancing tonight. I would be pleased, though, to receive a chocolate."

Drasten held out his arm. "I shall escort you, then."

Tristan looked at him. "No, you won't."

"Go find some other heiress, Dare. This one doesn't even like you."

Gasping, Georgiana stepped between them, shoving at Tristan's chest before he could unleash the fist he'd coiled. Her push didn't even budge him, but neither did he strike. "No," she said, catching his gaze.

The blue eyes that met hers were narrow and angry, but she didn't release her grip on his lapels. After a long moment, he let out his breath and grimaced. "I haven't killed anyone all month," he murmured, slight humor returning to his gaze. "No one will miss just one earl."

"I say, Dare, you can't talk —"

Moving with that deceptive speed of his, Tristan stepped around her and up to the earl. Grabbing the surprised Drasten's hand and shaking it, he leaned closer. "Go away," he murmured, very quietly. "Now."

The earl must have seen the same thing in Tristan's eyes as she did, because with a small nod he backed away and suddenly found another group of cronies to talk to. Georgiana drew a long breath. She sometimes forgot that when they'd first met, Tristan had had a reputation for hard drinking and harder wagering, and being a deadly shot. He had changed, and she wondered whether it was partly because of her.

"My apologies," he said, putting his warm hand over hers.

And now he was the easy, self-controlled Tristan again. For a moment Georgiana wondered if that wasn't the most significant change in him of all; he'd learned that his actions had ramifications not just for himself, but for others, and he let that knowledge guide him — for the most part.

"I'm glad to be rid of him," she returned, wondering whether he could feel the fast rush of her pulse. All he needed to do, apparently, was mention their being naked together and then threaten someone with bodily harm on her behalf, and her knees went weak. "Thank you."

"My pleasure."

She could feel the charged air between them, the sensation that not touching him and kissing him right then and there would cause physical pain. He seemed to sense it as well, and cast a look about the room as though he wished the rest of Almack's guests would disappear. Perhaps he wasn't as controlled as she'd thought.

"Georgiana," he said in a low voice.

"Will you please walk me . . . somewhere?" She could scarcely seem to breathe, she wanted him so badly.

"The coatroom?" he suggested. "You look chilled."

She was burning up. "Yes, exactly."

Considering that she wanted to run, they made their way across the crowded room in a fairly dignified manner. A footman stood watch at the coatroom door. As they approached, Tristan shrugged free of her grip on his arm, and put his hands behind his back.

"Would you please . . ." He trailed off. "Blast it, I've forgotten my gloves. Would you please find my brother, Bradshaw, and fetch them for me?" he requested.

The servant nodded. "At once, my lord."

As soon as he was out of sight, Tristan drew her inside the small room and closed the door. "You're wearing your gloves," she noted, looking at his hands.

He yanked them off and shoved them into a pocket. "No, I'm not."

Closing the short distance between them, he nudged her back against the door

304

and captured her mouth in a rough kiss. The electricity broke over them and she moaned, pulling his face down harder against her, trying to climb inside him.

His hands swept down her back and hips, closing around her bottom and tugging her against his body. She flinched. "Ouch."

"Wh . . . Damnation." He released her immediately, putting his palms against the door on either side of her shoulders. "Apologies."

"What about Bradshaw?" she asked, biting his lower lip. "That man's looking for him."

"It'll take a while. Shaw's not here."

Georgiana wanted to compliment him on his deviousness. With the small amount of time they were likely to have, however, that seemed less important than indulging in another hot, openmouthed kiss.

"I wish the damned door had a lock," he muttered against her mouth, kissing her until she felt nearly faint with wanting him.

"We couldn't, anyway." Sliding her hands around his waist, beneath his jacket, she kneaded the hard muscles of his back. "Could we?"

With one last, lingering kiss he pulled away. "No, we couldn't," he murmured, his voice husky with want. "If I intended to beat out the competition by ruining you, I would have done it a long time ago."

Georgiana leaned back against the door, trying to regain both her senses and her breath. "Then how *do* you intend to beat out the competition?"

He smiled, a slow, wicked curving of his lips that made her want to pounce on him all over again. "Persistence and patience," he said, running his fingers along her cheek. "It's not just your body I want, Georgiana. I want all of you."

A few weeks ago she would have doubted his sincerity. Tonight, looking into his intelligent, hungry eyes, she believed him. And that frightened and excited her down to her toes.

The door rattled. Cursing, Tristan flung himself onto the carpeted floor and grabbed one knee in his hands. "Damnation, Georgie, I only *asked* for a kiss," he snapped, then threw a glance at the footman as he stepped back into the room. "Did you find my brother?"

"N . . . no, my lord. I looked, but —"

"Never mind that. Help me up. Blasted flighty females."

Flushing, the servant hurried forward and pulled Tristan to his feet.

Trying to keep her jaw from falling open, Georgiana could only watch as Tristan sent an additional glare at her, then limped over to retrieve her shawl. "I suppose you'll want to return to your cousin now?" he asked, lifting an eyebrow.

"Y . . . yes. At once, if you please."

The footman stifled an amused look at Dare's back as, with elaborate caution, Tristan offered her his arm. She hesitated for effect, then took it.

As they made their way back into the main assembly rooms, Georgiana couldn't help looking at him. Any rumors resulting from their little adventure would be exactly as he intended — he'd tried to snatch a kiss, and she'd kicked him.

She'd known from the *ton*'s lack of reaction to their first tryst that he'd done something to keep the gossips at bay. What she hadn't realized until this moment was that he'd done so intentionally, and that he'd allowed it to sully his own reputation rather than hers.

"Thank you," she said quietly, looking up at his face.

He met her gaze. "Don't. When I lead you astray, I'm obligated to protect you from any gossip about it."

She wasn't certain how much leading

he'd done this evening. "Even so, it was nice of you."

"Then thank me by going walking with me in the morning."

She wondered briefly whether she could keep her hands off him for that long. "All right."

Chapter 17

Out, damned spot! Out, I say!
— *Macbeth*, Act V, Scene i

Amelia instructed the hired hack to wait at the end of the block for her, and paid the driver an extra five shillings to keep this visit and her identity — if he should realize it — to himself. Pulling her hood up close around her face, she slipped down the street and up the short front drive of Carroway House. She'd only seen the house from the outside, and the idea that soon the grand place would be hers created a shivering warmth deep inside her.

Her parents' house was opulent, but it wasn't on Albemarle Street. Only the oldest blue blood families had homes in this, the loftiest section of Mayfair. And soon she would be part of that elite circle, the one place where even her father's money couldn't gain them entry.

At two hours before dawn, she'd expected the house to be dark and everyone asleep. As she slowly pushed open the front door, which thankfully was unlocked, it seemed she was correct. The moon was full and would be late setting, and by its dim light through the windows she made her way to the stairs and ascended to the second floor.

Tristan had mentioned that the brothers had commandeered the bedchambers on the west side of the house, so she slipped down the hallway to that wing. This was going to be so simple, she wished she'd thought of it before. Lady Georgiana's plan didn't seem to be going at all well, so it was necessary to take matters — and anything else necessary — into her own hands. Amelia stifled a chuckle. The outcome would be to her benefit, certainly.

Behind the first closed door the room was dark and empty, and so closing it again softly, she proceeded to the next one. A dim heap of blankets took up the middle of the bed. Holding her breath, she crept farther into the room, then scowled. The face peeking out from the pile was too young and soft to be Tristan's — one of his younger brothers. He had far too many of them.

She recognized the sleeping occupant of

the next room as Bradshaw, a naval officer of some kind. He was handsome enough but without a title, or even a real hope of one, unless Tristan died without heirs. And he wouldn't do that if she had any say in the matter, which she would.

The clock ticking faintly down the hallway reminded her that she had only a short time before the servants began stirring. She pushed open the next door and peered inside.

Ah, success. She was glad it was Tristan stretched out on his back under the blankets and not the middle brother, Robert. On the one occasion she'd seen him, he'd made her uncomfortable and nervous, with his silence and his knowing eyes. He didn't look as though he ever slept, anyway.

Moving as quietly as she could, Amelia closed the door behind her and tiptoed toward the bed, shedding her cloak as she advanced. She couldn't hold back her smile. If Tristan was half the man his reputation claimed, tonight should be pleasant in more ways than one.

Tristan half opened one eye as delicate fingers trailed down his chest. At first he thought he was dreaming about Georgiana again, and, loath to wake, he sighed and closed his eye.

A tongue licked his ear, and the delicate fingers slipped below the blanket. He frowned. Even in his dreams, embracing Georgiana was scented faintly with lavender. Tonight, he smelled lemon.

Weight shifted and settled across his hips. Tristan opened both of his eyes.

"Hello, Tristan," Amelia Johns breathed, leaning forward, her dark hair spilling over her bare shoulders and bare breasts, to kiss him.

With an oath he shoved her off and scrambled out of bed. "What in damnation are you doing here?" he demanded, coming wide-awake.

She perched on the bed, her eyes luminous in the dim moonlight. Her gaze traveled down the length of him and focused below his waist, less startled than he would have expected from an innocent debutante. Apparently she wasn't as innocent as he'd been led to believe.

"I want to reassure you that I welcome your suit," she cooed, running her tongue along her upper lip.

He grabbed a blanket from the back of a chair and pulled it around his hips. Before Georgiana's return to his bed, he would have welcomed a midnight visit from a pretty female, but things had changed. Besides, he knew a trap when one pounced on him. And this was a good one. Completely naked, all she would have to do was yell, and he would be a married man.

The wholly male part of him acknowledged that she was quite pretty, and desirable — and, of course, wealthy. Swallowing, he returned his gaze to her face.

"I'm not certain what you're talking about," he said in a low voice, hoping no one else in the household had heard his initial outburst, and rather surprised she hadn't already roused witnesses. She would; of that he was certain. "But we can better discuss this over luncheon tomorrow, don't you think?"

Amelia shook her head. "I can satisfy you, as well as any other woman."

He doubted that, but under the circumstances it didn't seem a good time to argue. "Amelia, I'll discuss anything you like tomorrow, but this just isn't . . . seemly." Good God, he sounded like one of the women he used to seduce. He hoped it would work better on her than it had on him.

She scowled. "I know it's not seemly, but it's not as though you've given me any choice. You've barely even noticed me, lately. And I know why."

That sounded ominous. Whatever might be brewing in her pretty head, he had to make certain it didn't pass any farther than these walls. "Tell me why, then, won't you?"

"Lady Georgiana Halley. She warned me that you would make a terrible husband."

"She did, did she?" *That little interfering busybody.* Actually, he'd expected as much.

"Oh, yes. She said awful things about you. And then she promised me that she would teach you a lesson that would make you more appreciative of me." She slid off the bed and glided toward him, her bare skin milk white in the dim room. "So you see, she's only trying to make you look foolish."

He sidestepped her approach, wanting to have as much distance between them as possible if one of his family members or servants should discover them together. "I might say the same thing about you, Amelia."

She shook her head, full breasts peeking through the long waves of her brunette hair as she moved. "I don't want to make you look foolish," she breathed. "I want you to marry me."

Thank God Georgiana had been honest with him about her little lesson in behavior, or he might have been tempted to use Amelia to erase the feel of her against his skin. "That's very interesting," he returned, bending down to pick up her dress as they circled the floor, she stalking, he assessing. "Why don't you put this back on?"

"I don't want to."

"Nevertheless, it's very late, and if your parents awake to find you gone from their household, they'll be frantic."

Whether it was true or not, she slowed as she considered his words. Taking the opportunity, he held open the dress for her.

"If you please," he pressed, "you . . . distract me far too much, Amelia." He'd never worked this damned hard to escape sex before. "A discussion this important needs to take place in a more proper setting."

"No, it doesn't. I'm getting impatient, Tristan. You've been courting me for weeks, now. I think you should take me to bed, and —"

"There's always time for that later," he interrupted. His trousers hung over the back of a chair, and he dropped her gown and grabbed for them. "I'm actually very tired tonight."

"I could scream and wake everyone up," she said in her honeyed voice.

Tristan narrowed his eyes. *Bloody hell.* "And then you'll have to explain why you're in *my* bedchamber, and I'm not in yours. They'll say you're forward."

She pouted. "How can I be forward, or anything less than patient, when I've waited the entire Season for you to declare yourself?"

Amelia reached for his blanket. Tristan saw the move coming and grabbed her hand, holding her away from him. "If you make me angry," he said in a firm voice, "I won't marry you regardless of who gets ruined. My reputation would survive this."

"But your pocketbook wouldn't, because no one would want to marry you after the shameful way you've treated me."

"I'll risk it." As long as he could bluff her into believing that, he might make it until dawn as a single gentleman.

"Humph." Stomping her foot, she picked up the dress he'd dropped at her feet. "You know what I think? I think you're in love with Lady Georgiana, and when you declare yourself to her, she's only going to laugh at you. And then you'll have to beg me to marry you. And I *will* make you beg."

Turning half-away, he shrugged into his trousers and dropped the blanket. "I told you, we can discuss this over luncheon tomorrow. We'll both be calmer and more rested." *And more dressed.*

"Oh, very well."

"Where are your shoes?"

She pointed. "Over there, by my cloak."

He went to get them and light a lamp, while Amelia, annoyed and more than a little unsatisfied after seeing his fine form, yanked her gown up over her shoulders. As the lamplight flickered yellow into the room, she saw the toe of a woman's stocking hanging out of his bedstand drawer. Tristan was still occupied with gathering the rest of her clothes, so she stepped over and pulled it free. A note came out with it, and she opened it, reading it quickly.

No wonder the viscount was reluctant to give up Georgiana Halley. She'd been sharing his bed. And leaving him stockings as mementos. Glancing at his bare, broad back, she took the second stocking out of its quaint little box and stuffed both of them and the note into her pocket.

So much for Lady Georgiana teaching

Dare a lesson. That whore had planned to steal Tristan all along, and she was using the lesson as a ruse to keep her rivals from becoming suspicious. Well, she was in for a surprise now.

"All right, put on your shoes and cloak, and let's go," he growled.

For a moment she considered her original plan of rousing the household and forcing Dare into marriage. Her friends might laugh at her for being so desperate, though, after she'd spent weeks telling them how confident she was about his suit.

"I'm not very happy about this," she muttered for effect, stepping into her shoes.

"Neither am I." He didn't help her on with her cloak, but handed it to her from as far away as he could reach. "Do you have a coach?" he asked as he shrugged into his coat.

"I have a hack waiting around the corner."

"I'll walk you, then."

He was only worried that she would try something devious. She had his letter and the stockings, however. Holding one hand over her pocket to be certain nothing fell out, she preceded him down the stairs and out the front door.

"Remember, you are meeting me for

luncheon tomorrow," she said as they neared her hack. "I expect you to call on me at my parents' home."

"I will." Abruptly he took a step closer. "I'm not pleased with this, Amelia. I don't like tricks. Or traps."

"I'm only thinking of both of us," she returned, taking a half step away from him. She hadn't seen this side of him before. She found it rather arousing. "I want a title, and you want my money. But I do have other offers this Season, Tristan. Consider that tomorrow, too."

"I'll call on you at one o'clock."

She stepped up into the hack. "I'll be waiting."

Tristan slipped back inside the house and shut the front door. With a long exhalation, he leaned back against the sturdy oak and threw the bolt. That had been too damned close.

But Amelia's sudden appearance had answered a question that had been knocking about in his skull. She was still the logical choice for a wife; young, compliant — though not as compliant as he'd originally thought — and wealthy. And he absolutely didn't want to marry her.

With a slight smile, he pushed upright and headed for the stairs. He wondered what Georgiana would say if he simply proposed tomorrow. After she regained consciousness, that was.

And he and Georgiana *would* be married. She might very well be setting the stage for another humiliation for him, and if so, he would have to outmaneuver her. As long as she said yes, he could deal with the rest.

A dark form moved at the top of the stairs, and he tensed, fists coiling. If it was any other female besides Georgiana, he was going to throw himself off the balcony.

"Are you marrying her?" Bit's quiet, low voice came.

He relaxed. "Thank God it's you. And no, I'm not."

"Good." He turned on his heel and vanished back into the shadows. "Good night."

"Good night."

Whatever Robert had seen or heard, he obviously wasn't going to say anything. Tristan slipped back inside his room and fastened the latch on his door, then as an afterthought dragged a chair over to block the doorway. No more visitors before dawn. He had some thinking to do.

When Tristan arrived at Hawthorne House the next morning at precisely ten o'clock, he was dressed in a conservative blue coat and gray trousers, an elaborate cravat, and polished Hessian boots. Georgiana watched through her window as he came up the drive and rapped on the front door.

She still couldn't quite believe that he was there to call on her. Even when she'd hated and despised him, the sight of those blue eyes and that dark, curling hair just brushing his collar had made her heart beat faster. She'd told herself it was anger, and that she'd sought him out on every occasion to insult and injure him for the same reason. Now, she wasn't quite so certain.

What did that say about her, though, if she could remain attracted to a man who'd hurt and humiliated her? Did she only think he'd changed, or had he really done so? Was his calling on her another trick that would leave her heartbroken forever this time, or was he sincere?

"My lady, Lord Dare is here to see you," Pascoe said, from her sitting room doorway.

She turned to the butler. "Thank you. I'll be down in a moment."

"Very good, my lady."

Pulling on her gloves and retrieving her parasol, she took a last look at herself in her dressing mirror and made her way downstairs. Tristan was in the morning room, pacing as he always seemed to do in her aunt's house.

"Good morning."

He stopped. "Good morning."

As their eyes met, that familiar heat ran through her veins, and it was only with difficulty that she kept from striding up to him and pulling his face down for a kiss. That was new; in the past after her blood heated, she had wanted to stride up and put a fan across his skull. Perhaps that was part of the attraction: Wanting Tristan Carroway was dangerous. Liking him was even more hazardous.

"How is your . . ." He glanced behind her, at where Pascoe was lurking. "How are your injuries?" he amended.

"Much better. I'm only a little stiff, and a few interesting colors in some places."

Tristan grinned. "Glad to hear you're feeling better. Are you ready?"

She nodded. "Mary will accompany us."

"Very well. Are we to have an armed guard, as well?"

"Not if you behave."

His smile deepened. "Then perhaps you should send for one now."

Her pulse fluttered. "Oh, stop it. Let's go."

Mary waited for them in the foyer, and they descended the front steps and turned toward Grosvenor Street. Georgiana rested her hand on Tristan's arm, wishing she didn't have to wear gloves and that they could hold hands. She liked to touch his bare skin, and the scent of soap and leather and cigars that he always seemed to have about him intoxicated her.

"What?" he asked.

She looked up at him. "What do you mean, 'what?' "

"You're leaning. I thought you wanted to tell me something."

Georgiana blushed, straightening. "No."

"Ah. Well, I want to tell you something."

"Enlighten me," she countered, hoping he couldn't tell how very rousing she found his presence.

He gazed at her, his expression softening into a smile. "Edwina's cat has taken over the household. This morning, Dragon killed the fleur on Bradshaw's dress uniform hat and carried it into the aunties, as proud as if he'd killed an elephant."

"Oh, no. What did Bradshaw do?"

"He doesn't know, yet. Milly took one of the knickknacks off that gawdy ostrich hat of hers, cut it down, dyed it with ink, and sewed it to Bradshaw's hat."

Georgiana chuckled. "Are you going to tell him?"

"He's the keen-sighted naval officer. If he doesn't notice, it's his own damned fault, as far as I'm concerned."

"You're terrible! What if one of his superiors should notice?"

Tristan shrugged. "Knowing Shaw, he'll make it the new height of naval fashion. They'll all be wearing women's hats and baubles by autumn."

He glanced away as a coach passed them, and she took the moment to study his profile. "Is that really what you wanted to tell me?" she asked.

"No. But I imagine you receive compliments on your emerald eyes and sun golden hair all the time. I'm trying to be more original than that." He slid his eyes back to where Mary followed a few steps behind them. "Compliments about your fine breasts, though, probably won't help my cause."

Heat ran down her spine. "And what is your cause?" she asked in the same soft voice.

"I think you know what it is," he answered, "but I'm still trying to gain an admission from you that you really do trust me."

"I—"

"Dare!"

A jolly voice came from in front of them, and she started. Lord Bellefeld emerged from a clothiers to shake Tristan's hand.

"I've heard the most extraordinary rumor," the rotund marquis rumbled, bowing at her.

She thought Tristan stiffened. "And what rumor might that be?" he drawled. "I'm the object of so many of them."

"Ha! Indeed you are, lad. The one I heard is that you're in pursuit of this lovely young lady, here. Is it true?"

Tristan grinned at her, something in his eyes making her heart flip-flop. "Yes, it is true."

"Excellent, lad! I'm off to put ten quid on Lady Georgiana, then. Good day."

Her blood froze. Almost before she'd realized it, she'd ripped her hand from Tristan's arm and grabbed the marquis by the shoulder. "*What* —" Her voice shook, and she had to start over. "What do you mean, you're putting ten quid on me?"

Bellefeld didn't look in the least perturbed. "Oh, there's a board up at White's over who Dare'll end up married to. At the moment it's two to one that he'll be leg-shackled to that Amelia Johns female by the end of the Season. You're longer odds, but now I have inside information." He winked at her.

The blood drained from Georgiana's face, and she clutched Bellefeld's jacket to keep herself from collapsing in a dead faint. "Who . . . who else is on the board?" she managed.

"Eh? I don't remember all the names. Some chit named Daubner, and a Smithee or something. Almost a half dozen, if I recall. Ain't that right, Dare?"

"I wouldn't know," Tristan said after a moment, his voice oddly flat. "No one told me."

Finally, Bellefeld seemed to realize that he'd said something inappropriate. Rushing, he backed away. "No one means anything by it, I'm sure," he said. "All in good fun, you know."

"Of course," she said, releasing him. He stampeded away, but she stayed where she was. She couldn't turn to face Tristan. She wanted to run screaming back home and never look at anyone again.

"Georgiana," he said quietly, and she flinched.

"Don't you . . . dare —"

"Go home with Mary, if you please," he said in a black, angry voice she'd never heard before. "I have something to attend to."

She forced herself to look at him. His face was gray, as hers probably was. Of course he was upset; he'd been found out, his little plan discovered. "Going to put some money on me?" she forced out. "I wouldn't, if I were you — some inside information. And no, I don't trust you. I never — *never* — will."

"Go home," he repeated, his voice shaking. He held her gaze a moment longer, then turned and strode away in the direction of Pall Mall. Probably to change his wager to some more amenable chit.

"My lady?" Mary said, approaching. "Is something wrong?"

A tear ran down Georgiana's cheek, and she wiped it away before anyone could notice. It would never do if they thought she was crying because of Tristan's departure. "No. Let's go home."

"But Lord Dare?"

"Forget him. I already have."

She marched home, Mary trotting to keep up with her. Her bottom hurt, but she welcomed the pain; it gave her something else to think about. He'd done it again.

He'd seduced her, bedded her, and betrayed her. And this time she had no one to blame but herself.

Thank goodness she'd found out before she completely lost her heart to him. A sob ripped from her throat as Pascoe opened the front door. No, it didn't hurt, because she didn't care. Anything between them had been merely lust. She could put lust out of her mind.

"My lady?"

"I'll be in my rooms," she said as she hurried past the butler. "I'm not to be disturbed, for anyone or anything. Is that clear?"

"Y . . . yes, my lady."

The "board" at White's was actually a misnomer. It was a ledger book, where anyone admitted to the exclusive club could write down a wager with anyone else. Most of them were private wagers between two parties. On occasion, one appeared that garnered greater interest, or was made among a number of gentlemen.

As Tristan stalked into White's, shoving aside the doorman who tried to inform him that luncheon wouldn't be served for another hour, he made straight for the main gaming room and the ledger book sitting on its raised dais at one side. He'd run out of curses on the way over, but repeated a few choice ones as he caught sight of the book and the half dozen men standing around it.

"Dare, you dog," one of the younger ones said, grinning, "you can't wager on yourself, you know. Bad —"

Tristan coiled his fist and slammed the lad in the jaw. "Move," he said belatedly, as the fellow crumpled to the ground like a wet rag.

Footmen appeared from every direction as the rest of the spectators shuffled hurriedly out of his way. Without sparing them another glance, he flipped the heavy book to face him. " 'On the prospect of the marriage of Tristan Carroway, Lord Dare,' " he read to himself, " 'the female contestants are listed below. Please make your wager according to your choice.' "

No name claimed responsibility for the placement of the wager, but the list of females and their varied supporters already took up two full pages, and the wager had only been recorded yesterday. "Who did this?" he snarled, whipping around to face the growing mob.

"My lord, please come away and join me for a private drink," Fitzsimmons, the club's manager, said in a soothing tone.

"I said, 'Who did this?'" he repeated, fury boiling up from deep in his gut. The look on Georgiana's face when Bellefeld had spoken had nearly killed him. She *had* begun to trust him; he could see it in her eyes. And now she never would again. He could swear his innocence to heaven, and she would always believe he'd been responsible in some way, or at least that he'd known about it. Someone was going to pay for this — and with luck, someone would get bloody for it.

"My lord —"

"Who?" he bellowed. Grasping hold of the pages, he ripped them from the ledger.

A gasp went up from the gallery. *No one* removed pages from the wagering book. It simply wasn't done. Glaring down at the offending document, he tore it in half, and then in half again, and again, until it scattered like confetti from his fingers.

"Lord Dare," Fitzsimmons said again, his voice harder, "please come with me."

"Like hell," he snarled. "This wager is over. Is that clear?"

"I'll have to ask you to lea—"

"I won't be back — unless I hear of another wager concerning Lady Georgiana Halley. If I do hear of one, *ever,* I will burn

330

this place to the ground, so help me God." Before any of the more burly footmen could move in to escort him out of the club, he strode forward and grabbed Fitzsimmons by the cravat. "Now, for the last damned time, Fitzsimmons, *who placed this wager?*"

"It . . . . Your brother did, my lord. Bradshaw."

Tristan froze. "Brad . . ."

"Yes, my lord. Now please release m—"

Letting him go so quickly the man stumbled, Tristan stalked out of the club and hailed the first hack in sight. "Carroway House," he growled, slamming the door closed behind him.

The midmorning traffic was heavy, which gave him more time to contemplate just how much damage Bradshaw's wager had done. Of all the things he'd thought he might have to face with Georgiana, another wager hadn't been one of them.

When the hack stopped he jumped down, threw a shilling at the driver, and strode up to the house. For once Dawkins was at his post, and nearly received a bloody nose when Tristan shoved the door open faster than the butler could pull it aside.

"Where's Bradshaw?" he growled, flinging his greatcoat and hat to the floor.

"Master Bradshaw is in the billiards room, I bel—"

Tristan was up the stairs before Dawkins finished speaking. The billiards room door was halfway open, and he shoved it wide so hard, a painting in the hallway crashed to the ground. *"Bradshaw!"*

His brother straightened, a billiards cue in his hand, as Tristan hit him. They both went over the table and landed hard on the far side. Tristan was on his feet first, and slammed his fist into Bradshaw's jaw.

Bradshaw rolled under the table and came up on the other side, snatching up his billiards cue as he stood. "What in damnation is wrong with you?" he demanded, swiping his hand across his cut lip.

Tristan circled the table, too angry even to speak. Bradshaw kept pace with him, keeping the table between them. Dawkins had apparently alerted the household that something was afoot, because Andrew and then Edward appeared in the doorway. Robert arrived a moment later.

"What's going on?" Andrew asked, moving into the room.

"Get out," Tristan spat at him. "This is between Bradshaw and me."

"What is?"

"I don't have a clue," Bradshaw panted, wiping blood away again. "He's gone mad. Just ran in here and attacked me!"

Tristan lunged over the table at him and caught a glancing blow from the billiards cue. It knocked him off-balance, and he crashed into Bradshaw's shoulder instead of his chest. He wasn't sure what he was doing, except that he wanted Bradshaw to hurt, because he hurt, and because Georgiana had been hurt.

"Make him stop!" Edward shouted, running forward.

Robert grabbed him by the scruff of the neck. "Let the big boys deal with this," he said, and gave Edward to Andrew. "Take him downstairs."

Andrew flushed. "But —"

"Now."

"Damn."

Robert stepped inside the room and closed the door behind him, locking out the servants and any other onlookers. "Stay out of this," Tristan warned, shoving Bradshaw again.

"I will. Why are you killing him?"

"Because," Tristan answered, aiming another blow that Bradshaw ducked at the last moment, "he made a wager."

"I make wagers all the time," Bradshaw

exclaimed. "So do you!"

"You wagered about Georgiana, you bastard!"

Bradshaw stumbled over a chair leg and went down. Scrambling backward, he grabbed up the chair and held it in front of him. "What are you talking about? I made a wager about who you would end up married to. That's all, Tris. For God's sake, what's wrong with you?"

"She doesn't trust me — that's what's wrong. And now thanks to you, she never will. I want you gone from this house today. And I never want to set eyes on —"

"She blames you for the wager?" Robert interrupted from the far side of the room.

"Yes, she blames me for the wager."

"Is this about the other wager?" Bit pursued.

Tristan whipped around to face him. "When did you decide to speak? Leave off, and get out."

"If you send Shaw away," Robert continued, folding his arms, "he won't be able to explain anything. So which do you want: him gone, or an explanation for Georgiana?"

Considering his chances with her, it was a close decision. Damned Bit was making him think, though, making him slow down and look at what he was doing. Bradshaw held the chair out, keeping the legs pointed in his direction. He was breathing hard, his eyes on Tristan's face.

Tristan glared back at him. "Georgiana," he bit out. "She thinks I had something to do with the wager."

Bradshaw lowered the chair, but kept hold of it. "So I'll tell her you didn't."

"It's not that simple. My knowing about it is nearly as bad as my initiating it. Dammit, Bradshaw!"

"Then I'll tell her you didn't know, and that you tried to kill me when you found out."

It probably wouldn't matter to her. It was probably too late. "Get dressed," he ordered, and stalked out of the room. As he passed Bit, he reached out to grab him by the shoulder, but his brother dodged the contact. He didn't feel ready for the additional frustration of dealing with Robert today, but neither could he leave the miracle unaccounted for. "Explain," he said, continuing down the hallway to his bedchamber.

He'd ripped his sleeve, and Bradshaw had landed at least one blow. He needed to look semicivilized, or Georgiana would never listen to him.

Bit followed him. "Explain what?"

"Why you decided to get so chatty, that's what."

Silence accompanied them down the hall. Annoyed again, Tristan turned to face his brother.

"Is this a game, Bit?"

Robert shook his head, white-faced, the line of his mouth tense and straight. For the first time, Tristan realized that the intervention had cost his brother something. He faced forward again and continued into his bedchamber.

"Tell me when you feel like it, then. But go make sure Bradshaw hasn't escaped."

"He won't."

Taking deep breaths, Tristan tried to slow down the rampage of his emotions and recall some sense of logic. Much as he hated to admit it, Bit was right; if he was to have any hope of regaining a degree of Georgiana's trust, he needed Bradshaw to explain what had happened. And then he needed to do something he hadn't done in a very long time. He needed to pray, to anyone who would still listen to him.

Chapter 18

So will I turn virtue into pitch;
And out of her own goodness make the net
That shall enmesh them all.

— *Othello*, Act II, Scene iii

Amelia sat in the morning room, embroidering a pretty flower on the corner of a handkerchief. Her mother sat at the writing desk, sending out correspondence, and she knew her father was in his office pretending to do accounts.

Given the importance of the day, she thought she looked remarkably composed. The light blue muslin she'd chosen for the event was both demure and lovely, and it set off her eyes to great advantage while accenting the creamy complexion of her throat and arms. The double strand of pearls she wore was perhaps a bit much for a luncheon appointment, but she wanted to remind Tristan Carroway of precisely what she would be bringing to their union.

He'd been right about one thing; a formal declaration was turning out to be much more satisfying than a forced marriage to preserve her reputation. And this way her parents would be able to say that Viscount Dare had come to them, and not that she had tricked him into anything. Well, perhaps she had tricked him, but no one else need ever know that.

The clock behind her had just chimed the quarter hour, and she took a breath. She wasn't precisely excited; rather, she felt expectant. She had put in a good few weeks' work, and the rewards of that effort were about to materialize at the front door and make her a viscountess.

Coaches and pedestrians passed by on the street below, but she barely noted the noise. She didn't expect him to make his appearance early; he'd said one o'clock, and that was when he would arrive. She'd told her parents as much.

If anything, they had been more excited than she was, although they were of course careful not to mention what everyone expected to happen. Protocol was everything, and neither of her parents would utter the word "marriage" until Dare said it first. But they knew, as she did, that by the end of luncheon she would be a betrothed woman.

When someone scratched at her door just before one o'clock, Georgiana expected that it would be her Aunt Frederica with a cup of herb tea. "Please go away," she said, rocking in the chair by the window, a throw pillow clutched to her chest. She'd probably have to get rid of it; it was soaking wet with tears.

"My lady," Mary's voice came, "Lord Dare and his brother are here to see you."

Her heart jolted. "Tell Lord Dare that I do not wish to see him," she managed, "ever again." Even saying his name hurt.

"I'll tell him, my lady."

Avoiding him in London would be nearly impossible, since they traveled in the same circles. No, this time she would go home to Shropshire, as she should have done the moment she left his bed. She would never run across Dare there.

The scratching sounded again at her door. "My lady, he's quite insistent that he and his brother speak with you."

For a moment she wondered which brother he'd dragged here with him. Probably Edward, since he knew that she had a soft spot for the boy. He was not going to wear her down with adorable children, though. What he'd done this time was worse than inexcusable. "Tell him no, Mary."

The maid hesitated. "Yes, my lady."

This time when Mary reappeared at her door, her voice was agitated. "He won't leave, Lady Georgiana. Shall I fetch Gilbert and Hanley?"

Part of her would enjoy seeing Dare removed from Hawthorne House by the burly stable hands, though it wouldn't be as easy as Mary seemed to think. But telling him to his face to leave her alone and never call on her again might be even more satisfying. "I'll be down in a moment."

"Yes, my lady." Mary sounded relieved.

Her body shook as she climbed to her feet. Lead seemed to fill her shoes, and every step took an effort. Concentrating on walking helped, and she kept her mind focused on putting one foot in front of the other as she left her room and went downstairs, Mary at her heels and looking exceedingly worried.

"Where are they?" she asked.

"The front sitting room, my lady. Pascoe wouldn't let them any farther into the house."

Good for Pascoe. Squaring her shoulders and hoping that her eyes weren't as red and puffy as they felt, she pushed open the sitting room door, ready to say something devastating and final — and then forgot what it was.

Tristan, a bruise on the left side of his face, stood close to the doorway. Bradshaw was seated on the couch, one eye black and swollen almost shut, and his lip puffy and bruised. Neither man looked at the other as she entered.

"Georgiana," Tristan said, his face deadly serious, "give me one minute, and then do what you will."

"You're assuming, Lord Dare," she said, amazed that her voice sounded crisp and businesslike as she closed the door on Mary and Pascoe, "that I think you deserve one minute. I do not."

He opened his mouth, then closed it again, nodding. "Very well. Then please give Bradshaw one minute."

The look he sent his brother, dark and full of anger, surprised her. She'd never seen him express anything less than warmth and affection for all the members of his large family. "One minute."

Bradshaw stood. "I placed a wager in the books at White's yesterday," he said

341

in the same flat tone his brother had used, "about whom Tristan would end up marrying. I thought it would be amusing. He didn't know anything about it. In fact," he touched his fingers to his lip, "he was very unhappy when he learned what I'd done. I apologize, Georgiana, if I've done anything to hurt you. That was not my intention."

A tear ran down her cheek, and she brushed it away. "Did he put you up to this?" she asked, refusing to look at Tristan.

"He made me accompany him here. He said if I didn't, he would send me packing." He slid his gaze sideways, sending Dare another angry look. "Other than that, no, he didn't put me up to anything."

"Georgiana," Tristan said urgently, "I've been an idiot in the past, but I hope you know that I would never do anything like this — to you, or to anyone else. I have learned my lesson."

He hadn't said she should trust him, but that was what he meant. She reluctantly met his gaze. Blue eyes searched her face, his expression worried. Did it bother him that much that she might send him away for good? She was probably being a thrice-cursed fool, but she did trust him. She trusted him because she wanted to do so, and because it would hurt too much if she decided once and for all that she could not.

Slowly she nodded. "I believe you."

As though released from invisible chains, Tristan strode forward and wrapped his arms around her, kissing her forehead, her cheeks, her mouth. "I'm so sorry," he whispered. "I'm so sorry."

She kissed him back, seeking the heat and comfort of his warm, lean body. If he had been planning a trick, this wasn't it. And given his reaction, she began to think that perhaps he wasn't playing, at all. If he wasn't . . .

"Ahem."

With a gasp she pulled backward, but couldn't escape far because Tristan caught hold of her arms. Bradshaw wore an expression of supreme curiosity and surprise.

"Did I miss something along the way?" he asked, folding his arms.

"That's obvious, isn't it?" Tristan returned, his gaze not leaving Georgiana.

Seeing Bradshaw standing there reminded her that he wouldn't be the only one speculating about her. She shuddered. "What about the wager?" she asked.

"It's gone."

Bradshaw frowned. "What do you mean, 'it's gone'? It's on the books at White's. Much as I hate to say it, those wagers don't just go away, Tris."

"This one did."

"And how did you manage that?"

"I ripped it out of the book and destroyed it." Tristan ran his fingers along Georgiana's cheek. "Got myself banned from White's in the process. That's probably a good thing, when I consider it. I wouldn't want to be a member of a club that would allow people like me through its doors."

She chuckled, though it came out sounding a little soggy. "On behalf of myself and the other ladies involved, thank you." Looking at Bradshaw, she scowled. "And shame on you."

"I've learned my lesson, too," he said. "And I'll be remembering it for quite some time, I can assure you. Next time you pummel me, take off your damned signet ring, Dare."

Tristan still looked more angry than conciliatory. Rather than let another fight break out, Georgiana pulled free from his grip and summoned Pascoe. "Would you gentlemen care to stay for luncheon?" she asked them.

Bradshaw started to nod, but Tristan looked abruptly uneasy. "What time is it?"

"A quarter past two, my lord," the butler supplied.

"Damnation. I would like to stay," he said, turning for the door, "but I have a previous engagement for which I'm very late." He stopped, looking again at Georgiana. "Wycliffe's hosting a dinner tonight. You'll be there, won't you?"

"Yes, I'll be there."

His expression still serious, he sketched a bow. "Then I'll see you this evening."

Bradshaw trailed after him, his gait a little stiff. He touched Georgiana's shoulder as he passed. "I've never seen him like that. Thank you for forgiving me."

She pursed her lips. "If he hadn't blackened your eye, I would have, Bradshaw."

"Fair enough."

People would still speculate about the wager, especially now that Tristan had terminated it in such a spectacular manner. But he'd done it to protect her honor — and because it had upset her. Whatever else had happened over the past six years, one thing was becoming rather clear: Tristan Carroway had indeed learned his lesson.

Her relief when Bradshaw had explained

the wager made something else equally clear: Her heart, her desires, and her dreams had ceased to listen to any kind of reason and sense. All she could do was hope that this time she and Tristan had set off down a different path, and that she would end up somewhere besides ruined.

By the time Tristan returned to Carroway House, swore Bradshaw to secrecy, changed clothes yet again, and climbed back on Charlemagne to head for the Johns residence, it was nearly three o'clock. Hopefully, if he managed to be sufficiently tactful with Amelia, nothing more would come of last night's visit. And he was going to do his damnedest to be extremely tactful.

The Johns butler showed him into a downstairs sitting room close to the front door. It was beginning to look as though no one in London wanted him in the depths of their household today. That was fine with him; after his last encounter with Amelia, the closer to an avenue of escape he was, the safer he would feel.

Amelia entered a few minutes later, and he sketched her a shallow bow. "I owe you an apology," he drawled with a smile. Charm generally worked with young ladies.

She tilted her head at him, and for once he couldn't read her expression. When they'd first met, he'd thought her a naive, grasping little chit, hardly more than a girl and willing to sell herself for a title. As a wife she would have been petty, pretty, and easily ruled. What she'd attempted last night, however, had taken planning, courage, and determination, which made him distinctly uneasy. It had either been a fluke, or he'd been badly mistaken in his estimation of her character.

"We sat for luncheon without you," she said, gesturing for him to take a seat.

"I'd hoped that you had. Again, my apologies. Something of . . . utmost urgency came up."

He sat on the couch, allowing her to dictate the conversation for the moment. Even so, the hairs on the back of his neck pricked, and he kept one eye on the doorway, just to be sure it remained open. She'd caught him off-balance once; he wouldn't allow her to do it again.

"I'm very angry with you," she said, taking the seat opposite him.

"I don't doubt that. I'm not entirely happy with you, either."

The butler stepped through the door. "Shall I bring tea, miss?"

She smiled. "Would you like tea, Lord Dare?"

He would have preferred whiskey. "Tea will be fine. Thank you."

"At once, Nelson."

"Yes, miss."

Her smile remaining, she folded her hands in her lap, the very vision of a prim, proper debutante. If he hadn't seen her disrobed in his bedchamber last night, he never would have believed the tale. And that, he sensed, could become a very large problem.

"I want to ask you a direct question."

"Please do."

"Are you going to ask me to marry you, Tristan?"

"No, I'm not."

She nodded, not looking the least bit surprised. "Why not?"

"I had at one time considered a marriage with you," he said slowly, trying to spare her feelings and realizing that he was doing it because of Georgiana's damned annoying little lessons, "but after coming to know you, I think I would make you a miserable husband."

"Shouldn't I be the one to make that decision?"

"No, not really. I'm twelve years older

than you are, and my experience is far greater. I —"

"I think you should ask me anyway," she interrupted, her prim hands folding into fists.

Tristan shook his head. "In six months, when you're happily married to any of a hundred other gentlemen who would be exceedingly pleased to have you as a wife, you will thank me."

A footman scratched on the open door and entered, a tea tray in his hands. Amelia's smile reappeared as if by magic, and Tristan wondered that he'd ever thought her guileless and innocent. As soon as the servant left, the smile disappeared again.

"I understand why you think I might be happy elsewhere, but I really do have my heart set on becoming the Viscountess Dare. It has a very nice sound to it, don't you think? Dare is a 260-year-old title, and a very well respected one."

"You've done your research."

She nodded. "I have, on all my beaux. And after careful study, I have selected you."

Now he was beginning to wonder whether she was unbalanced. Tristan glanced at the teapot. It probably had arsenic in it. "Amelia, I value your admiration and your friendship, but you and I will not be married. I'm sorry if you misunderstood my attentions. That was very shoddy of me. And now, I think I should leave you to more pleasant contemplations." Tristan stood.

Her voice rose. "I have your letter."

He continued toward the door. "Unfortunately, Amelia, in my long and lamentable past, I have written letters to quite a few young ladies. On rare occasion, even poetry has crossed my pen."

"Not a letter you wrote to me. A letter written to you."

Tristan stopped. "And which letter might that be?"

"Well, it's not precisely a letter. More of a note, though it is signed. It's rather crumpled, as well, I'm af—"

"What does it say?" he interrupted, pure fury running through him. She couldn't have *that* note. Not that one.

"I think you know what it says," she answered in a calm tone. "I have the little gifts she left you, as well. You may not have wanted *me* sharing your bed, but I know who *was* there, Tristan. And here you had everyone thinking you two were enemies."

A hundred responses flashed through his mind, most of which would have landed him in Newgate Prison, charged with murder. "I suggest you return to me anything you might have stolen from my home, Amelia," he said very quietly.

"Don't you wish to know what I want in exchange for the return of Lady Georgiana's very personal items?"

"You go too far," he hissed, taking a step toward her. He could accept Newgate Prison, if it saved Georgiana any more pain.

"I will be happy to return them to you," she said in the same calm tone, though her eyes darted toward the doorway, "to dispose of in any manner you wish."

"Then do so at once."

"Not until the day we are married, Lord Dare. I assure you, I will keep them safe in my chest of drawers until that day."

By God, she was a devious little bitch. He needed a plan, and time enough to come up with one. "And what assurance do I have that you'll do as you say?"

Her smile returned. "The assurance that I want to be Lady Dare." She stood, smoothing her skirt. "Shall we tell my parents the happy news?"

Out of his limited patience, Tristan grabbed her arm and drew her up hard against him. "Do not presume too much,

Amelia. I will cooperate to a point. But if you ruin her, I'll ruin you. Is that clear?"

For the first time she looked less than serene. "We will be married," she said, pulling her arm free, "and the betrothal will be announced. You may choose the timing, but we both know that you'll need my money before the end of summer. I will give you three days, Lord Dare, to propose to me in a proper and flattering manner."

Tristan turned on his heel and left. As he rode back to Carroway House, one thought kept rolling through his mind: Georgiana needed to know about this, yet he wouldn't be able to stand seeing the pain in her eyes again.

He would make this right. He had to, for both of them.

Chapter 19

The course of true love never
did run smooth . . .
— A Midsummer Night's Dream,
Act I, Scene i

Sitting for half an hour with slices of cucumber over her eyes finally left Georgiana feeling that she could reemerge from her bedchamber without frightening small children. Her heart felt lighter as well, though Tristan's intentions and her own response to what he might ask of her gave her an aching head and a craving for a large glass of spirits.

Since she'd returned to Hawthorne House she'd attempted to take up her usual tasks to assist her aunt, but she'd been woefully haphazard about it. That would have to stop. This late in the afternoon, the dowager duchess would be sorting through her correspondence and party invitations.

Georgiana found her aunt in the sitting

room as she expected, but Frederica wasn't doing her correspondence. Neither was she alone.

"Lord Westbrook," she said, curtsying. "What a pleasant surprise."

The marquis stood. "Lady Georgiana. Her Grace told me that you weren't feeling quite the thing. I'm glad to see you've recovered."

"Yes, I had a bit of a headache. What brings you here, this afternoon?"

"Actually, I came to see you, my lady." Stepping forward, he took her hand and brought it to his lips.

Nodding, she ran her appointment book through her head, but she didn't recall making any plans with the marquis for this afternoon. "May I offer you some tea, then? Or a glass of claret?"

"Claret would be splendid."

Her aunt stood. "I'll see to it. Excuse me, my lord."

Georgiana frowned in suspicion, wiping the expression away with a smile as she met Westbrook's gaze. Aunt Frederica acted like a mother bear when Tristan was anywhere in the vicinity, yet she volunteered to depart with Westbrook's arrival.

"Her Grace is very generous, to share you with me," the marquis said, smiling.

He still gripped her fingers. This was beginning to feel familiar, though she couldn't place Westbrook in the same category as most of her other suitors. John didn't need her money; and in a sense that made his presence much more problematic. Unless she was misreading his intentions, which was entirely possible. The havoc Dare created within her seemed proof enough that most of the time she had no idea what she was doing.

"Why did you want to see me, John?" she asked.

"Because I'm unable to resist doing so." He squeezed her hand, then released her, an uncharacteristic sheepish look crossing his handsome features. "I'm not certain how to say this without sounding like a . . . nodcock, but I *do* need to say it."

"Do so, then, by all means."

"Yes. Georgiana, as you know, I am a single gentleman with a considerable fortune. I don't say that to brag, but only because it's the truth."

"A well-known truth, my lord."

"Even so. Because of my circumstances, I have been given my choice of young ladies to marry. I have met them all, and studied their character, prospects, and appearance. What I am here to say is, I am . . . desperately in love with you, Georgiana, and I ask you to be my wife."

She waited for a flutter of her pulse, a speed in the beat of her heart. All she felt, though, was doubt that Westbrook had ever been desperate about anything in his life — much less her.

"John, I —"

"I know you may not feel the same way about me, but I am willing to wait." He grimaced. "I also know that Dare has been forcing his presence on you the past few weeks, and that with his influence you may be . . . uncertain of the course your future should take."

"I don't understand."

"I am trying to speak as a gentleman regarding another gentleman, but for your sake I'll be blunt. I have become suspicious that Dare is still obsessed over the wager he made six years ago regarding your virtue, and that he may be attempting still to lead you astray."

Oh, dear. If Westbrook only knew the truth about how far astray she'd gone, he would be appalled. He would also withdraw his proposal in an instant. "Do you have any proof of this?"

"I am relying on my intuition and my

personal knowledge of Dare. He is a known blackguard and a rake. In addition, his properties are nearly bankrupt, which leads me to further doubt his motives regarding your person."

"You mean you believe he intends to ruin me and then marry me for my money," she said.

"That is my fear."

If she'd been left with one thing over the past six years, it was a severe dislike of rumors, especially those that concerned herself or Tristan. "Are you promoting your own cause, John, or sabotaging Lord Dare's?"

"I am only concerned for your well-being, and I know your judgment may not be entirely sound where Dare is concerned. Logically, you know I am the better choice."

Her head knew he was correct, even if her heart said otherwise. "John, you said you would wait. Will you give me a few days to consider my answer?"

"Yes, of course." The marquis approached her again. "May I request a kiss, to signify that my intentions are serious?"

Shaking off the annoying idea that she was somehow being untrue to Tristan, she nodded. Other than his statements that he wanted more than just her body, Dare had never made any sort of direct declaration to her. She owed it to herself to have all the facts necessary to make an informed decision.

With a slight smile Westbrook placed a hand on either side of her face, leaned down, and touched his lips to hers. The kiss was brief, civilized, and very polite, a chaste kiss as befitted the chaste young lady she was supposed to be.

"May I call on you tomorrow, Georgiana?"

She blinked. "You may."

"Then I shall take my leave. Good afternoon, my lady."

"Good afternoon."

Minutes after he departed, Aunt Frederica swept into the room. "Well?"

"Very subtle, Aunt Frederica."

"Never mind that. Did he propose to you?"

"Yes, he did."

"And?"

"And I told him I would think about it."

The dowager duchess sank into a chair. "Oh, Georgiana."

"Well, what did you expect? I don't love him."

"What does that signify? You don't

follow the advice of your lungs or your kidneys, do you?"

"What —"

"Then don't listen to your heart so much. Dare is *not* someone a proper lady with magnificent prospects marries."

Georgiana put her hands on her hips. "Did you put Westbrook up to this?"

"Of course not."

"Good. If there's one thing I don't need, it's one of the few people whose counsel I rely on turning into a matchmaker."

"I only want you to be happy. You know that."

With a sigh, Georgiana relented. She certainly didn't want to be at odds with her formidable aunt, of all people. "I know that. Come help me choose a gown to wear to Grey and Emma's dinner."

The evening felt like one of the magical ones Georgiana remembered from when Tristan had first begun his pursuit of her, when she'd been a naive debutante fresh out of finishing school. Those dinners had been at Aunt Frederica's rather than Grey's, and not all of the Carroway brothers were usually in town at the same time, but it still felt familiar.

She and her aunt were the first guests to

arrive at Brakenridge House, and went upstairs to find Emma attempting to teach Grey how to play the harp. From the high color in Emma's cheeks that hadn't really been what they were doing, but given her own recent behavior, she wasn't about to comment on it. At least Grey and Emma were married.

Grey released his wife and the harp and strolled over to kiss Frederica, and then her. "Now tell me," he said, taking her hands and guiding her away from the other ladies, "do I allow Tristan into the house this evening or not?"

His gaze was both curious and concerned, and she couldn't help smiling at him. "At the moment, we are friends," she said. "Whether that will last through dessert or not, I have no idea."

Her cousin tucked her arm around his and escorted her to the garden window. "Did you hear he was banned from White's?"

"Yes, he told me."

"And he told you why?"

Georgiana nodded. "Don't feel as though you have to protect me from him, Greydon. Your friendship shouldn't suffer because of me. And I assure you, I am quite capable of taking care of myself."

"You aren't as jaded as you pretend, my dear. Nor am I as obtuse as you and my mother like to think." The duke sent a warm glance at his wife, who sat chatting with Frederica. "Ask Emma. I figured her out."

"Yes, and nearly ruined fifty schoolgirls in the process."

" 'Nearly' being the operative word, Georgie. Don't change the subject."

"All I can tell you is that if I need help, I will ask."

"You'd better. Never forget that I'm larger and meaner than you are."

"I couldn't possibly forget. I still have nightmares of leeches attached to my nose."

The duke laughed, the sound rolling warm and rich from his chest. She couldn't help grinning in return, and squeezed his arm. "I'm glad you're happy," she said. "You deserve it."

His smile faded. "Are you happy?"

She shrugged. "At this moment I'm mostly confused."

"Confused isn't all bad, cousin. You're too used to thinking you know the answer to everything, anyway."

"I don't know about th—"

With the timing of a playwright, Tristan

strolled into the room, Milly on his arm and the rest of the Carroways trailing behind him. Even Robert had come, she noted with some surprise. True, their two families had known one another for years, and they would be the only guests tonight, but it still warmed her heart to see him.

As Tristan approached her, though, the warmth skittered into something hotter. "Hello," she said.

"Hello."

He took her hand, brushing his lips across her knuckles, and straightened again. His eyes met hers, and along with the tingling arousal she always felt in his presence, something colder touched the edges of her heart. "What's wrong?"

"We need to talk sometime this evening." Emma and Bradshaw approached, and he released her hand. "Not now, though."

That was enough to set her mind flying in all directions. Knowing Tristan, anything might have happened. Someone had pieced together the wagering sheet, and the mess had begun all over again, or someone had realized that more than personal affront had caused Lord Dare's angry reaction to the wager, and by morning she would be completely ruined. Or he'd learned of Westbrook's proposal, and had killed the marquis.

All through dinner and their subsequent games of Commerce and charades, she worried. Tristan seemed his usual charming, witty self, and even drew reluctant laughter from Aunt Frederica. This was too hard. Being in love wasn't supposed to be so difficult. Of course, that was probably only true when the two people in question were completely unspotted and had never hurt, argued with, or deceived one another. Georgiana sighed. Westbrook had offered her that, and she had the feeling it would be deathly boring.

She was seated on the floor helping Edward sketch Bradshaw's ship, which he'd decided to call the *Storm Cloud*, when a hand touched her shoulder. Even though she'd been expecting it all evening, she jumped.

"Excuse me, Runt," Tristan drawled, "but I need to speak with Georgie for a moment."

"But we're drawing Bradshaw's new ship," Edward protested.

"Did I lose my old ship?" Bradshaw asked, leaning over to view the picture as Tristan helped Georgiana to her feet.

"This is the one for you to captain," his youngest brother explained.

"Then might I suggest more lifeboats?" Shaw returned, sending a glance at Tristan as he slid down to take Georgiana's place on the floor.

She felt the eyes of all the room's occupants on her back as she and Tristan exited the drawing room, but no one said anything. She wondered how much they really knew about her convoluted relationship with Lord Dare. By now they had at least to suspect.

Her heart began thumping even harder when Tristan led her into Grey's billiards room and latched the door behind them. "Please tell me what's happened before I have an apoplexy," she asked, trying to read his expression.

He strode up to her and took both her shoulders in his hands.

"What —"

Tristan leaned down and kissed her, tilting her head back with the ferocity of his embrace. Her hips went back against the edge of the billiards table, reminding her that she'd been thrown from a horse recently, but she didn't want him to stop. No one but Tristan made her feel so . . . possessed, and made her enjoy the sensation so much.

He devoured her, left her breathless and weak-kneed, as though he'd embraced her with his entire being instead of just his mouth. When he finally drew back, she leaned into his chest, wrapping her fingers into his lapels. "My goodness," she breathed. "And I thought all your secrecy meant something ill was afoot."

"Something ill *is* afoot," he said quietly. "You won't like it, or me, after I tell you, and I wanted to kiss you this one last time, at least."

"Now I'm worried," she said, still clutching him. Dread wrapped cold fingers around her heart. "Tell me."

Tristan drew in a deep breath. "I had a visitor last night. Early this morning, actually."

"A visitor?"

"In my bedchamber."

"Oh." He'd found another lover. Deep, sharp jealousy stung her, and she let him go. "Thank you for telling me. At least you did it in private, which is more than I exp—"

"Wh . . . No! No. That's not . . ." He took another breath. "It was Amelia Johns, Georgie. She pounced on me while I was dead asleep."

"Amelia? I can't believe that! She's just a child."

"No, she isn't."

"But —"

"Trust me — I can lay that misconception to rest. She's very much full-grown." He ran his fingers along the neckline of her gown, as though he couldn't stop touching her, as if he didn't even realize he was doing it.

"What happened, then?"

"I shrieked in a very ungentlemanly manner and threw her out of the house."

Thank God. Georgiana tugged him forward, touching her lips to his. "Good." She'd never felt she had much in common with Amelia, other than Tristan, and found she didn't like the girl very much at all. She wondered how *he* would react, if she told him about Westbrook's proposal.

"It doesn't end there. She took something from my room."

Georgie shook him, though she might as easily have moved a mountain. "What, for heaven's sake?"

"Your letter. And your stockings."

"My . . ." She blinked, a sudden roaring in her ears so loud she couldn't hear, couldn't think. Her knees buckled.

Cursing, Tristan caught her up against him, lifting her so she sat on the edge of the table. "Georgiana," he whispered urgently, "don't faint. Please don't faint."

Resting her head against his shoulder,

she drew in a shaking breath. "I won't. Oh, no. *Oh, no.* Why would she do that, Tristan?"

"Because she wants me to marry her."

Georgiana looked up, light-headed and dizzy and beginning to think that safe, dull love might have some advantages, after all. "I don't understand."

"Who would have thought I was such a desirable catch?" he asked with a grim half smile. "She intends to reveal your — and my — indiscretion to the world unless I make her Lady Dare."

"Why would she think she had to threaten you — me — like that?"

"Probably because I told her that I have no intention of marrying her." He kissed her again, soft and slow, as though the embrace was something precious. "How could I tell her anything else, when you and I . . . when . . . I don't want to ruin this?"

Tears welled in her eyes. She had her answer for Westbrook now.

"I have three days before I give her an answer, but you needed to know," he continued.

Georgiana shook her head, searching madly for any logical reason that would mean this wasn't happening. "She knows I was trying to help her. Even if you've changed your mind about her, she has to know that I didn't intend for any such thing to happen."

"I don't think she cares about that, Georgie."

"Of course she does," she insisted. "You probably threatened her or something, didn't you?"

He frowned. "Not at first."

"You see, you just frightened her. She must have felt she had to keep those . . . items to protect herself from further injury by you."

Tristan began to look annoyed. "I did not —"

"I'll go see her, and explain that they don't mean anything, but that I need them back to protect myself from scandal."

"They don't mean anything?" he repeated, tilting her chin up so she had to meet his glittering gaze.

Georgiana swallowed. "That's what I'll tell her. She's a female; she'll understand."

"She's closer to a dragon than a female, but I don't suppose I can talk you out of this."

"No, you can't."

He kissed her again. *My goodness.* She could become very used to having him touching her and holding her. Sighing, she kissed him back, sliding her hands around his waist, under his jacket.

"You're not angry with me?" he asked, kissing her again, more deeply.

"I'm not happy with this, of course, but I'm not mad at you. And I have something to tell you, too."

"What?"

"Lord Westbrook proposed to me."

His expression darkened. "Today?"

"This afternoon."

"And you turned him down."

"Tris—"

He kissed her again. "And you turned him down," he repeated, again making it a statement rather than a question. "Tell me."

He'd told her about Amelia, and she had to be equally honest. "He didn't want an answer. He wanted me to think about it."

"And will you?"

Georgiana swallowed. "I have a few other things to worry over, at the moment."

He smiled a little grimly. "You're right, of course. I still don't like it."

"And yet no threats of violence. You almost sound like a proper gentleman."

Tristan chuckled. "We'll have to remedy that." He pushed her knees apart and stepped in close against her. Everyone was just two doors down the hall, but as he slid her long skirt up past her knees, there was no mistaking his intentions.

"Someone will hear," she said, gasping as his warm hands caressed the insides of her thighs.

"Not if we're quiet." He grinned. "And quick. The door's locked. See how cautious I am now?"

"This is not caution. This is —"

"A very good idea."

She wasn't so certain of that and would have protested again, mostly because she didn't want to have to hurry. As she opened her mouth, though, his knowing fingers dipped between her thighs and inside her. She arched her back, her protest becoming a barely stifled moan.

"You want me," he murmured, his voice shaking a little.

"I can't help myself."

She hadn't meant to say that, it seemed like such an admission of weakness. Tristan only chuckled, reaching around her shoulders to unbutton the top fastenings of her gown.

"I don't know if it's the sex, or just touching you," he said, tugging the front of her dress forward so he could slide his left

370

hand into her bodice and fondle her breast. "You'll be the death of me, Georgiana Elizabeth."

She couldn't breathe any longer. "Hurry," she gasped, unbuttoning his breeches.

Kissing her openmouthed, Tristan freed himself, drew her forward again, and entered her. She threw her head back, the sensation of him filling her so extraordinarily satisfying that it stole her breath away. Flinging her arms back behind her to keep her balance, she sent billiards balls rolling across the table.

"Ah, yes," she moaned, wrapping her ankles behind his hips. "Oh, Tristan."

"Shh," he said, holding her thighs as he pumped his hips strongly into her. "Oh, God." His eyes caught and held hers as she spiraled into release.

He followed with a deep groan, and bowed his head against her shoulder. Shaking, Georgiana sat up straighter again. "Good heavens," she sighed, twining her fingers through his hair.

"I told you we could be quick," he said against her shoulder, his voice deep and rich with amusement. "And you play a fair game of billiards, as well."

"Quick is nice," she agreed. "But we

have been gone from the others for quite a while."

"Not that long." He cupped his fingers around her breasts again.

"We can't," she said regretfully. It was difficult to be firm when all she could think of was how good he felt.

"Right." He pulled away from her, rebuttoning her gown and slipping her skirt back down. "We'll tell them we've been arguing."

Tristan fastened his trousers and tucked his shirt back in. Making love — on Grey's damned billiards table, yet — had been unwise in the extreme, but he couldn't regret it. He would never regret being with Georgiana, whatever the consequences.

She spun a slow circle, trying to look at the back side of her dress. "How do I look?"

"You look beautiful."

Deeper color touched her cheeks, already flushed from their lovemaking. "That's not what I meant. Am I put back together?"

"Quite well, Georgiana," he murmured. Even now he wanted her again, though at the moment it felt more like the need to protect her. Giving in to the urge, he pulled her into his arms, tucking her head against his shoulder.

She sighed, relaxing against him and settling her arms around his waist. "I'm glad you told me," she said. "If you hadn't, I —"

"You would never have trusted me again," he finished. "And why did you tell me about Westbrook?"

"For the same reason, I suppose."

The next step was a simple and obvious one: He needed to ask Georgiana to marry him. But he didn't want her to think that he was simply jealous, or trying to escape from Amelia and using her as the most convenient method to do so.

So, with deep regret, he released her. "We should get back, or we'll miss cake and strawberries. I find myself quite famished."

Her eyes twinkled. "Yes, you do seem to have an appetite."

"Only around you, these days."

At least he'd made her forget for a few moments that someone else now possessed her stockings and her letter, but as she took his arm and they exited the gaming room, the sated amusement in her eyes faded, replaced by the ill-concealed worry that he so often saw there. He knew that, because he couldn't keep his eyes off her as they rejoined the others, and she went to check on the progress of Bradshaw's ship.

He wanted to see that look of worry leave her eyes once and for all. And he wanted to wake up in the morning with her beside him, and to be able to touch her and kiss her without having to drag her into coatrooms to do so.

"Is everything all right?" Grey asked from behind him.

Tristan turned around, pasting a look of jaded amusement on his face. "Nothing a glass of whiskey couldn't cure," he drawled. "Why?"

"Because you and Shaw look like someone's beaten you half to death, and you've been banned from White's. Not exactly your usual day."

"Hm. It's been fairly uneventful, I thought."

"Fine. Don't tell me, then. But just know," the duke said, taking a step closer and lowering his voice, "that if you hurt Georgiana again, you will regret it."

After what Tristan had been through that day to avoid just that, he'd had enough. "I assure you," he said in the same hard tone, "that I am taking all of this very seriously. And if you ever threaten me again, you'd best do so over a pistol."

Grey nodded. "Just so we understand one another."

"I think we do."

With a faint scent of lavender, Georgiana appeared between the two of them. "My goodness," she said, "you two are stomping and snorting like bulls. Do behave, or take your little battle out to the pasture, won't you?"

"Snort," Grey said, and strolled over to rejoin his wife.

"I was going to say that," Tristan protested, unable to keep from taking her fingers in his. "Worried about me?"

"Emma just had this room refurnished. I didn't want you to break anything."

Her eyes warmed, and the sudden dryness in his throat made him swallow. No one but Georgiana could make him feel like a green schoolboy.

"Come and see the galleon Edward's drawn," she continued, tugging on his hand. "He's going to be the cabin boy, you know."

"And we'll all join the crew as pirates, no doubt."

Edward popped to his feet. "Could we?"

Tristan lifted his eyebrow. "No."

"Oh, I'd like to be a pirate," Edwina chimed in. "We could all wear trousers and curse."

"Yes!" Edward galloped over to his aunt. "And Dragon could be the ship's mascot!"

"Dragon?" Emma asked, chuckling.

"My kitten," Edwina explained.

"And I could ride my pony on deck!"

"Good heavens," Georgiana choked, laughing breathlessly, "we'd be the scourge of the seven seas."

"We'd be the laughingstock of the seven seas, you mean," Tristan corrected, his heart beating a fast tattoo at the sight of her smile.

"Well, if word gets out to the Admiralty that my first command would feature kittens and ponies and the aunties in trousers, I might as well become a pirate," Bradshaw said dryly. "I suppose you'd want to knit our skull and crossbones, Aunt Milly?"

"Oh, heavens no. Not a skull. Perhaps a teacup. That's much more civilized."

Even Frederica was chuckling now. "You should suggest that to the East India Company, then."

"Can't you hear the screams of terror as we hoist the teacup flag?" Andrew, who'd been sitting beside Aunt Milly, chimed in.

"I'd be screaming, myself." Tristan pulled out his pocket watch. "Children and pirates, it's nearly half past midnight. I think we need to take our leave."

If it had been he alone, he would have stayed all night, or at least as long as Georgiana remained. After the past few weeks, he didn't even like letting her out of his sight. Too many things could still go wrong.

She and Frederica decided to leave, as well, so at least he was able to escort her down the stairs and out the front door. "Take care," he said, wishing he could kiss her good night.

"I will. And I'm going to call on Amelia tomorrow."

"Good luck." He reluctantly released her hand as she disappeared into her aunt's coach. "Let me know what happens."

"Oh, I will. You can wager on that."

"Not at White's," the dowager duchess said as a footman closed and latched the door.

If being banned from White's were his only problem, he would be a happy man. Sighing, he ushered his family into the pair of coaches they'd commandeered. Edward was so sleepy that he allowed Bradshaw to hoist him over one shoulder. They could all use some sleep. He, of course, had to do his monthly accounts tonight so he could meet with his solicitor in the morning and determine how many days he had remaining before he either had to marry or begin selling off property.

Dire as that was, he was still more concerned about Georgiana's meeting with Amelia. The chit had surprised him with her venom, and he could only hope that Georgie had more luck than he. With the way things had been going, though, he doubted she would. So he would have to come up with another plan.

Tristan smiled as he settled back in the darkness of the coach. After tonight, he thought he knew just what that plan would entail.

Frederica Brakenridge preceded Georgiana upstairs to the second floor of Hawthorne House. Someone needed to say something, and as her niece's parent in absentia, the task seemed to have fallen to her.

She stopped in the doorway of her bedchamber. "Georgiana?"

Her niece halted, an absent half smile on her face. "Yes, Aunt?"

"Is he going to ask you to marry him?"

"What?" Georgiana flushed. "Tristan?"

"Westbrook already asked, and you put him off. Yes, Dare. Is he?"

"I don't know. Heavens, what would make you say such a thing?"

"Goodness knows why, but you've had a *tendre* for that man for years. And I know he broke your heart once. Are you going to allow him the opportunity to do so again?"

Her niece laughed. "I am much older and wiser these days. And I haven't even decided if I like him, yet."

"Really," the duchess said, unable to keep the skepticism from her voice. "It looked to me as though you'd already made up your mind about that."

Georgiana's smile faded. "Do you have something you wish to say to me, Aunt Frederica?"

"Just a few days ago, you were in hysterics over him. I'll admit he seems to have matured since his father's death, but do you really think he's someone to whom you can give your heart, my dear?"

"That is a very good question. I'll let you know when I have an answer." Georgiana turned away again, heading off toward her own bedchamber. "I do wish my heart and my head would make the same decisions, though."

Frederica frowned. This was even worse than she'd thought. "Don't we all."

Chapter 20

I tell you, he that can lay hold of her
Shall have the chinks.
— *Romeo and Juliet*, Act I, Scene v

Tristan wanted to bang his head against something hard. "I know it's bad," he grumbled, settling for glaring across the desk at his solicitor. "I see the numbers just as plainly as you do."

"Yes, my lord, of course you do," Beacham said in a soothing voice, pushing his spectacles back up to the bridge of his nose. "What I meant to say was, the situation is *very* bad. Untenable, almost."

"Almost," Tristan repeated, springing onto the word and holding on for dear life. "It's salvageable, then."

"Eh, well, you see —"

"*What?*" Tristan hammered his fist against the desk.

The solicitor jumped, his spectacles sliding down his nose again. Swallowing, he shoved them back into place. "The Glauden estate at Dunborough isn't entailed, my lord. I know of several nobles, and even one or two merchants, looking for a small piece of land in Scotland. For hunting, you know."

Tristan shook his head. "Glauden's been in my family for two hundred years. I will not be the one to lose it." And Robert had spent last winter there. If Bit felt comfortable someplace, he wasn't about to take it away from him.

"To be honest, my lord, even knowing your . . . skill at wagering, and even after seeing the resulting figures, I'm not certain how you've managed to keep solvent. It's something of a miracle to me, really."

"What matters is that *I* won't be the one to begin selling off any of the familial properties. Give me another option."

"You've already sold off the majority of your personal possessions. Your stable, with the exception of Charlemagne, your yacht, that hunting lodge in Yorkshire, the —"

"Be helpful, Beacham, for God's sake," Tristan interrupted. He knew precisely what he'd given up, and that it wasn't enough. "What will it take for me to be able to keep paying my taxes, my staff, and my food bills for the next three months, say?"

"Another miracle," the solicitor mumbled, running a hand over his nearly bald head as though that would stimulate his brain activity.

"Pounds and pence, if you please."

Beacham sighed, leaning forward to flip open one of his seemingly hundreds of ledger books. "Three hundred pounds a month."

"That's steep."

"Yes. Most of your creditors will continue to honor your papers for another few months, but only if you don't incur any further debt."

Tristan supposed that was good news, yet he felt as though someone had just summoned a priest to deliver last rites. "All right. I can manage three hundred quid." He had no idea how, but he would do it, because it was necessary.

"Yes, my lord."

"And now for the bad news," Tristan continued. "Paying off all my creditors, bringing in enough blunt for seed, stock, everything. How much?"

"Everything, my lord? Don't you wish to set your sights on a more . . . . practical figure?"

"I am holding my breath in anticipation of your finally answering a question without some commentary attached," Tristan said, glaring. If he began smashing things, poor Beacham might expire from fright.

"Yes, my lord. In order to return all of your properties and yourself to a state of solvency, all at once, you would need approximately seventy-eight thousand, five hundred twenty-one pounds."

Tristan blinked. "Approximately," he repeated. At least when Beacham delivered a death blow, he did it with power and precision.

"Yes, my lord. It may be done in increments, of course, which is probably a wiser and more easily achieved course of action, but that will ultimately increase the amount of money needed."

"Of course."

The amount was close to what he'd expected, but hearing someone else confirm the number made it somehow worse. "How long do I have to acquire the three hundred pounds for this month?" he asked, sitting back in his old, comfortable chair.

"A week, would be my guess, or two if you manage to . . . wager against the right people. And win, of course."

"I haven't had much time for wagering, lately." There was also the matter of being banned from White's, where he always found his wealthiest opponents.

Beacham cleared his throat. "If I may be so bold, I had heard, my lord, that you were pursuing a young lady with the idea of marriage. Given that you refuse to sell any property, that may be your only viable alternative."

"Yes, I do have someone in mind, but she will need some convincing."

Fate might be fickle, but it also seemed to know what it was doing. Lady Georgiana Halley had an annual income of nearly twenty thousand quid, and even without her dowry, he happened to know that she'd been investing very wisely over the past six years. All of his family's estates would be saved within one second of her saying her vows to him. The problem was, he didn't know whether he could convince her to say them.

His determination to make her his wife had more to do with need and desire than money, but if she'd been a pauper, his obsession with her would probably have ended with him in the Old Bailey for bankruptcy. If she turned him down . . . He simply wouldn't think about that.

The solicitor stirred, and Tristan shook himself back to the present. "Thank you, Beacham. Let's set our next meeting for Tuesday, and we'll see if I'm in better or worse condition than today."

"Very good, my lord."

From the solicitor's expression, he didn't expect anything to improve. Tristan had his own doubts about that as well.

He would have to tell Georgiana precisely how desperately he needed her money before he proposed. They'd danced around true feelings and true issues for years. It was well past time for the truth.

The damnedest part of it all was that he *wanted* to marry Georgiana. When Amelia had told him about the letter and the stockings, that had become the most important item on his agenda. He needed to protect Georgiana from any rumors that might surface.

The idea of living without Georgiana was completely unacceptable. Even if it meant selling off every last damned stitch of clothing he owned, he couldn't consider marriage with someone else. It would be she, or no one. And it *would* be she.

One thing he'd learned in all this mess was simple: He needed to tell her the truth, however angry or hurt it might make her. He could woo her, he knew, if he had the time to do it. She needed to see, over and over, that he'd changed.

But three months didn't seem enough time to prove himself, much less the two days left under Amelia Johns's ultimatum. With four brothers, two aunts, and a handful of properties all staffed by people who looked to him for the food on their tables and the clothes on their backs, he didn't have much of an alternative.

He went upstairs to dress for the House of Lords. As he passed the open door of Bit's bedchamber, he glanced inside, expecting to see his brother sitting by the window, reading. Instead, Robert was shrugging into a riding jacket.

"Bit?" he said, stopping dead.

His brother glanced over his shoulder at Tristan, then pulled on a pair of riding gloves. "What?"

"What are you doing?"

"Dressing." Continuing to do so, Bit settled a blue beaver hat on his black, too-long hair.

"Why?"

The old Robert, the one before Waterloo, would have made some comment about not wanting to go out into the streets naked on such a chilly day. This Bit, though, just brushed past him.

"Are you all right, at least?"

"Yes."

That would have to do, though Tristan wished he had time to shadow Robert and make certain he truly was all right. Following him about wouldn't accomplish anything, however. Besides being very good at not being followed, Bit needed help, and Tristan had no idea what sort of help, or who could best provide it.

"Blast it all," he muttered, continuing on to his own bedchamber. Georgiana was the only one with whom Bit seemed able to converse in full sentences, and she was on her way to negotiate with Amelia Johns. What a bloody wonderful day they were all having.

"And where are you off to?"

Georgiana started, nearly ripping the button off her pelisse as she whipped around. "Aunt Frederica, you startled me."

"I can see that." The dowager duchess continued gazing at her, settling for lifting an eyebrow at her niece's choice of attire.

Georgie glanced down at her gown. Pale green and very simple, it was probably the most demure dress she owned. Looking as innocent as possible had seemed a good idea.

"I have a few errands." That didn't seem to cause her aunt to continue on down the hallway, so she smiled. "Did you want anything from Mendelsohns?"

"Ah. They had some new lace I wanted to look at. Do you mind if I come along?"

Drat. She couldn't very well drag her aunt with her when she went to Amelia's to ask for the return of her stockings. Well, that was what she deserved for trying to deceive her. "Of course I don't mind. I only thought you'd find it dull."

"Nonsense. I'll get my reticule." Frederica left the doorway just as Pascoe appeared in it.

"Lady Georgiana," the butler enunciated, "you have a caller. Shall I inform him that you are out?"

Him. A male caller could be anyone, and she knew for a fact that the Marquis of Westbrook would be calling later that afternoon. But of course her pulse sped anyway, just on the chance it might be Tristan. Her aunt had stopped again, though, and Georgiana stifled a sigh. Subterfuge was far more difficult than she would have imagined. "Yes, please convey my apologies, Pascoe."

"Very good, my lady." The butler headed back downstairs.

Cursing to herself, Georgiana watched him descend. "Pascoe, who is it, by the way? You didn't say," she called.

The butler stopped. "He had no card, my lady, or I would have given it to you. It is Robert Carroway, I believe. All the gentleman said was that he wished to speak with you."

"*Robert* Carroway?" Georgiana hurried down the stairs. "Do you mind waiting, Aunt?" she called over her shoulder.

"Never mind, dear. I'm going to luncheon with Lady Dorchester. Your schedule is far too erratic for me."

"Thank you!" Georgiana smiled as she reached the sitting room doorway — and nearly collided with Bit as she charged into the room. He stepped back, avoiding her, though it looked as though he'd been on his way out. That didn't surprise her.

"Bit, good morning," she said, backing up to give him room.

"Apologies," he muttered, as though it hurt him to speak. He strode past her into the foyer. "My mistake."

"I was just about to go for a walk," she said to his back, throwing her reticule to Pascoe, who caught it and put it behind him with nothing more than a raised eye-brow. "Would you care to join me?"

He slowed, nodding the back of his head at her. She needed a chaperone. Mary was upstairs mending the gown she'd worn to Grey and Emma's last night, which had mysteriously lost two buttons. A downstairs maid, her arms full of table linens, emerged from a doorway. "Josephine, please put those down and join me for a walk."

"M . . . me, my lady?"

Pascoe stepped forward. "Do as Lady Georgiana says, Josephine. At once."

In less than a moment they were out the door, Robert walking so quickly that Georgiana didn't even take the time to collect her bonnet or parasol. "Robert," she said, trying to catch up to him without breaking into a run, "your pace is somewhat brisk for a stroll."

He slowed at once, allowing her to draw even, but his jaw was clenched so hard she didn't think he could have spoken even if he'd wanted to. Well, if there was one skill she'd learned from the duchess, it was how to talk about nothing until the other person felt comfortable enough to speak in turn.

"I meant to tell Edward last night," she began, "that he should sign and date all of his drawings. When he looks back on them later, they'll have more value to him if he knows when he drew them."

"I have trouble remembering things myself, sometimes," he said in his low, quiet voice.

Success. "So do I, though it depends on what it is," she returned, after giving him a moment to continue if he chose to. "I'm good with faces, but as for what happened where and who said what, my mind has more holes in it than a yard of lace."

"I doubt that, but thank you for saying it." He took a breath, letting it out in a sigh. "Did I ever ask you to marry me?"

"No. You were one of the few who didn't."

"I was an idiot."

She chuckled, though a breath of uneasiness went through her. Being involved with his brother was difficult enough, and she didn't want to hurt him. "You were — and are — refreshingly independent."

"So independent I can't make myself leave the house, most days."

"You're here today."

What might have been a smile touched his mouth. "You like Dare today. I wasn't sure you'd want to talk with me, tomorrow."

"I would always talk with you, Robert. No matter what might happen between Tristan and myself."

He nodded. "Good. And you can always talk to me. I'm told I'm a good listener." Bit glanced at her sideways from beneath long black eyelashes, as though to make certain she understood that he was teasing. "You haven't lost your sense of humor, I see."

"Not entirely."

They had reached the east edge of Hyde Park, teeming with riders and coaches in the late morning. Though he didn't say anything about it, she could sense that he was growing more and more uneasy at the sight of the crowds. "Have you ever had a pastry at Johnston's?" she asked.

"No."

"I'll buy you one, then." Georgiana headed south, angling away from the park.

"No. I need to go." A muscle in his cheek jumped, his stance equal parts wary and angry — at himself, she thought. The Carroways were proud men, and he had to hate that she could see his distress.

They turned back along Regent Street, walking side by side in silence, Josephine trailing behind them. She wanted to ask Bit if there was a particular reason he'd decided to come by today, or if he had some specific thing he wanted to tell her. Yet she didn't want to drive him away or make him uncomfortable enough that he wouldn't want to return.

Once they reached Hawthorne House, she had a groom bring Robert's horse back around. "I am glad you came by," she said. "And I'm serious; anytime you feel like chatting, I will be available."

His deep blue eyes held hers for a long moment, leaving her with the unsettling feeling that he could read her thoughts. "You're the only one who doesn't make me feel like Pinch," he finally said.

She frowned. " 'Pinch'?"

"You know, from *The Comedy of Errors*. 'They brought one Pinch, a hungry lean-faced villain, A mere anatomy, a mountebank, A threadbare juggler, and a fortune-teller, A needy, hollow-eyed, sharp-looking wretch; A living-dead man.' "

The quote, and the deep, flat tone of his voice unsettled her. "For someone who says he has trouble remembering things, you recalled that quite well."

The faint almost-smile touched his mouth again, then vanished in a shudder. "I spent seven months in a French prison. I memorized that play; an old playbook was the only thing we had to read. We were . . . encouraged to remain silent. At all times."

"Robert," she murmured, reaching a hand toward him.

He backed away. "There is . . . nothing worse. Don't let yourself be trapped, Georgiana, whether it means being with Tristan or not being with him. Don't give in because it's easier. If you do, there's nothing left. That's what I came to tell you." He swung up on his horse and clattered down the drive.

Disquieted, Georgiana sat down on the front steps. Robert didn't say much, but when he did . . . "My goodness," she whispered.

Awful as what he'd said had been, it did help clarify matters. She wouldn't allow someone else to dictate how she lived the rest of her life. Amelia Johns had something that didn't belong to her — and Georgiana meant to get it back.

The Johns's butler showed Georgiana into a downstairs sitting room, where a dozen young ladies of Amelia's age sat giggling and eating sandwiches.

Amelia rose to greet her, a smile on her pretty oval face. "Good afternoon, Lady

Georgiana. I never expected to see you here."

"Well, I needed a moment to chat with you about something, Miss Johns," Georgiana said, feeling ill at ease. Other than Tristan, Amelia was the only person who knew what she'd done — and had the means to ruin her in Society.

Looking at her, though, with her pretty, innocent gaze and her giggling friends, Georgiana couldn't help but think Tristan must have misinterpreted her reasons for keeping the letter and the stockings. Perhaps Amelia was merely jealous. After all, Tristan had paid attention to the girl, and he was devastatingly handsome, and Georgiana *had* promised her assistance. In a sense, all of this was her fault.

"Certainly we should chat," Amelia returned, "but won't you have some tea first?"

Georgiana forced a smile. "That would be lovely. Thank you, Miss Johns."

"Oh, do call me Amelia. Everyone does."

"Very well. Amelia it is."

Her hostess faced the other girls in the room. "Everyone? I'm sure you know Lady Georgiana Halley. Her cousin is the Duke of Wycliffe."

"Ooh. I heard that he married a governess," one of them chirped. "Is that true?"

"Emma was the headmistress of a girls' school," Georgiana said. The feeling in the room seemed . . . odd. Hostile, almost. The hairs on the back of her neck pricked. "And cousin to a viscount," she added, accepting a cup of tea from a footman.

"And now she is a duchess," Amelia took up, motioning Georgiana to sit down beside her. "So nothing in her past signifies in the least."

The look she gave Georgiana seemed full of secrets, as though she was prompting Georgie to say something in defense of a woman's character. Beginning to feel annoyance creep in, Georgiana sipped her tea. She might be outnumbered here, but she was by no means unarmed.

Though she'd seen them at the various events of the Season, she didn't know most of the young ladies at all well. They were daughters and nieces of barons and knights, mostly, and a granddaughter or two of a higher-ranking nobleman thrown in for good measure.

The girls began chatting again, silly things about fashion and weather, and she relaxed a little. Perhaps she was just nervous and was misreading things.

"Lady Georgiana," Amelia said softly. "I am surprised to see you here."

"I wanted to apologize to you," Georgiana returned.

"Really? Whatever for?"

"For Lord Dare. My plans have gone distressingly astray, I'm afraid."

"How so?"

After seeing the note, Amelia had to know already. If she wanted to hear another apology, though, Georgiana was willing to accommodate her. Glancing at the other girls, she said, "I think this conversation requires a bit more privacy, if you don't mind."

"Hm. I suppose my guests can spare me for a few minutes." She stood, drawing Georgiana up with her. "Excuse us for just a moment, won't you?"

The tittering and giggling didn't diminish as Georgiana followed her hostess out of the sitting room and down the hall to a smaller room that overlooked the quiet street. "Your home is truly lovely," she said, taking in the expensive, tasteful decorations again.

"Thank you. Now, did you really come here to apologize for your . . . indiscretions with Tristan? It's not necessary, I assure you."

Georgiana swallowed down her retort. Amelia had a right to be angry. "It *is* necessary, because I told you that I would help you win him as a husband, and I've done anything but that."

"Nonsense. You're the reason I *will* win him as a husband."

Be polite, Georgiana reminded herself. "This has all been a terrible misunderstanding, and I feel awful about it. I only wanted to help you. You must believe that."

"I don't believe it for an instant," Amelia replied, the calm smile still on her face. "But as I said, it doesn't signify. I have set my sights on Lord Dare, and I will marry Lord Dare."

"Through blackmail?" she bit out, before she could stop herself.

The girl shrugged. "I'm not so silly that I wouldn't use something that came my way."

Direct questions and indignation seemed to be netting her better results. "You stole them."

"And how did Tristan get them, pray tell?"

Georgiana started to snap out an answer, then closed her mouth again. Yelling wouldn't help anything. "Amelia, what happened between Tristan and me was completely unexpected, but I do not intend to let you use it to harm either of us. Surely you wouldn't do something so . . . unnecessary, that would harm both your friendship with Tristan and with me."

"We are not friends, Lady Georgiana. We are rivals. And I have won."

"I don't think this is a contest, Am—"

"And my actions *are* necessary, because Tristan already informed me that he has no intention of marrying me." She sighed. "I suppose he still doesn't have to do so, but what happens next will be *his* fault, then. I told him that you were playing a trick on him and teaching him a lesson, so he won't want you now, anyway. Once he and I are married, I'll give your nasty little items back to you, and we can all be happy."

And to think Georgiana had thought her a naive, helpless young girl. For a long moment they gazed at one another, then Georgiana took her leave.

Her first instinct as she climbed into her aunt's coach was to go tell Tristan that he'd been right, and to find out if he had come up with any sort of plan.

As she considered the problem, though, one thing kept coming to mind. She really had done all of this to herself. First she'd decided Tristan needed to be taught a lesson, and that she was the only one who could do it. Then she'd failed miserably at it, entangling her life with his all over again.

But she wanted Tristan Carroway. As Robert had said, she couldn't simply give up and accept the future someone else left for her. They needed to talk, so she could decide whether she could ever trust him as much as her heart desperately wanted to.

Georgiana leaned out the window. "Hanley, please take me to Carroway House," she called. "I would like to call on Miss Milly and Miss Edwina this afternoon."

The driver nodded. "Very good, my lady."

Chapter 21

What say you? Can you love the gentleman?
— *Romeo and Juliet*, Act I, Scene iii

When Tristan returned home for the afternoon break at Parliament, he went straight to his office. He knew damned well that he'd never find nine hundred quid over the next three months, but he needed enough blunt to give himself a few days of breathing space — to plan how in the world he would maneuver Georgiana into marrying him, without ruining her in the process.

"My lord?" Dawkins scratched at the office door.

"What is it?"

"I am to inform you that Lady Georgiana is here, visiting Miss Milly and Miss Edwina."

Tristan bolted to his feet and strode to the door, slamming it open so quickly the butler nearly toppled backward. "Who told you to inform me about this visit?"

"Lady Georgiana did, my lord. They are in the morning room. She has been there for some time, but I don't believe she was aware that you had returned."

"And why didn't you tell her I was here?"

"I was in the pantry, my lord, reviewing the larder contents."

"You mean you were sleeping in the pantry."

The butler snapped up straighter. "My lord, I —"

"Never mind."

If she was here, then she'd spoken with Amelia. Part of him hoped she'd convinced the chit to give up the stockings and the letter; with nothing held over Georgiana, he could ask for her hand today. The other part of him, the part that wanted to sweep in like a medieval knight and free his damsel from the dragon, hoped that Amelia had turned her down. He'd done little enough for her that this felt like his responsibility.

"Good afternoon," he said, strolling into the morning room.

She was seated between the aunties, all of them laughing. As she met his gaze, though, he knew that she'd been unsuccessful. Whatever she might try to tell him, her eyes never lied.

"Good afternoon," she answered. "Your aunts have just been telling me about Dragon's antics."

"Yes. Thank God he's not any larger, or he'd be tearing the house down around our ears." He walked closer. "Aunties, may I steal Georgie for a moment?"

"Oh, I suppose so," Milly said, chuckling. "You always steal away our prettiest visitors."

"Really?" Georgiana murmured, as she moved past him into the hallway. "And how many pretty visitors have you stolen?"

"Just you. What happened?"

Georgiana glanced up and down the hallway. Reading her reluctance, he motioned her into the library and shut the door behind them as she sat on the couch.

"Tell me."

"I thought you might be here when I arrived," she said, her expression agitated. "I completely forgot about Parliament today, and I was late going to see Amelia after my stroll with Bit. She was holding a luncheon party for her friends, and I don't know what she might have said to them, but —"

"Just a moment," Tristan said, sitting back on the arm of the couch. "Could you go back to 'my stroll with Bit'?"

"Oh." Humor reappeared briefly in her

eyes. "I take it you didn't know he came to see me, then."

"He never talks. How am I supposed to know anything?"

"You might have told me that he was held in a French prison and not permitted to utter a sound," she countered. "No wonder he finds it difficult to do so now."

Tristan sat where he was, trying to absorb what she'd said and reconcile it with what he'd observed in his brother. "My God," he muttered.

She touched his arm. "You didn't know, did you?"

"No. I didn't. How long was he . . ."

"Seven months."

Seven months. "Was he even at Waterloo?"

"I don't know. Does it matter?"

He fought a scowl, anger at the damned politics which had sent his brother to France and had created a bureaucracy so ineffective he hadn't even been aware that Robert might have been missing from his company for seven damned months. "Only because they pulled five musket balls out of him, and I'd like to know how they got there. Jesus."

"Tristan," Georgiana murmured, "he's alive, and he'll tell you when he's ready."

Drawing a deep breath, he nodded,

wrapping his fingers around hers. "Thank you."

"No need."

Tristan shook himself. Bit would come around; Georgiana's problem was more immediate. "Just tell me you have good news about your mission."

Concern became exasperation in her green eyes. "You know, when I first saw you and Amelia together I thought that the poor dear didn't stand a chance, and that she desperately needed to be rescued," Georgiana said, twining and untwining her fingers with his. "I had no idea she was the person least in need of rescuing in all England."

"She wouldn't return your things."

"Oh, she's more than happy to return them, once the two of you are married."

The glance she sent him spoke more strongly than words ever could. She wanted to know if he intended to marry Amelia, and she didn't want him to do so. Tristan's heart jolted. It would kill him if she slipped out of his fingers again.

"Then we need an alternate plan, because I am not going to marry that witch."

"Hm. And what would you suggest?" She smoothed her skirt. "If it's all the same to you, I would prefer that the . . . secrecy of our relationship to this point remained secret."

"The plan I have would make keeping that secret very difficult," he said slowly, his heart beating so quickly he thought it would burst from his chest.

"Then you must think of something else, Tristan. I couldn't stand . . . Oh, it's all my fault, anyway. Perhaps I deserve to be ruined."

"No, you don't," he said softly, kneeling at her feet.

Her throat contracted as she swallowed. "Tristan, what —"

"Marry me, Georgiana. That news will drown any gossip she might attempt to spread."

She stood so quickly she nearly knocked him onto his backside. "But that —"

"But that what?" he repeated, standing. "It's perfect."

"But . . ." She paced to the window and back, wringing her hands. "But when you were so nice to me after . . . that night, I thought you might be . . . trying to engage my affections again to get revenge."

Tristan blinked. "At the beginning, the thought might have crossed my mind, but for God's sake, Georgiana, can't you tell now that I'm sincere? That I've been sincere for quite some time?"

Facing him again, she nodded. "But we can't do this," she whispered.

The blood drained from his face. "Why not? Why in damnation can't we marry?"

"Because I won't marry you to avoid gossip or blackmail, Tristan. With the way we began, I couldn't stand wondering whether either of us had been forced into marriage for any reason."

A muscle in his jaw clenched. Georgiana wished she hadn't said it, but it was true. If they married for either guilt or protection they would always resent one another, and she would never be able to trust him completely.

"There's always a reason for marriage," he said, holding her gaze. "You can't hope to avoid all of them."

"But I can avoid this. I won't let you attempt to save me this way. I can save myself."

"Georgiana, don't —"

"No," she broke in, turning for the door. She needed to leave now, before he saw her crying. "I can't marry you, Tristan. Not under these circumstances."

He grabbed her shoulder and spun her around before she was even aware that he'd closed the distance between them. "But under other circumstances, you would."

It wasn't a question, but a statement, and almost a plea. "I might." She pulled away from him and fled out the door.

For politeness's sake she should take her leave of the aunts but, blast it all, tears began rolling unbidden down her cheeks again. She hurried downstairs, snatched her bonnet and shawl from a very startled Dawkins, and fled into Aunt Frederica's coach. "Take me home."

"Yes, my lady."

She needed to talk to someone, to tell them what a muck she'd made of everything. If she told Frederica, though, her aunt would probably tell Grey, and then Grey would go after Tristan, and one of them would get hurt. The same would happen if she went to her brother or Emma, and she couldn't go to one of Tristan's brothers. Above everything else, she didn't want to return home weeping yet again. If events would just stop spinning for a few moments, she might have half a chance of getting her bearings.

"Hanley," she said, leaning out of the window again, "please take me to see Lucinda Barrett."

The driver didn't even look perturbed that they'd now set out for Hawthorne

House twice and detoured halfway across Mayfair both times. "Yes, my lady."

She would have trusted Evelyn, as well, except that Evelyn always insisted on believing the best about everyone, which would have been little help at this point. Lucinda was nearly as skeptical as she was, and at times more devious. That was exactly the sort of friend she needed right now.

"Lady Georgiana!" Madison, the Barretts' butler, exclaimed as he opened the door. "Is something amiss?"

Georgiana wiped at her damp face. "No, no, Madison. I'm fine. Is Lucinda in?"

"I'll inquire, my lady, if you'll wait in the morning room."

He showed her in, then vanished. Too agitated to sit, she paced from one window to the other, twisting her hands. This was too much. This entire day was just too much.

"Georgie? What's going on?" Lucinda swept into the room, dressed in her afternoon best.

"I'm sorry," she said, tears obscuring her vision again. She tried not to blink, but that only made it worse. "I didn't realize you were going out. I'll leave."

Lucinda intercepted her and guided her

back to the couch. "Of course you won't. Madison, have someone bring us some tea, if you please."

"Yes, miss."

"I don't know why I'm crying," Georgiana said, forcing a smile and swiping at her tears again. "I'm just very frustrated, I suppose."

"Tell me everything," Lucinda said, stripping off her gloves and dropping them onto the end table. The butler reappeared, a footman bearing a tea tray following, and she motioned for them to set down the tea and leave. "And Madison, if Lord Mallory should come calling this afternoon, please inform him that I am regrettably indisposed."

"Yes, Miss Lucinda."

"Mallory?" Georgiana broke in as the door closed, leaving them in private. "I thought you'd told him you weren't interested."

"I have, several times, but he lets me drive his horses." Lucinda reached over and took Georgiana's hand. "Now, what's happened?"

Now that the time had come, Georgiana wasn't certain how much she wanted to say. She'd spent the last six years keeping her secret; speaking about it was more difficult than she'd expected.

Lucinda seemed to realize that. "Just tell me what you want," she said quietly. "You know nothing will pass outside these walls."

Georgiana took a deep breath. "Tristan proposed to me."

"*What?* He what?"

"He asked me to marry him."

Standing, Lucinda poured herself a cup of tea. "It is times like this, I wish women drank brandy. What did you tell him?"

"I told him I couldn't marry him. Not under these circumstances."

"And what circumstances might those be?"

"Oh, dear. I . . . gave Tristan some items," she began, fidgeting, "and someone else took them. Now if he refuses to marry this person who took the items, this person will use them to ruin me."

"I see." Lucinda took a sip of her tea and added a lump of sugar. "I'm not trying to pry, but it might be easier for me to help you if you used more nouns and fewer pronouns."

Taking a short breath, Georgiana nodded. "The items are a pair of stockings and a letter. The person who took them is Amelia Johns."

"I thought Dare intended on marrying her, anyway."

"He thought about it, at one time."

"But now he wants to marry *you*."

When Lucinda said it, the statement seemed to carry even more significance. He *did* want to marry her. He'd truly wanted *her*. "Yes. That's what he said, anyway."

"And when did this happen?"

"Twenty minutes ago." Georgiana could sympathize with her friend's confusion. "Do try to keep up, Luce," she said, with a small smile.

"I'm attempting to. But other than Amelia Johns trying to blackmail Dare with your things, which doesn't quite make sense at this point, you *would* marry him?"

"My heart wants to," Georgiana whispered, her eyes filling again. "My mind isn't certain yet."

"So marry him, and then whatever Amelia does won't really matter."

"It's not that simple. Several years ago, Tristan participated in a wager that . . . hurt me. Somehow we managed to keep anyone from gossiping about it, but I'm afraid to tr—"

"To trust him," Luce finished. "Do you think he would use your things against you?"

"No. He would never do that. But until this is resolved, I can't trust that any decision either of us makes would be the right one."

"So get your stockings back, Georgie."

"Amelia won't return them. Not until she and Tristan are safely married."

"And I repeat — get them back."

Georgiana sat back, looking at her friend. The idea of sneaking into someone's home and stealing them . . . Of course, they were hers in the first place. And if she had them back, and misplaced guilt truly wasn't the reason Tristan had proposed to her, perhaps he would propose again. And then she could say yes — though that would take even more courage on her part than sneaking about strange houses. At any rate, she wanted her stockings back.

"Do you want help?" Lucinda asked.

"No. Any problem that arises is going to be mine alone, Luce. And so will the decision to do it — or not do it."

They finished their tea, chatting about other, more normal things. Lucinda was trying to calm her down, and she was grateful for the effort, but the entire time, she was mulling over what she would do about Amelia Johns.

It was easy enough to say she would storm Johns House and take back what belonged to her. But deciding whether she could make herself do it was something else entirely. She would be saving Tristan from a marriage he didn't want, and she would be saving herself from scandal. At the same time, she would be sending a clear message to Tristan that she wanted to marry him. If he still bore any thoughts of revenge, he could easily take that moment to destroy her heart.

Stronger than her fear and uneasiness, though, she wanted to hear Tristan propose to her not because he felt obligated to do so, but because he wanted to.

As she returned to Hawthorne House, she made up her mind. The next evening would be the Everston soiree, and Amelia was sure to attend. She, on the other hand, would be making a detour to Miss Johns's home, to retrieve her stockings and her letter.

The first thing to do in preparation, Georgiana decided, was to find the appropriate clothing. She rummaged through her wardrobe until she found an old muslin gown of dull brown and gray that she'd worn to the funeral of a friend's distant relation. It still fit, though it was rather tight across the bosom. As Tristan had reminded her, she was curvier now than she'd been before.

Georgiana smiled at the memory, then caught sight of herself in her dressing mirror. That smile was the look of someone in love. How she'd come so far in a few short weeks she had no idea, but she couldn't deny how she felt.

The true test, she supposed, would be when she presented Tristan with the stockings and the letter. She would either be proved a great fool, or he would propose to her again — and she would decide once and for all whether she could trust her heart to him, or not.

Mary appeared in the doorway, and she flung the old gown back into the wardrobe. "What is it?"

"Lord Westbrook is here to see you, my lady."

Oh, no. She'd been so concerned with Tristan and her stockings that she hadn't even taken the time to think about Westbrook's proposal. "Blast. I'll be right down."

When she reached the sitting room, she paused in the open doorway. Westbrook sat at one end of the couch, a bouquet of roses in his hands and his gaze on the fire crackling in the fireplace. That could be her future: calm, serene, and peaceful. They would keep separate bedchambers, of course, and give just the right number of dinner parties each Season for just the right people. In the evenings he would do paperwork and she would embroider, and he would tell her nothing of his day which might upset her delicate sensibilities.

Georgiana shuddered. She wanted passionate nights, and laughter, and having discussions about prices and politics and nonsense just because she found them interesting. If that came with anger and arguments, so much the better.

She watched him for another moment, but he didn't even fidget. Tristan couldn't keep from pacing while he waited for her. Georgiana cleared her throat.

"Georgiana," he said, rising as she entered. "You look well."

"Thank you. I apologize for keeping you waiting."

"No need."

"May I offer you some tea?"

"Thank you, no. I . . . wonder, have you considered my offer?"

"I have. John, I'm not quite sure how to say this."

A slight frown crossed his face, then cleared again as he lowered the bouquet. "You're refusing me."

"You are a wonderful, thoughtful man, and any lady would be lucky to have you as a husband. I —"

"Please, Georgiana. You've made a decision; please do me the courtesy of not explaining why one or the other of us is deficient. Just leave it as a refusal, and I'll be on my way. Good day, my lady."

Still looking nothing but calm, he stepped past her, collected his hat, and left. Georgiana sat on the couch. That had been so easy that it actually left her feeling better. He'd been a perfect gentleman, bloodless and correct. He couldn't have been remotely in love with her, much less madly so.

And so she was back where she started: hungering for a man with an old but tarnished title, a black reputation, no money, and a delight in chaos and mischief. Only this time, perhaps he wanted her as much as she wanted him.

That evening she played whist with her aunt and composed a letter to her mother that mentioned nothing of Tristan or multiple marriage proposals or anything but the latest fashions of the Season. With three other daughters to marry off, one beginning next Season, her mother had several times mentioned that fashion was the most essential information Georgiana could provide her. Thankfully Lady Harkley seemed convinced, as most of the *ton* was, that her second daughter would never wed, and she'd stopped pestering Georgie about it.

"Are you all right, dear?" Frederica asked.

Georgiana shook herself. "Yes, of course. Why do you ask?"

"You've barely won a hand all evening, and we both know you're a more calculating player than I am. Your mind seems to be elsewhere."

"I'm trying to lure you into a trap," she answered, making a renewed effort to concentrate on the game.

"Georgiana," her aunt continued, placing a hand over hers and stopping her shuffle, "you are a daughter to me. You know that. Tell me anything you wish, and I will do what I can to help."

"You are a mother to me," Georgiana replied, her voice breaking. "But I have found that there are some things I need to take care of on my own."

"People are talking about you and Dare, you know. They're saying that the old enemies appear to have reconciled."

"He has changed in a great many ways," she said, dealing out the cards.

Frederica nodded. "I have noticed some changes. But don't forget, some things don't change. That entire family is in dire financial straits, my dear. I would hate to think that you're being manipulated into thinking a certain way about things simply because he wants your money."

"As I said," Georgiana countered, the muscles across her back stiffening despite her effort to remain relaxed, "I will take care of this on my own." She knew money was involved; that was one thing he'd never dissembled about. And thank goodness for his honesty, or the additional doubts would have been enough to topple her resolve.

"Just as you took care of Lord West-brook."

"I told you I didn't love him."

"And I told you that you might consider security and comfort over your heart."

"I'm trying to."

"Try harder."

Aunt Frederica finally relented, and they played the rest of the game with amiable chatter. When she excused herself to go up to bed, though, tension spread its fingers across Georgiana's shoulders again. Tomorrow night she would have to take matters into her own hands. And if she acted in as transparent a manner as she had tonight, anyone would know that something was afoot.

"Stop it, stop it, stop it," she muttered to herself. If she continued driving herself toward hysteria, the Johns family would find her passed out in a dead faint on their front steps.

That made her smile. It would certainly cause Amelia a moment or two of difficulty, anyway.

The next day she met Evelyn and Lucinda for luncheon at their favorite street corner café, and though Luce tried several times to discover whether she'd come to a decision or not, Georgiana thought she deflected the inquiries quite well. Evie's curiosity was much more difficult to turn aside.

"All I'm saying," her friend mused, slicing a peach, "is that I thought the lesson you were going to teach Lord Dare had to do with the danger of trifling with ladies' hearts."

"That's precisely what it was, my dear."

"Then why is everyone saying he's pursuing you?"

She blushed. "That is not —"

"Evie," Lucinda interrupted, "I heard your brother would be returning from India before the end of the year. Is that true?"

Their dark-haired friend smiled. "Yes. I have to admit, I've actually missed Victor, despite his annoying habit of thinking he knows everything. All of his stories have been so romantic. Did I show you the scarf he sent me from Delhi?"

"Yes," she and Luce answered in unison, then laughed. "It's lovely. You should wear it for his homecoming," Georgiana continued.

Surprisingly, that elicited a frown from Evelyn. "My mother wants me to choose a husband before he returns," she said glumly. "She thinks Victor will never approve of any of my suitors, so if I've made a match before he can naysay it, it'll be too late for him to do anything."

"That's awful! Please say you won't settle just to please your mother," Lucinda said, taking Evelyn's hand.

"I don't want to, but you know how she can be. How both of them can be." Evie shuddered.

A waiter approached with more lemonade, and Georgiana smiled fondly at her two dearest friends. More than anyone else, she could rely on them to pull her out of the doldrums, and not to pursue questions she didn't wish to answer.

"Georgie," Lucinda whispered urgently, "behind you. It's D—"

"Good afternoon, ladies." Tristan's low drawl curled deliciously down her spine.

Without waiting for an invitation, he took the fourth seat at their table. He was wearing the light gray jacket that made his blue gaze deep as twilight.

"Good afternoon, Lord Dare," Lucinda replied, offering him a cucumber sandwich.

He shook his head. "My thanks, but I can't stay. Parliament's meeting this afternoon."

"Regent Street seems a bit out of your way, then, my lord," Evelyn said.

"Whom did you bribe to find out my whereabouts?" Georgiana asked, smiling at him.

"No one. I used my intuition after Pascoe said you'd gone out to luncheon. I happen to know you're fond of cucumber sandwiches, and I happen to know that you prefer the ones here. Ergo, here I am."

"And why were you calling on me, when you are expected in the House of Lords momentarily?"

"It's been nearly a day since I last saw you," he said, leaning his chin on his hand to gaze at her. "I missed you."

Georgiana blushed. She knew she should reply with something coy and witty, but it was difficult to think logically when most of her was occupied with keeping herself from pouncing on him and smothering his mouth with kisses.

"That's a very nice thing to say," she settled for, and saw the swift look of surprise in his eyes, quickly blanketed.

"You seemed out of sorts when you called on my aunts yesterday. They were concerned about you. May I pass anything on to them?"

"Yes. Tell them . . ." She stopped, because while the message she wanted to give Tristan was that she felt better, that would never do when she cried off going to the soiree tonight. "Tell them I was sorry to cut my visit short, but I had a bit of a headache."

He leaned closer, apparently forgetting that her friends sat directly beside them, and that they were in a crowded outdoor café with a hundred interested witnesses. "And how do you feel today?"

"Better, but tired," she said in a low voice. "Now go away, Tristan."

A sensuous smile curved the corners of his mouth. "Why?"

She decided that he couldn't help being desirable and exciting. "Because I find you very annoying, and you're interrupting my luncheon."

The smile deepened, touching his eyes. "I find you very annoying, too," he replied softly. Sitting back and glancing at her companions, he pushed away from the table. "Good day, ladies. I expect I'll see you this evening?"

"Oh, yes, the Everston soiree," Evie said. "Until then, Lord Dare."

His gaze remained on Georgiana. "Until then."

"Oh, my," Lucinda said, as he strolled away. "My butter's melted."

Georgiana laughed. "Lucinda!"

She knew what her friend meant, though. The conversation had felt sensuous and intimate, and somehow very significant. He'd come just to find out how she was feeling, and to let her know that he still meant to pursue her, whatever happened with Amelia.

It left her feeling more optimistic, and more courageous. She would regret not seeing him tonight, but she had a crime to commit.

Chapter 22

Lovers and madmen have such seething brains,
Such shaping fantasies, that apprehend
More than cool reason ever comprehends.
— *A Midsummer Night's Dream,*
Act V, Scene i

Georgiana sent Mary to inform Aunt Frederica that she wouldn't be attending the Everston soiree, and then strode as fast as she could back and forth in her bedchamber for the next fifteen minutes. Pausing at the doorway at the end of each circuit to listen, she hitched up the skirt of her shift and went over to the window and back again.

Frederica would wait until the last possible moment to come and see her, in case she changed her mind. Of course her aunt would think that she declined to attend because of Dare — which was correct, but not in the way her aunt could possibly have imagined.

At last she heard the dowager duchess

coming down the hallway, and she sprang over to lie on her bed. She was out of breath and flushed, which was what she'd intended, but that coupled with her supreme nervousness made her worry that everyone would think she was having an apoplexy.

"Georgiana?" Frederica cracked open the door and leaned her head in.

"I'm sorry, Aunt Frederica," she said, trying to keep from running out of air. "I just don't feel well."

The dowager duchess approached the bed, leaning down to put her hand across Georgiana's forehead. "My goodness, you're burning up! I'll have Pascoe fetch a physician at once."

"Oh, no! Please don't. I just need to rest."

"Georgiana, don't be silly." She hurried to the door. "Pascoe!"

Oh, dear. This would never work. "Aunt Frederica, wait."

Her aunt faced her again. "What, child?"

"I'm lying to you."

"Oh, really?" A delicate eyebrow arched, the sarcasm in her voice difficult to miss.

"I spent twenty minutes striding about so I could tell you that I didn't feel well." She sat up, motioning her aunt to the edge of the bed. "All of that nonsense about my being able to take care of everything myself is just — well, nonsense."

"Thank goodness you've finally realized that. Now we'll stay in tonight, and you'll tell me all your troubles."

Georgiana squeezed her hand. "No. You look so . . . lovely, and I truly just want to sit about and read a book and not have to do anything."

That was the truth, whether it was what she actually intended to do this evening, or not. Aunt Frederica kissed her on the forehead and rose. "Read then, my love, and I shall enjoy the attention I'll receive from telling everyone that I fear you're on your deathbed."

Georgiana chuckled. "You are very wicked, but please don't tell that to Grey or Emma. They'll charge over here and frighten everyone to death."

"True enough." The duchess paused in the doorway, putting up a hand to stop Pascoe as the butler charged into view. "Any particular instructions regarding Lord Dare?"

Frederica Brakenridge was quite possibly the most astute person she'd ever known, and after everything she'd put her aunt through — not just over the past weeks, but over the past six years — pretending now that there was no connection between herself and Tristan would be an insult. "Please tell him the truth, Aunt Frederica. He'll know, anyway."

"Yes, I think he might."

"Your Grace," the butler panted, "my apologies, but did you require —"

"Yes, I require you to escort me down the stairs," the duchess said, favoring him with a smile that actually made him blush, the first time Georgiana had ever seen the butler out of countenance. Frederica sent her a wink and closed the door, leaving her in calm silence.

At least the silence was calm, because she certainly wasn't. The evening was far too young for her to slip out yet; even though Amelia and her parents would be at the soiree, their servants would still be awake and sure to notice a stranger in the upstairs rooms.

She assumed that was where her stockings and the note would be, so she would begin her search in Amelia's bedchamber and hope for the best. If her things weren't there, she had no idea what she would do. She wouldn't have the opportunity to make another search later, since two days from now Amelia would begin to let other people — no doubt her tittering, giggling friends — know about the items she'd acquired.

For the next three hours Georgiana wandered from room to room, attempting four different times to sit down and read, and almost immediately giving up again. She couldn't sit still, much less concentrate on anything. When the glances the butler and the rest of the household staff sent her began to look pained, she apologized and dismissed them for the evening.

She was willing to wager that by now the Johns household was already dark and quiet, too. Georgiana drew in a deep, shaky breath. *It was now or never.*

She pulled the dowdy brown muslin out of her wardrobe again and donned it. Her most practical walking boots followed. She tied her hair back in a simple knot that hung down her back, both so it wouldn't get in her way, and so if anyone happened to see her, they hopefully wouldn't recognize her.

This wasn't just for Tristan; this was also for her. The last time someone had wronged her, she had sat still and wept and felt sorry for herself. Tonight, she was taking action.

Blowing out the lamp on her bed stand, she tiptoed into the hall and closed her door. Pascoe had left the downstairs door unlocked for Aunt Frederica, and she slipped outside and down the front steps without anyone hearing or seeing her. She had a few moments of trepidation when a hack didn't stop for her at once, but when she made her way down to the better-traveled corner, a beat-up old coach pulled up beside her.

"Where to, miss?" the bearded driver asked, leaning down to yank open the door.

She gave the address and climbed in, sitting stiffly in one corner as the hack rocked into motion again. Her heart beat a fast, steady hammer against her ribs, and her fists were clenched. Georgiana forced herself to relax, and grabbed on to the tendril of excitement buried somewhere deep under her skin that told her this was going to be the most daring thing she ever did.

She felt naked, for she'd intentionally left Hawthorne House without a shawl or reticule, carrying just enough money for the hack. Bringing a reticule to a robbery had seemed too silly, and quite possibly dangerous if she lost it somewhere. Her pockets were large enough to carry the stockings and the letter.

The coach lurched to a halt, and the driver yanked open the door again. Taking another deep breath, Georgiana clambered out, handed the driver up the correct change, and watched as he drove back into the darkness. "Here we go," she said to no one in particular, and slipped up the dark drive to Johns House.

All of the windows were dark. That left her feeling a little more confident, and she climbed the shallow front steps, remembering to stay in the shadows, and pushed down on the handle of the front door. It didn't budge. She pushed down again, harder. Nothing.

"Damnation," she whispered. How were the Johns supposed to return home if their front door was locked? What a shabby lot of servants they had. Perhaps, though, the family came in through the kitchen door, closer to the stable.

She descended the steps again and ducked into the small garden on the south side of the house. Halfway toward the stable, she stopped. One of the windows on the bottom floor was cracked open. "Thank goodness." She pushed through the shrubbery and grasped the bottom of the window. With a shove it slid up — too far and too fast.

Gasping, she froze. No sound came from the house, and after a moment she let her breath out shakily. Hiking her skirt to her knees, she clambered over the sill and into the dark house. The hem of her gown caught on the window latch, and as she freed it she nearly lost her balance. Catching herself up against the solid bookcase that abutted the window, Georgiana tried to collect her fraying wits.

The hard part was finished, she told herself. Now that she was in the house, it would merely be a matter of searching through a few empty bedchambers until she found the correct one. She took a step away from the bookcase, and then another, almost feeling her way toward the even darker doorway. Then something moved in the corner of her vision, and she drew in a breath to shriek.

A hand clamped over her mouth. Georgiana struck out blindly, her fist meeting something solid, and then she lost her balance, falling facedown to the floor with a heavy form on top of her.

"Georgiana, stop it," Tristan's familiar murmur sounded in her ear.

With a muffled half sob she relaxed, and he removed his hand from her mouth. "What are you doing here?" she whispered.

He shifted off of her and helped her to her feet. "The same thing you are, I would imagine."

In the deep gloom she could make out little more than a large dark form and faintly luminous eyes, and a set of white teeth formed in a smile. He *would* think this was amusing. "How did you know it was me?"

"I smelled lavender," he answered, running his fingers through the tail of hair that hung over her shoulder. "And then I heard you curse."

"Ladies don't curse," she returned in the same, nearly soundless voice. His presence calmed her immensely, but his touch set her nerves fluttering in a completely different, much more pleasant, way.

Belatedly, it dawned on her that he *was* here for the same reason she was. Tristan had broken into Johns House to steal back her things so no one could hurt her with them. Georgiana rose up on her toes and touched her lips to his. He kissed her back, drawing her up against him.

"What was that for?" he whispered. "Not that I'm complaining."

"To thank you. This is quite heroic of you." She felt more than saw his sudden frown. "Don't thank me, Georgie, This is my fault."

"No, it's n—"

"I'll take care of things from here," he

continued, ignoring her protest. "Go home, and I'll let you know when I have your items."

"No. *You* go home, and I'll let you know when I have my things back."

"Georgi—"

"They are my things, Tristan. I want to do this." She grabbed him by the lapels and shook him a little. "I need to do this. I won't be someone's victim again."

He was silent for a long moment, until finally, she felt him sigh. "All right. But follow me, and do exactly as I tell you."

She started to protest again, but thought better of it. She knew from personal experience that he'd snuck about in dark houses more than she had. "Fine."

"You saw Westbrook yesterday," he murmured, taking her shoulders in his hands. "What did you tell him?"

"This really isn't the time or place for that conversation."

"It's the perfect place for it. Tell me that you told him no."

Georgiana looked into his shadowed eyes. Comfort and peace had their merits, but they were nothing compared with the heat and humor of Lord Dare. "I told him no."

"Good. Let's go, then."

Tristan took Georgiana's hand and led the way into the hall. The servants had put out every light on the ground floor, making traversing the hallway to the stairs difficult. At least if a servant appeared, he and Georgie would have a good chance of hiding before they were seen.

At the top of the stairs he hesitated. Georgiana bumped into him from behind, and uttered another barely audible curse.

"Do you know where you're going?" she whispered.

He faced her. "And why would I know the location of Amelia's bedchamber?"

"You knew where mine was."

"That was different."

"How so?"

"Because I was half-mad for you. Now be quiet. I'm thinking."

" 'Was'?" she repeated.

"Am. Hush."

Amelia, despite her willingness to shed all of her clothes in his bedchamber, was always fully covered when she went out-of-doors. She'd said something about strong sunlight disagreeing with her delicate complexion, as he recalled.

"Her room will be in the west wing, I think."

"We could find it faster if we split up."

He shook his head, tightening his grip on her fingers as they crept along the balcony toward the west-facing bedchambers. Stunned as he was by her sudden appearance in the Johns sitting room window, her skirt hiked up past her knees, he wasn't about to let her out of his sight now. "They won't be home from the soiree for hours. We have time."

At the first door he hesitated, making certain Georgiana was well behind him. He took hold of her shoulder, pulling her close to him. "If anything happens, head back to the window and out through the garden," he murmured. "Don't go back out to the street straightaway. That's where they'll look first."

"You too, then," she returned, her soft hair brushing his cheek.

Tristan closed his eyes, breathing her in, then shook himself. He couldn't afford to be distracted now. Taking a breath and holding it, he slowly turned the knob and inched the door open. The rooms would be unoccupied, but he didn't want to risk a squeak alerting the upstairs servants.

The faint scent of lemon wafted toward him on the night air. "This is it," he mouthed, lips against her ear.

He released her hand so he could feel his

way inside. Luckily the curtains were slightly parted, letting a faint sliver of moonlight fall across the center of the floor. The wardrobe stood behind a vanity screen and a full length dressing mirror, and he slipped behind them, Georgiana close on his heels.

Amelia had said she would keep the stockings safe in her dresser, and as he inched the heavy top drawer open, he sent up a silent prayer that she hadn't been lying.

A light flared by the bed.

Tristan froze, his arm buried up to the elbow in the dresser drawer. Beside him Georgiana stood wide-eyed as she stared at him, not even breathing. The light dimmed, settling into the more even flicker of a lamp. His fingers touched the edge of a piece of parchment, and he gripped it, not daring to move any further in the deep silence of the room.

"Luxley?" Amelia's sleepy voice came, barely more than a whisper.

He and Georgiana exchanged glances. " 'Luxley'?" she mouthed.

"You naughty boy, are you there? Where have you been?"

Sheets rustled, and at the sound Tristan yanked his hand free, pulling the stockings and the note with him, and pushed Georgiana into the corner beside the wardrobe. He crouched beside her, hoping the vanity screen and the mirror would keep them in deep enough shadows that Amelia wouldn't be able to see them.

Bare feet padded to the window, and the curtains were pushed aside. Now would be their best chance to escape. Showing the stockings to Georgiana, he shoved them in a pocket and took her hand again.

The window rattled and opened.

"Amelia, my flower," Lord Luxley's melodious voice came, followed by a grunt and a heavier thumping sound as the baron entered the room. "Your groundskeeper needs to have a care about that trellis. I nearly broke my neck."

The unmistakable sound of kissing followed, and Tristan glanced sideways at Georgiana. She met his gaze, her expression a mixture of horror and deep amusement.

"Close the curtains, Luxley, for heaven's sake," Amelia's soft voice said, and bare feet padded back toward the bed.

Curtains shifted, and the room light yellowed again to the lamp's glow as heavier footsteps made their way to the bed. More kissing sounds followed, together with some throaty groans from both parties. *Good God,* Tristan thought, settling down more comfortably in the corner and pulling Georgiana up against his shoulder. Unless Luxley lived up to his reputation for brevity, this might take a while.

"We can't leave now," she whispered into his ear.

"I know," he replied, turning his head to return the favor. "We'll have to wait until they settle down again, or get too busy to notice us."

"Oh, dear," she murmured back, then slowly and unmistakably licked the curve of his ear.

Tristan swallowed, surprised into stillness as the sound of boots hitting the floor and the bed creaking with additional weight came from beyond the screen. Clothes shuffled to the floor a moment later, followed by the unmistakable sound of muffled groaning and sucking.

He looked at Georgiana again, his amusement warring with something much deeper and more intense. Just seeing her aroused him. Tonight, the combination of darkness, danger, and the obvious sounds of sex were enough to put him over the edge. She sank against him, kissing him on the throat. Tristan took her face in his hands and captured her mouth, kissing her roughly.

Luxley was making small sounds of enjoyment on the bed, and Tristan didn't need to see to know precisely who was servicing whom. And he'd thought Amelia a novice? Shaking himself, he tore his mouth from Georgiana's and captured her hands, tucking them into his. They needed to concentrate, to wait for the moment they could escape.

The rest of him, though, particularly the lower part, was concentrating on the slender, curvaceous figure beside him and the sounds of sex just a few feet away. Georgiana looked both embarrassed and excited, her lips parted, begging for his further caress.

The figures on the bed shifted, accompanied by some very naughty words he'd never imagined Amelia would even know, much less utter aloud. Then a rhythmic thumping began, to the accompaniment of Amelia's moans and Luxley's grunts of effort. The baron didn't seem to be much for small talk or foreplay.

Tristan kissed Georgiana again, hot and openmouthed. Somehow the fact that they couldn't make any noise made their touching even more intense, and his fingers crept beneath the neckline of her tight bodice, cupping her breast and teasing her nipple between his thumb and forefinger. Her eyes closing, she leaned into his hand, running her fingers through his hair and pulling his face forward for another plundering kiss.

She intoxicated him, made him feel drunk with lifting, soaring emotions he hadn't even known he possessed before he'd touched her the first time. Loosening the top buttons running down her back, he tugged the front of her dress down to catch her nipple in his mouth. Her body trembled against him, making him ache and yearn for more. She was his, and he wanted no one else, ever.

The sounds on the bed grew louder, the rhythmic thumping faster and harder, and Georgiana's wandering, seeking hands found the fastening of his breeches. Unbuttoning them, she reached inside, fondling him as he fondled her breasts. His heart thundering, Tristan threw back his head, thunking it against the wardrobe.

At the same time Georgiana gave a shuddering gasp, pushing closer against him. A vase on top of the wardrobe rocked and toppled, hitting the vanity screen and knocking it sideways. Tristan had an unforgettable view of Luxley's buttocks pumping with Amelia's delicate heels locked around them, before all hell broke loose.

Amelia screamed, Luxley bellowed, and Tristan extracted his hand from the front of Georgiana's dress and yanked the material back up. Shooting to his feet despite an intense discomfort in his aroused nether regions, he pulled her up beside him and held his trousers closed.

"What the devil?" Luxley blustered, looking over his bare shoulder and clearly torn between finishing his work and defending his honor.

The door burst open, followed by Mr. and Mrs. Johns and a handful of servants. "What is — *Amelia!*"

Obviously the Johns family had either stayed home or had returned early. For some reason, the entire episode suddenly seemed hilarious. Tristan took Georgiana's hand as she tried to hide behind him. "Run," he gasped, and sprinted for the door.

They barreled past the Johnses and their startled staff and ran downstairs, Georgie holding up her sagging dress and he trying to button his trousers without falling and breaking his neck. The sitting room window was still open.

As lights and raised voices flared upstairs and in the servants' quarters, Tristan lifted Georgiana so she could scoot out, then followed behind her, grabbing her hand again as they ran through the garden and emerged around the corner, out of sight of Johns House. Together they ducked into the shadows of a neighboring stable.

Breathing hard, he stopped, and Georgiana doubled over beside him. Alarmed, he knelt at her feet, looking up at her. "Are you all right?"

A strangled laugh answered him. "Did you see their faces?" she chortled, collapsing into his lap and throwing her arms around his shoulders. " 'Amelia!' They were so shocked!"

He laughed, relieved as he cradled her against his chest. "I don't suppose she wanted to be a baroness, but it's a bit late for that now." Of course, if *they'd* been recognized, Georgiana was thoroughly ruined, too, but he had the perfect solution for that.

"Oh, she'll have to marry Luxley. He has no chance of escape."

"He wasn't in any condition to escape. I almost wasn't, either." Still holding her close, he buttoned up her gown. Tonight was not the night to risk nudity in the middle of Mayfair.

"Do you think they saw us well enough to know who we are?" Brief concern touched her gaze again.

"I'm not sure. Amelia will figure it out, but the rest of them had, ah, several other things to occupy their attention." That wasn't quite true; in trying to defend her honor Amelia would of course identify them, and her parents would be desperate for someone else to share some of the blame and the gossip. He would take what steps he could to minimize the damage, so letting Georgiana worry about it tonight wouldn't help anything.

"As much sympathy as I'd like to feel for her, I can't help thinking she got what she deserved."

"And Luxley, too," he agreed, anger touching him, "for courting you and bedding her, the bastard."

Lifting her head, she kissed him. It was a light kiss, full of laughter and affection, and it stopped his heart. "This was a very interesting evening," she said, chuckling again.

"I love you," Tristan whispered.

Her smile fading, she met his gaze. Then she touched his cheek. "I love you," she said, in the same soft tone, as though neither of them dared to say it aloud.

"We'd best get you home, just in case all hell does break loose." He helped her to her feet again. "How did you get here?"

"I hired a hack." She leaned her head against his shoulder, wrapping her hands around his arm with an easy intimacy that left him almost breathless. "It's only a few blocks. Might we walk back?"

If she'd asked, he would have carried her across the Pyrenees in his arms. He had a pistol in one pocket, which would offer them ample protection against any ne'er-do-wells wandering Mayfair in the middle of the night. That, though, wasn't what he was worried about.

"No. I want you back and safely in bed in case Johns rides to Hawthorne House demanding an explanation."

The concerned look came into her eyes again. "Do you think he'll do that?"

"Actually, I think he'll be more concerned with Luxley, and then with my presence. You may come up in conversation eventually, though, so everything where you're concerned must be as proper as possible."

He whistled down a hack. "Take her to Hawthorne House," he said, giving the direction as he handed her up and tossed the driver a few coins.

"Tristan . . ."

Reluctant to stop touching her, much less let her out of his sight, Tristan took her fingers and kissed them. "I will call on you in the morning, Georgiana. And then you and I will resolve some things."

She smiled, then sat back in the dark as the coach lurched off into the night. Tristan looked after the hack until it turned the corner and passed out of sight. He took her smile as a very good sign. She must know what he meant, and she hadn't objected. Whistling, he waved down another coach to return to Carroway House.

As he sat on the worn leather, the paper in his pocket crinkled. He pulled out her stockings and the note, and read it again. She'd given him her stockings and thought to be rid of him. Tomorrow he would return her stockings, and ask for her, instead.

And he prayed that she wouldn't come to her senses and realize what a poor catch he was. If she didn't say yes . . . Tristan couldn't even contemplate that. Not if he wanted his heart to keep beating until he saw her again.

Chapter 23

Julia Your reason?
Lucetta I have no other but a
woman's reason: I think him so,
because I think him so.
— *Two Gentlemen of Verona*,
Act I, Scene ii

The rumors arrived before the milk.

Danielle threw open the heavy curtains far too early, and Frederica Brakenridge sat up to glare at her personal maid. "What in the world is going on?" she demanded. "And you'd best say the French have invaded."

The maid curtsied, worry and nervousness in every line of her rotund body. "I'm not certain, Your Grace. I only know that Pascoe spoke with the vegetable girl a minute ago, and then he said I must go awaken Your Grace at once."

Pascoe wasn't known for frivolousness, so Frederica pushed the blanket aside and stood. "Then help me dress, Danielle."

Years of experience had taught her that any situation, no matter how dire, could be improved with proper attire. So, although she keenly wanted to know what had overset her stoic butler, she took her time with her hair and her morning toilette.

As she emerged from her private rooms Pascoe was waiting for her, and a great many of the household servants seemed to have found items in the hallway in need of dusting or polishing. Georgiana's bedchamber was only two doors down, and if the girl had managed a good night's sleep, she wasn't about to disturb it this early in the morning.

"Downstairs," she commanded, leading the way.

"Your Grace," the butler said, following on her heels, "I am truly sorry to have awakened you so early, but I have learned something which, whether factual or not, desperately needs your attention."

Frederica stopped just inside the morning room door, motioning the butler to accompany her. "What is it, then, that has upset everyone at this ungodly hour?"

The butler worked his jaw for a moment. "I have been informed, by a certain very unreliable source, that . . . something occurred in the Johns household last evening."

She frowned. "The Johns household? What does that have to do with my waking early enough to view sunrise?"

"The, ah, something which occurred concerned Miss Amelia Johns being caught *en flagrante delicto* with Lord Luxley."

Frederica lifted an eyebrow. "Really?" Luxley was one of Georgiana's most persistent suitors. As of now, however, he was officially out of the running.

"Yes, Your Grace."

"And?"

"And, ah, another couple was seen . . . in the same room, though they immediately fled into the night."

A stone of dread hit the pit of Frederica's stomach. Dare had been absent from the soiree last night, as well. If he had betrayed Georgiana's trust again . . . "Which other couple, Pascoe? Out with it."

"Lord Dare and . . . and Lady Georgiana, Your Grace."

"*What?*"

Swallowing, the butler nodded. "This person also informed me that Lord Dare and Lady Georgiana were in a certain state of undress."

"Un—" For a moment, Frederica wished

she didn't believe that fainting was for weak minds. "Georgiana!" she roared, heading for the stairs again. "Georgiana Elizabeth Halley!"

Georgiana forced open one eye. Someone was calling her name, she thought, though it might have been a dream. The call repeated, reverberating through the house.

"Uh-oh," she muttered, making the other eye open and sitting up. Aunt Frederica never yelled.

Her door burst open. *"Georgiana,"* Frederica said, her color high as she strode into the room, "tell me you've been here all night. Tell me at once!"

"What have you heard?" she asked, rather than answering.

"Oh, no, no, no," Frederica groaned, sinking down on the bed. "Georgiana, what in heaven's name happened?"

"Do you really want to know?" she asked quietly, her heart thumping with nervousness for the first time. She might not care any longer what the *ton* thought, but she cared about what her aunt would think.

"Yes, I really want to know."

"This is between us," Georgiana pressed. "You may not say anything to Grey, or to Tristan, or to anyone else."

"Stipulations, my dear, don't apply to family members."

"They do this time, or I'm not saying anything else."

Her aunt sighed. "Very well."

She had almost hoped that Aunt Frederica wouldn't agree to her terms, so she would have an excuse not to explain anything. No doubt, however, her aunt had also anticipated that outcome. "Very well. Six years ago, I was the object of a wager," she began.

By the time she finished, Aunt Frederica looked as though she very much regretted agreeing to any conditions at all. "You should have told me earlier," she finally said, her jaw clenched. "I would have shot him myself."

"Aunt Frederica, you promised."

"Well, at least your antics will have made Lord Westbrook feel better. That's something, I suppose."

"I suppose so."

Her aunt stood. "You'd better get dressed, Georgiana. I won't be the only one hearing rumors today."

"I don't care," Georgiana said, lifting her chin.

"You've been well respected by all of Society, and sought after by all the eligible men. That will change."

"I still don't care."

"You will. Your Lord Dare doesn't have a promising tendency to stay about."

"He said he would be here this morning," she answered, a tremor making her fingers shake. He'd promised; he would come.

"It *is* morning. Early, but morning. Get dressed, my dear. The day will only get worse, and you need to look your best when you face it."

The more Georgiana thought about it, the more nervous she became. Mary helped her dress in her most demure morning gown, of patterned yellow-and-green muslin, but if the news had already spread here, by midmorning everyone in London would know that she and Tristan had been seen, half-naked and with her hand down his trousers, in Amelia Johns's bedchamber. A demure dress wouldn't stop those rumors.

She and Frederica sat down for breakfast, but neither of them had much of an appetite. The servants were as precise and polite as always, but she knew quite well that they had been the first to hear, and that they had been the ones to pass the information on to her aunt. How many other servants were chattering to their employers this morning?

The front door burst open. A heartbeat later the Duke of Wycliffe strode into the breakfast room, Pascoe on his heels and catching gloves, coat, and hat as her cousin flung them off.

"What in damnation is going on?" he demanded. "And where the hell is Dare?"

"Good morning, Greydon. Have some breakfast."

He jabbed his finger in Georgiana's face, angrier than she'd seen him since he'd rescued Emma from utter ruin. "He *will* marry you. If he doesn't, I'll kill him."

"What if I don't want to marry him?" she asked, thankful that her voice was steady. No one was going to dictate her future for her.

"You should have thought of that before you joined an . . . orgy in Amelia Johns's bedchamber!"

She stood, shoving her chair backward and feeling red heat flood her face. "It was no such thing!"

"That is what everyone is saying. Good God, Georgie!"

"Oh, shut up!" she growled, stomping out of the room.

"Geor—"

"Greydon," his mother's stern voice came. "Stop bellowing."

"I am not bellowing!"

Georgiana kept walking, hearing the argument continuing behind her, until she reached the morning room. She slammed the door closed and leaned back against it. Everything had been so clear last night. Hearing Amelia and Luxley had been . . . arousing, but even more so had been the sense they might be caught any moment, and the headiness of being trapped there with Tristan pressed up against her. She had literally been unable to keep her hands off him.

She always felt that way around Tristan. Even when she was angry with him, she needed to be touching him, if only by slapping her fan across his knuckles. She wanted to touch him badly at the moment. She wanted to feel the way she'd felt last night, when he'd held her and told her that he loved her. Where was he? He had to know the rumors were flying everywhere.

Someone knocked at the door, and she jumped. "Go away, Greydon," she snapped.

"Truce," he said, turning the handle and pushing.

She pushed back. "Why?"

He was much bigger and stronger than she was, but he only nudged at the door again. "Georgie, we're family. I may want to wring your damned neck, but I'll refrain from doing so."

"Georgiana," her aunt's voice came, equally close, "we must present a united front."

"Oh, very well." She allowed them to enter. They were right; her disgrace would affect them, as well, though their titles and power would protect them from most of it. She had no such protection. If Tristan didn't come . . . She paced by the window, clasping her hands together.

"What's our story going to be?" Grey asked, watching her stalk back and forth.

"Obviously, it has to be that whatever those idiot Johnses and their servants think they saw, Georgiana was home with a cold. It was dark, and late, and they were distressed at seeing their daughter's . . . indiscretion. Understandable, but for heaven's sake, they should know better than to accuse anyone of good family of anything so atrocious."

Georgiana stopped pacing. "No."

Frederica looked over at her. "You don't have much choice, dear."

"Aunt Frederica, I will not use someone else's error to improve my own situation. Not even if the someone is Amelia Johns."

"Then you are ruined," Frederica returned in a calm voice. "Do you under-stand that?"

A cold shiver of dread ran through her. "Yes, I do. I will accept that."

"Just a damned minute," Grey growled, standing. "You mean to say you actually *did* what they say you did?"

"Not the orgy part, no," she retorted.

"I'll kill him."

"You will do no such th—"

The door opened just as he reached it. "Your Graces, Lady Georgiana," the butler announced, "Lord D—"

Grey grabbed Tristan by the shoulder and yanked him into the room, slamming the door closed in Pascoe's face.

"You son of a b—"

Using one hand, Tristan shoved Grey sideways. "I'm not here to see you," he said, his face hard and set.

His gaze found Georgiana, frozen by the window, and she made herself breathe again. The reason he'd used one hand was that he gripped a bouquet of white lilies and a box wrapped with ribbon cradled in the other.

"Good morning," he said in a softer voice, a small smile touching his sensuous mouth and darkening his sapphire eyes.

"Good morning," she breathed, her heart skittering.

"Dare," Grey growled, approaching again, "you are going to do the right thing. I will not tolerate your inexcusable behav—"

"Shut up, dear," Frederica interrupted. Rising, she took her son by the arm and led him toward the door. "We'll be in the breakfast room if you should require our presence," she said, opening the door.

"I am *not* leaving them alone," the duke growled.

"Yes, you are. They promise to remain fully clothed this time."

"Aunt Frederica!" Georgiana exclaimed, flushing.

"Get on with it." Sending her a brief, encouraging glance, the dowager duchess closed the door.

Georgiana and Tristan stood for a moment, gazing at one another in the sudden silence. "I hadn't realized the news would spread this fast," he said in a low voice, "or I would have been here earlier. Amelia and Luxley aren't nearly as interesting to everyone as I'd thought they would be, obviously."

"I was hoping everyone would be so occupied with talking about them that they would forget to mention us."

Tristan cleared his throat. "I need to ask

you a question. Two questions, actually."

If her heart beat any faster, she was going to faint dead away. "I'm listening," she replied, feigning calmness as best she could.

"First," he began, handing her the bouquet, "do you trust me?"

"I couldn't believe you remembered that I liked lilies," she said, holding on to them so she would have something to do with her hands.

"I remember everything, Georgiana. I remember how you looked the first time we met, and I remember the look in your eyes when I betrayed your trust."

"But you didn't, really," she returned. "You hurt me, but no one else ever knew. How did you keep it quiet, with a wager resting on the outcome?"

He shrugged his broad shoulders. "Creativity. Georgiana, do you —"

"Yes," she interrupted, meeting his gaze. "I trust you."

If he'd been waiting for a moment to get his revenge, this was it. She'd spoken the truth, though. She did trust him, and just as importantly, she liked him. She loved him.

"Well, then," he said, as though he hadn't been certain what her answer would be, "this is for you, too."

He held out the box. The size of a box of cigars, it was bound with a single silver ribbon, tied in a bow at the top. Swallowing, Georgiana set aside the lilies and took it in her hands. It was lighter than she expected.

"It's not another fan, is it?" she asked, trying to joke.

"Open it and find out," he replied.

She thought he looked nervous, and it made her feel a bit sturdier to realize that he wasn't invulnerable. She tugged on one end of the ribbon, and it fell away. With a swift breath, she flipped open the lid.

Her stockings lay neatly folded side by side, the rolled-up note in between them. She started to thank him, then noticed what held the missive in its tight coil. A ring. Tristan's signet ring.

"Oh, my," she whispered, a tear running down her cheek.

"And now for my second question," he said, his voice not quite steady. "Some people will say that I'm asking you this because of your wealth. And I do need what you have in order to save Dare. Other people will say it's because I have no choice, and that I am obligated to save your reputation. We both know there's far more to it than that. I need *you*. Even more than your money, Georgiana, I need you. Will you marry me?"

"You know," she said, wiping another tear away and torn between laughing and crying, "when this first began, I only meant to teach you a lesson about the consequences of breaking someone's heart. What I didn't realize was that you had something to teach me, as well — about how people can change, and about how sometimes you *can* trust your heart. My heart's been in love with you for a very long time, Tristan."

Tristan took the box from her and set it on the table. Removing the ring from the parchment, he reached for her hand. "Then answer my question, Georgiana. Please, before I expire from the suspense."

She gave a teary chuckle. "Yes, Tristan. I will marry you."

He slipped the ring on her finger, then pulled her up against him, touching his lips to hers. "You've saved me," he murmured.

"I'm happy my money can help with Dare," she said. "I always knew that would be part of any arrangement I entered."

Sapphire eyes held hers. "No, Georgiana. You've saved *me*. I kept wondering how I could even think of marrying someone else, when I compared every female I met with you. But I knew you hated me, and —"

"I don't anymore." She sighed. "I'm not certain I ever did."

Tristan kissed her again. "I love you, Georgie — so much that it frightens me a little. I've been wanting to tell you that for a while, but I wasn't certain you would ever believe me."

She'd worried about the same thing. "I believe you now. And I love you."

He took her hand, looking down at the overlarge ring on her finger. "I suppose we should tell your family, before they shoot me." His eyes met hers again. "And please, tell me you're through with lessons."

Georgiana chuckled again. "No promises. I may feel the need to continue your education later."

"Heaven help us both, then," he whispered with a smile, and kissed her.

Why, man, she is mine own,
And I as rich in having such a jewel
As twenty seas, if all their sand were pearl,
The water nectar, and the rocks pure gold.
— Two Gentlemen of Verona,
Act II, Scene iv

461